paris 1969

Paris 1137

Nonfiction Books by Linda Tatelbaum

CARRYING WATER AS A WAY OF LIFE:
A Homesteader's History
(1997)

WRITER ON THE ROCKS—
Moving the Impossible
(2000)

YES & NO

Linda Tatelbaum

A Novel by Linda Tatelbaum

About Time Press
Appleton, Maine

for my students

⌒

Yes and No is a work of fiction. Resemblance to people living or dead is coincidental. Even the facts bear only a resemblance to what really happened. Who can know? History, too, is a work of fiction.

Many books were consulted in the formation of this novel, among them: Etienne Gilson, *Heloise and Abelard* (University of Michigan, 1960); Betty Radice, *The Letters of Abelard and Heloise* (Penguin, 1974); Helen Waddell, *Peter Abelard* (Viking, 1959).

Printed and manufactured by J.S. McCarthy, Augusta, Maine, USA

Cover design by Ribeck & Co.
Cover photograph by Mel Curtis / Getty Images
Text set in Goudy Old Style by Lurelle Cheverie
Author Photo by Bonnie Farmer

First Printing
ISBN 0-9654428-2-9
Library of Congress Control Number 2003090594

About Time Press
1050 Guinea Ridge Road
Appleton, Maine 04862
(207) 785-4634
www.colby.edu/~ltatelb

Thank you

TO faithful readers, you keep About Time Press alive and well.

TO Kalman Winer and Noah Tatelbaum Winer, for love,
laughter, ideas, good food, and careful reading.

TO Harriet Frank Tatelbaum, for patience and pluck,
and the late Milton Tatelbaum, for longevity,
but it had to end sometime.

TO Sylvia Frank, sorry you died without reading the next one.

TO Harold Winer, you recognize perseverance when you see it.

TO Jean Donovan Sanborn, I can't believe you read all the drafts.

TO Colby College, for all kinds of support and opportunity.

TO the many friends who listened, read, encouraged, questioned,
and assisted with this novel-in-progress over the fifteen
years of its genesis:
Kate Barnes, Bill Carpenter, Diane Charney, Geri Coughlin,
Stephanie Erber Darien, Judy Daviau, Mike Dorward,
Stephanie Davis Dorward, Lisa Frank, Gabriel Freiman,
Joan Freiman, Aklilu Gebrewold, Jill Gordon, Bill Halpin,
Roderick Hook, Susan Kenney, Bob Levey, Phyllis Mannocchi,
Lyn Mavrinac, Pat Onion, Marilyn Pukkila, Fred Ribeck,
Erika Sayewich, Alix Kates Shulman, Tobin Simon,
Carol Sloane, Susan Sterling, Jackie Tanner, Larissa Taylor,
Catherine Torphy, Linda Trichter Metcalf, Grace von Tobel,
Susanne Ward, Deborah Weisgall.

TO anyone I've omitted (sorry, it's been such a long road).

first one must eat stones and dream them into form.
First one must write a book without words
and swim upriver to the end of time.
And you? How will you begin?

Stand on the corner of Rue Monge and Rue des Ecoles on a chilly Paris morning. Watch for a girl to come out of her hotel carrying a briefcase, wearing knee socks and a triangular scarf on her head, a London Fog raincoat. You'll recognize the young American with long brown hair parted in the center. Her blue eyes observe everything without knowing what to do about it. You don't know what to do either, so you follow her.

She walks briskly, noticing trees, stooping to pick up a chestnut by the curb. The wind plays with the slit at the back of her raincoat, revealing a brown wool skirt. Follow her around the corner and enter the café across the street from the one she's heading for. Settle down in the front window with a *demi* of espresso. Throw off your trenchcoat and tug the edge of your beret over one ear. Then pull out your notebook, and begin the research you've been planning for ages. There's something buried that leaves you hungry. This girl you've never met might lead you to your subject, because she is young and not yet flavored with bitterness.

Time is a soup, you've always thought. History is simmering, still unfinished. You can toss anything into the stockpot. First choose the perfect young vegetables from the garden to scrub and peel and dice. Add them to the stock with garlic and bay leaves, thyme and peppercorns, flageolets and onion, a splash of wine. Someone will recognize that *soupçon* of sage you threw in as an afterthought. Someone like the girl, who doesn't yet know what she will do for you, nor do you. Nothing is lost, not even work you can't remember without her help.

If emptiness can be called pain, there must be a memory to fill that space. Pain will not stand in for memory and still satisfy. The flavor of an untold story seeps up from the bottom of the kettle where it sits on a low flame, for centuries it seems. No words can express a self when no one hears. There are only bubbles struggling up through thick stock and escaping as steam. The trace of what can't be named has long since faded from the knife edge, the chopping block, the fingernails. She who peeled and diced, she, you, was once an I, giving the pot a stir, wiping hands on a smock and returning to write the story no one heard. The story was lost, and with it yourself, expunged by the pumice of time.

And so, alone as always, and looking for what has been misplaced, you are drawn to the girl going into the café across the street. She leans against the counter with a *chocolat*. The proprietor brings a croissant on a small white saucer. You can't see her there beyond the glass, any more than you can speak the memory. Nevertheless your pain is real, and your view of her grows real in your notebook. This time the story will not be effaced.

She sips in silence to hide her American accent from Monsieur Montreux, as if he wouldn't know by the knee socks. He polishes the mahogany bar with a damp cloth, eyeing her sideways. He stops to smoothe the thin line of his black moustache and tightens the white apron around his portly waist. She's like a daughter from the provinces, so refreshing after these Parisian women who parade past the café in high boots. This one is shy, new, this one is lonely. She licks the rim of her empty cup and gathers the last crumbs of croissant with a wet finger.

"Au revoir," she mumbles, tying a scarf under her chin. She pulls open the door. "Merci."

You, in the Café des Etoiles across the way, know what she hopes, what he thinks, what she says, what he feels. All is simmering on the burner. You stir with the one kind of language left to you, the deep song of time, earth, vegetables. You dissolve the old residue into her fresh young story, which begins now as she emerges from Chez Montreux and heads for the Sorbonne. She is lost from view in the sharp morning mist, but you know where she's going and what she will do. The story you once wrote down is lost, but hers you can record in a notebook empty of your own faded details. This girl, properly prepared, can speak where you have been silenced, can persevere where you have faltered.

You smile as she merges with the growing crowd at the open market, disappears between the cheese merchant and a stand loaded with onions. You feel the queasy lurch of her stomach as she passes through the iron gates of the Sorbonne and climbs the dim stairway to the lecture hall. Your pen takes over and begins to depict a life into which you might find your way. These Left Bank streets, labyrinthine and narrow, with their uneven cobblestones centuries old, are as familiar to you as the pain which has no name.

You go to the counter for another espresso. Back at the little round table, you take off your beret and shake loose your hair. You ignore the man at the next table who watches you as only a Frenchman can watch a woman. He doesn't know the importance of your research, as you reach for the core of time itself. How could he know what it means to suffer erasure before words ever reach your lips, or your pen? How could he know the joy of reading the forgotten story of your own life, spoken in a young woman's voice? He sees you as the body of a woman, but that is his story, not the one you need to retrieve. Voice...the voice...this story requires breath, tongue, and someone to listen. Requires I, which you lack. Requires grammar and vocabulary, an unfolding plot.

You glance at him. He smiles solicitously, waiting for you to put down the empty cup so he can offer more. But no. You shake your head. No more. You sip the last of your bitter coffee and turn to a new page. This is a story that requires a new page.

*first
folio*

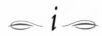

I t's a matter of finding out what you need her to do. She can provide the life. Just follow Naomi Weiss up the stone stairway of the
Ecole des Chartes. Once she steps over the threshold of the Sorbonne's
famous school of paleography, it could be eight centuries ago. Pale
daylight seeps through high windows onto the benches of a scriptorium.
Scribes shiver in their robes, copying manuscripts from dawn till dusk.
This morning in 1969, Naomi hugs a black briefcase close to her racing
heart and waits for the other students to slide along the bench. She
ends up too near the lectern, too far from the aisle, but like a monk, she
accepts her position and tries not to wonder what brought her here.

Even though your pen seems to shape her life story on the page
before you, in truth she's the one who chose to come here from the
cheerful lecture halls and intimate seminar rooms of Cornell
University. She's the one who enters the ancient hall where no one
knows her successes, her fears. She is as unsure of her plans as you are.
But you recognize that a girl whose skill with medieval scripts propelled
her to this venerable institute, yet whose professors have cast her loose
with no work to pursue, is a girl without a teacher. You, invisibly at first,
can be the teacher she doesn't know she needs. You can provide the
work. And she, with her curiosity and knowledge, will give you what
you've lost. She will give you your name.

This girl, this Naomi, snaps open the briefcase that holds only a
blank notebook and ballpoint pen. The French students have fountain
pens, and little jars of black ink. They sit reviewing their old notes. The

sour tang of authority flavors the hall on this first day of fall term. Last fall, the French schools hadn't yet recovered from "the events of May '68" that sent students raging into the streets. Today, students who once threw rocks and built barricades now try to place each script in the proper time period. They point anxiously at their notes with small magnifying glasses, uttering nothing more radical than "merovingienne…carolingienne…non, c'est çà, oui oui…"

Poor girl, this innocent graduate student, she lets these serious young men and women in dark turtlenecks and black berets intimidate her. Shyness chokes her, and not speaking French as well as she ought to. She leans down to pull up her knee socks, and opens the Cornell spiral notebook. She's forgotten how much she knows, how perfectly she's learned these medieval scripts, which is why she is here and not back at Cornell doing research for old Herr Professor Kurtzmann. "My dear," he said, "you simply must go to Paris, and get a chance to handle the real manuscripts, and not just these copies!"

Of course you would find a girl like this. You have bent to the soil, sun on your back, in order to forget the body. You've made it a gardener's tool for praising earth. And you've succeeded in forgetting all but the heft of a carrot yanked from the ground. This is a girl who wears her soft body like an impediment, an excuse, among these young intellectuals so comfortable in their own skin. She is, grâce à dieu, the perfect choice for your work.

"Quelle heure est-il?" a man whispers to Naomi. His hot breath makes a blush rise under her hair. What time is it? She looks at her watch, tries to formulate the answer in French, but she is too late. All heads bow as a grim elderly man stands in the doorway, a sheaf of tattered notes pressed against his rumpled suit. Professeur Emile Mauriet. The man she came here to study with. Silence draws over the hall like a drape slowly closing as the eminent man strides to the front. He mounts the high lectern like the Archbishop of Paleography and begins without looking up, "...l'écriture du moyen âge..." drifting out from somewhere above his crooked tie.

All she's managed to write so far is "13 octobre 1969." The student next to her takes down the professor's every word, something about ninth-century calligraphy. She can't even read his spidery handwriting, so how will she ever identify the old scripts Mauriet is lecturing about? Every time he thumps his magnifying glass on the lectern, the students write down some fact codified by nineteenth-century European paleographers. She knows these facts, the clues that reveal a manuscript's source and date. Kurtzmann wanted her to come learn every dot and curlicue. Working for him has been a game. But what a stale game it seems, now that she's here. Everything old. Old evidence, old assumptions, an old past.

She looks down the row of scribbling students. Did last year's revolt leave no mark on them? Hey, you guys, couldn't 1968 change the way we read these old words? She raises her eyes toward the lectern, where only the part in Mauriet's oily white hair is showing as he drones on. She doodles an impatient row of Carolingian capitals in the margin.

Suddenly the professor looks up from his notes. Everyone in the room jerks to attention. Naomi stops doodling. Her heart plunges to her stomach. She feels the blood drain from her cheeks. The French students know that one failing mark can end their ambitions for a career as scholar, historian, curator, professor. Indeed, their rebellion last year began as a protest against France's "sudden death" exams. Now, their evident fear of Mauriet marks a clear defeat.

Not that she's such a triumphant rebel. Her friends back at Cornell had picketed against a life-or-death exam held to determine which male graduate students could keep their draft deferment, and which would go to Vietnam. Her best friend Sharon pressured Naomi to boycott her doctoral orals, scheduled the same day the men filled the huge armory at Barton Hall to take the exam. "Are you going to let those imperialist pigs get away with murder?" Sharon screamed. It's not the professors' fault, Naomi insisted, and besides, I'm here to study. "Yeah, go ahead," Sharon accused, "escape into the past."

She wipes her sweaty brow with the back of a hand and looks down the aisle. Her new peers tilt pale faces toward Mauriet, who surveys the hall from under white eyebrows. Maybe it *is* the professors' fault. Look how Mauriet's power survived the world's most prominent student uprising. They joined forces with labor unions, and the strike caused the French government to fall. And now, Mauriet's up there, the same as always.

While these students took to the streets, and her friends joined SDS to protest Vietnam, she was working with the old librarian. Herr Kurtzmann tested her like a playful grandfather, challenging her with obscure questions, grinning and calling her brilliant when she returned to his sixth floor office with the answer. He sent her to the Ecole des Chartes to learn, not to be examined, even suggesting she matriculate here as an auditor. Thank goodness she won't have to face sudden death like her French colleagues! She resumes doodling in her notebook.

"Mademoiselle," booms the professor from the lectern. Horror! Emile Mauriet pointing his magnifying glass—right at her! Is he pointing at someone else, please God? She turns to see a hall full of students exhaling smugness from every Gallic nostril.

"Mademoiselle," he demands, "la signification de cette abbréviation?"

What does it mean? Which abbreviation? This one, the pp with a line through the stem? She hears her panicked voice say, stupidly, "Moi?"

He waves the magnifying glass irritably, "Oui, oui, c'est çà, allons…"

She plucks the itchy brown sweater away from her damp breasts. Not this panic again. The first week of graduate school, sitting around a seminar table high up in Olin Library, Kurtzmann had called on each of them to translate a Latin manuscript filled with difficult abbreviations. Naomi had to hold her icy hands under the table to keep them from shaking. She was the youngest, just 20 years old, a fresh B.A. from Cornell, and the only woman. The old professor took pity on her. He saved her for last, then sat with one wrinkled hand on his jaw, looking out over the Cayuga Valley as he listened to her. She came to the end of the formulaic salutation, "To the venerable bishop of Chartres from his servant in Christ, greetings," and began haltingly on the text itself. She felt Kurtzmann turn his keen ears toward her as she came to the bottom of the first column. He put on thick trifocals to watch her go on. She ended, "from his servant who sends prayers and greetings in the name of Our Lord," and all her colleagues let out their breath. The benign old professor smiled with pleasure, "Very *good*," and took off his glasses to inspect her blushing face.

Now, everyone in this hall is staring, waiting for her to fail. She opens her mouth. Nothing comes out. Finally, "Pardon, Monsieur, uh, Professeur, mais, uh, je suis auditrice."

Auditor! Mauriet shoots her a look of disgust, as if she were a filthy pauper crawling across a stone floor on her knees to beg his forgiveness, and he, holding onto a heavy cross that hangs from his neck, waves her away with a ringed hand. He moves on to the next student.

He'll never call on her again. She'll sit on this bench all term, mute and invisible now. And she knew the answer! She wants to blurt, "Two p's with a line crossing the tail—is *propter*!" But what good is an answer that comes too late?

She tumbles out onto Rue St. Jacques after lecture with the crowd of exuberant students. They lean against the iron fence, faces no longer pale. The men push up their sleeves and the women cluster around them, making plans that don't include her. They all troop off toward the Jardin du Luxembourg. Naomi stands in front of a bookshop window filled with volumes of poetry, watching the reflection of old Mauriet tottering down the steps of the Ecole des Chartes. By the time she turns around, the students have disappeared around the corner and she is alone in the narrow street. She walks to the Jardin and buys a crêpe spread with jam from a vendor. She sits down on a bench next to a middle-aged woman who holds an unopened notebook in her lap.

So. Saved from disgrace—yet totally disgraced. She knew the answer! How could she not? Carolingian minuscule is so easy! She bites her crêpe and flicks a tear from the corner of her eye with the unsticky end of a little finger. Of course good old Charlemagne would make sure his monks left a legible record of his reign. Without schools, without writing, who would remember the suffering and triumphs of all the great men?

Naomi looks around the broad park, chestnut leaves turning russet, branches loaded with spiky burrs, thinking about Charlemagne and how she does not want to be a monk transcribing alphabets. She sneaks a glance at the woman tossing crumbs to the pigeons. She wants to be free like her. Like you, for it is you who've followed her here, to taste again her promise. The professor has pushed your subject to her crushing moment, which you need in order to extract the fullness of her, just as basil must be bruised to bring out the flavor. She stares at your profile, the wisp of light brown hair escaped from your beret, the delicate wrinkles on your cheeks. She eyes the notebook on your lap, wondering what you're working on. The notebook is mostly blank, dear girl, except for a memory that taunts like a whiff of broth.

Do not look over at her, do not smile. Let her life remind you what you're searching for. Lead her to the place where you buried it, and let her dig up the words. The girl looks away. She finishes the crêpe and licks jam off her wrist.

$\backsim ii \backsim$

A teacher can't lead until she can follow. So let Naomi leave her chilly room on the fifth floor of the Hôtel Plaisant, where she hunches over books at a rickety table covered with a plastic tablecloth. A gauze curtain sways in the draft seeping under the French doors. She huddles in a sweater and hat, hands tucked beneath her legs. A little yellow desk lamp she bought gives the only warmth. Let her abandon the cramped room, the faded pink wallpaper, the damp bed with its stained grey bedspread and uninviting bolster. Today's mail, again, did not bring the stipend check from Cornell, leaving her with overdue rent and barely enough francs for two slim meals a day, mostly bread, never meat or wine. Instead have her try the Sorbonne library, hoping, like you, to forget how hungry she is.

She'll find out everything about the Latin Quarter that Kurtzmann failed to tell her. The Sorbonne is nothing like the American university that welcomed him during the war. His Naomi Weiss browses freely in the Cornell stacks. She has her own carrel where he leaves clues and messages stuck in her books. Here in Paris nothing is free, nothing is easy. Your Naomi Weiss will begin by waiting in line at the Sorbonne library, at a turnstile where a grey man looks down his nose at each student's pass, all of them blue except Naomi's. Hers is pink. Her eyes are the only thing blue about her, and her mood, and her usually rosy skin, mottled blue now with cold. The little sour man admits one blue pass after another, and she begins to lose heart. She's already waited in line at the Bibliothèque Nationale, shown her Carte d'Identité, asked for the Abélard manuscript Kurtzmann told her to look at. But *non, non, pas possible, Mademoiselle,* not without a letter from Cornell to certify she is an auditor.

She's starting to think there's only one place in Paris that doesn't require a Carte d'Identité, and it is the laundromat on Rue des Carmes. She likes to lean against the drier, comforted by her pink flannel nightgown appearing and reappearing in the round window. She lugs the warm bag of clothes up Rue des Bernardins, up the five spiral flights to the top floor, racing the timer that clicks the hall light off. Her north-facing garret abuts a building with bars on the windows, making Rue des Bernardins a dead end. Through the railing of her narrow balcony, she can see a fenced triangle of grass across the street, and beyond that, the busy Rue Monge. A bathroom in the hall looks down on the landlady's courtyard clothesline, and out across the chimneys of the Latin Quarter.

The turnstile creaks as each student flashes a blue card and presses through. Naomi steps to the gate just as the phone rings. The grumpy man covers one ear and shouts, "Allô?" While his back is turned, she slips through. What the hell. In Pierre Abélard's time, the early 1100s, there was no university. No turnstiles, no blue passes. So what's the big deal? Scholars argued philosophy in taverns, and paid their teachers only if they liked what was taught. Abélard, with his charismatic style, managed to spirit away his rivals' students. They couldn't stop him. Only after the King founded the Sorbonne by official decree did teachers have to be approved—by the Pope. Academic freedom? Already a lost cause here by 1203!

She sits down at a table, breathless from her heresy at the gate. She'll never be able to penetrate the next level of this hell—the closed stacks. No one can, least of all an American auditor with a pink pass. She shivers, and hears her cough magnified by the domed ceiling. Her briefcase makes a loud snap as she opens it to pull out a tattered copy of Abélard's autobiography, *Historia calamitatum*. She scans the familiar opening pages. Born in 1079, oldest son of a noble family in Brittany. Gave up his birthright and "withdrew from the court of Mars to kneel at the feet of Minerva." The goddess of wisdom led him on a crusade through every school of theology in France. Logic was his sword; his enemy, those who put faith in what authorities say. "We must question!" was his battle cry, "we must prove! *Intelligo ut credam*—I think so that I might believe. Else why did God give us mind?"

The first text Naomi will ask for from the locked stacks is Abélard's *Sic et non.* Where is the truth of God, Abélard demanded, when evidence from Church Fathers can prove a proposition both true *and* false, yes *and* no? He runs his sword through all their proofs—

> that faith is based on reason, and that it isn't
> that God knows all things, and He doesn't
> that marriage is good for everyone, and not
> that God is three, and He is one

—dangerous stuff! He scoffed at his old masters who taught only by lecture, clearly a method that dies hard. Abélard scorned Anselm of Laon, "famed by tradition, but a nobody before a questioner." He cornered his mentor, William of Champeaux, in a heresy that forced William to resign. Oh, he was fierce in his battles, Minerva at his side. Finally they banished him from the Latin Quarter. He climbed Mont Ste. Geneviève, the hill behind the Sorbonne, and started his own school. Kurtzmann told her to look for the site. Imagine! Abélard walked these Left Bank streets!

Wonder what he'd think about this library, this stone monument to tradition? By day, these students say Yes to their books. At night they rally in the Jardin and say No. The only scar left in this *quartier* from "the events of May" is a festering welt of paddy wagons parked along Boul' Mich every night, just waiting to nab a student. This explains their tight, fearful handwriting, and the youthful vigor that propels them out onto Rue St. Jacques after class.

How she hates the thin, terrifying wail that pierces the evening air, as chilling as the river mist. The sirens bring out the coward in her. She's not like other students, both here and at Cornell, protesting academic oppression, war, capitalism, the rule of elders. What would she risk arrest for? Each night she slips unseen through the dark streets of the Latin Quarter down by the Seine, after a cheap dinner at a student restaurant. Sometimes she stops at the corner pâtisserie for an éclair to take back to her room, where she studies and writes until sleep overcomes her. What would she willingly die for? A millefeuille, a Napoléon, a cream horn? Certainly an apricot tart. She licks her lips, smoothing down the page of Abélard's story.

She'd die for a look behind the most famous of his calamities, the love affair with his young pupil Héloïse, for which he was punished with castration. Kurtzmann would not approve what she really came here for. Manuscripts, sure, of course. But why do scholars insist that whatever doesn't reach words is lost? What they call "history" can't be all that's left! There must be something more. Something known with the heart. She can barely say it—the heart!—after what happened in Dante seminar that time, when the great Mario Grappone blew up at her for imagining her way into the "Purgatorio." It felt good to try on the faith of Dante. But, "You don't have to believe it, you know," Grappone snorted.

That shut her up for the rest of the semester. And sent her off into Latin paleography, where Kurtzmann offered objective knowledge, a kind of treasure hunt that depends on your eyes, not your...heart—she can hardly say the word without flushing. But still she wonders. Has she wasted her time mastering the written clues, if she only seeks the unwritten? She closes the *Historia calamitatum* and cradles its spine against her palm. Somewhere between the lines of all these manuscripts she hopes to be examining soon, this written record of the philosopher Pierre Abélard, there's got to be a jaunty Pierre singing his lyrics on the river bank, a young Héloïse walking from the marketplace with a basket of leeks.

Grappone could have his fantasies, could believe his own arguments, entertain his own doubts. But a young scholar, a woman, must stick to the text. Only to be condescended to, only to be patronized, only to be…condemned: Guilty!…if she steps out of the text into some other way of knowing. The hell with that.

It's one thing to stand up to him now, in her head. She busies herself gathering her notebook, her Latin dictionary. Why is she here, anyway? She'd been mesmerized by Grappone's broad stooped shoulders, his prominent skull passing back and forth before a blackboard covered with Italian, Latin, Provençal, arrows, circles, and, above all, spirals. The whole class had been seduced by their master who was all questions, no answers. But the more she took down his every word in a Cornell notebook and in the margins of *La Divina Commedia*, the more she became convinced that the scholarly Grappone, ploughing the texts with devotion, was a man who knew the answer as deeply as Dante knew it. That kind of belief doesn't fit, in academe. No wonder he favored the students who doubted, intelligently and loudly, mostly the men. He liked her well enough, and gave her A's, but she was never part of his "group." No matter how early she showed up for the four-hour seminar, "the group" would already be arguing with their perplexed master in the smoke-filled room. Grappone looked like he hadn't slept in weeks, or if he had, he'd been wearing the same crumpled white shirt day and night. The seat of his pants, she noticed when he got up to dash "concatenation" or "solipsism" on the board, was shiny, and his middle-aged paunch strained the buttons. He held the chalk between stained fingers like a cigarette, and once in a while he absently took a puff of chalk, or tried to write on the board with a butt. He kept a box of sugar cubes on the seminar table, and in between smokes he sucked sugar. Lost in thought he would suck, scratch his bald spot, and then forget to stop scratching as he pondered a line from the "Inferno" while everyone sat and waited, also sucking sugar.

She didn't suck sugar, maybe that was the problem. She listened, read, studied, and never checked her watch, even when the four-hour seminar trailed into five or six. She turned the onionskin pages of the *Commedia* carefully at first, and then, as the margins filled up with her notes, she turned them more confidently. They reached "Purgatorio" at mid-term. That's when she dared to be the Dante-who-believes. And Grappone recoiled. From what? What had her blue eyes seen in his deep brown ones? He is a scholar, a Great Man in the field, objective, clever, ambitious. He has tenure, and a long list of publications. He lectures in Italy. His recommendation can make or break a young scholar. And she is so young, so horribly young.

"You don't have to *believe* it!" Her colleagues squirmed on their hard wooden chairs. He could be unpredictable, Grappone, he could be fierce, despite that velvet laugh. Naomi flushed, and then goose bumps raised the hair on her arms. She looked down at the gold medallion of Dante's profile embossed on the dark blue cover. Dante's head swam on the far side of her tears. Grappone's smoke choked out all the air in the room. Perhaps she'd faint. She swallowed, and picked up her pen, still staring at Dante's wobbling profile without blinking, to hold back the tears. And the seminar went on, to reach "Paradiso" in spring. But she wasn't part of his following after that, and didn't like Dante anymore. She'd pass Grappone's office and hear his thick voice, see the smoke curling out the door. She was crushed, extinguished. Ashamed. Of what? Now that she is here alone, in another country, holding a book she truly wants to enter, now she demands to know: was her crime really so great? She'd had the gall to *feel* something! To *know* through feeling! Perhaps the greatest crime of all: she recognized *him*!

Naomi sweeps Abélard's calamities into her briefcase, and shoves the chair back with a screech across the marble floor. At the gate, oh, no, the grey man is checking passes. You can't go in *or out* without the right credentials! She digs into her briefcase, and holds out the card. Enraged by the pink intruder, he sputters insults that bounce off the domed ceiling. And not one student looks up from reading to watch an American girl being sent to the Bastille. *Ne pas revenir!* This much she understands. *Don't come back!*

She rushes through the dusky courtyard of the Sorbonne, under the iron gateway. Kicked out! She stumbles over rugged cobblestones past the bookshops, through the marketplace, past kiosks plastered with radical slogans. Where to turn…how to be a historian without books? How to follow the trace…a silence she knows isn't empty…some other Abélard who was more than what he wrote…some Héloïse still lingering in the *quartier*…

From the window of the Café des Etoiles, you watch the girl rush by on the other side of Rue des Ecoles. You mean to stay invisible, but her distress takes you to the layer of story that isn't hers. It's tempting to peel back the last stubborn onionskin, to strip the yellow-white flesh and release tears. You can tell by her headlong stride back to the Hôtel Plaisant, and by her burning cheeks, that she wants never to show her face again. *Ne pas revenir*, as the librarian decreed, never to return. Never again to be the girl you were just now, rushing past the window, holding onto tears until the last spiral of stairs. You'll jump right into the damp bed, knee socks and all, and stay there with your head under the covers. But you can't escape a thing. When hunger pangs rouse you at 7 o'clock, who will you be then? And me? Who will I be as I follow, beshadowing you with my past?

A rueful smile plays at your lips as you swallow a spoonful of rich onion soup. The warmth rushes down your throat and spreads in your chest, and you see that you've just found a voice, in speaking to her. If she is called *you*, then you are… *I*? Perhaps. You put down the spoon and follow your pen across the white page and up the spiral stairs and into the miserable bed.

~ *iii* ~

Dunking a heel of bread into the watery stew, Naomi makes up her mind. As soon as Kurtzmann's letter of introduction arrives, she'll show it to Mauriet. Then she'll be admitted to the Bibliothèque Nationale. She'll see those Abélard manuscripts for herself. Especially the letters between him and Héloïse, though her dissertation proposal ran more to his ethical philosophy. She has a hunch that living with the consequences of his love affair with Héloïse helped evolve the ethics. Naomi eats the bread and wipes her chin. No grey little man will keep her out when she flashes a letter from Werner Kurtzmann.

Over the rim of her water glass, she watches the row of French students on both sides of the long table, gulping cheap wine. The *prix fixe* ladleful of stew and a half-loaf of bread is all she can afford. Wine is extra. Conversation and friendship are extra, something else to renounce. She, too, is living with consequences, cut off from her parents by the choice to study such a Christian era, when they'd hoped for a good Jewish daughter. She throws back the last of her water and, just like that, she decides. Letter or no letter, it's time to begin. She stands up and brushes bread crumbs off her lap. No one notices as she opens the door, letting in a gust of chill air.

She shivers and pulls her collar up. There's no money for the after-dinner trip to the pâtisserie tonight. She always looks forward to pointing her finger like a child at a glistening tart, or a mountain of custard swirled with chocolate, and watching the woman wrap her treat in a pyramid of pink paper and string. She sighs, walking from the old quarter near St. Severin and the river, and up Boulevard St. Germain toward her room, which will be lonely with no pastry for company. The wail of sirens from over by Boul' Mich seems distant from this end of the fifth *arrondissement*, where only the hum of traffic along Rue Monge breaks the quiet. Her narrow Rue des Bernardins ends with an abandoned building, bars on the windows.

The room is warm for a change, and she is warm from racing the light timer up the spiral stairs. She opens the French doors to the night. Leaning over the railing, she can smell the yeast of tomorrow's long loaves at the boulangerie around the corner, and see the bright café across Rue des Ecoles where Parisians sip wine, espresso, and cognac every evening. She never goes there. She likes the deserted quiet of her street. Hearing more sirens, she steps back into her room and closes the glass doors. Not a soul in Paris can disturb her here. She settles down at the desk with the new notebook she bought with her pastry money this afternoon. She sighs again, then leans over to sniff the new paper. Behind her, a rare hiss from the lukewarm radiator, in front of her the glow from the little yellow desk lamp. She tucks up her feet, ready to begin.

Begin what? The new notebook is for figuring out something. She holds the pen, unsure if this will be worth the price of a pastry, then writes: *"Pensées de la Nuit." Paris. 29 octobre 1969 –* . There. A title. That's a start. She turns to the next page. She stares at the pink wall, fiddling with a pile of paperclips. A chair scrapes across the floor on the other side of the wall. Someone lives in that dark building, then, someone is there at night? She assumed it was a warehouse, with its dark windows, no sign of life on the sooty façade. No geranium, lamp, curtain, cat. Her heart beats fast. Someone in a chair just beyond the wall. Who? She listens. Nothing.

Not a soul in Paris knows me, she writes to reassure herself. *Je suis toute seule.* All alone. She sucks the end of her pen, and adds, *J'aime ma solitude.*

Is this a lie? Does she really love her solitude? She will try not to tell lies in this notebook. So much of what she has to write is a lie. *Ma solitude.* She is lonely, but it suits her, and it sounds better in French anyway. Solitude lets her meander through wordless space. To discover...what? The meaning of history. Merely that! Her pen draws a fancy H embedded in curves. She chuckles, picturing herself at an oral defense. History as Wordless Space. Grappone would love that one! At the thought of him her blush rises again, the hurt and shame still fresh. Okay. They want words, she'll give them words, though really what she's after is the shape of the invisible. Which you can't see to defend.

History, yeah. How *they* define it. She taps her pen on the cover of Etienne Gilson's classic *Heloise and Abelard*, a book she brought from Ithaca. She opens to "Chapter 6. The Mystery of Heloise." Abélard's life they call "a story"—of "calamities" no less. Gilson dismisses Héloïse's as "a mystery" because "no text comes down to us." But how can you dismiss this exceptional girl who, at 15, could read and write not only French, but Latin, Greek, and Hebrew? Héloïse who, though pregnant by her 37-year-old mentor, tried to talk him out of marriage because it would ruin his brilliant career. Héloïse who gave birth to a son, Astralabe, and left him in Brittany with Abélard's sister. Who finally consented to a secret marriage, hiding among the nuns at Argenteuil. When her Uncle Fulbert found Héloïse gone, he sent his cronies to castrate Abélard in his bed. All through the Latin Quarter the cry went up, the beloved master! In shock and pain, Abélard forced Héloïse to take the veil.

Héloïse never wrote this story down. Gilson marvels at her silence, which fills him with desire. To him, Héloïse is "a learned young woman seduced by the famous master." He interprets her silence as devoted obedience to her mentor, her lover, her husband, her "brother in Christ." Gilson would want the same from her, wouldn't he, if he were the mentor, the lover? Nothing in writing. No evidence. Denial. Silence. Death—to the woman—and continued life and work, fame even, for the man. A mystery, he calls it. "If it is to this conclusion that history brings us," he ends, "history will never take us any further. Perhaps history is posing a problem here that is itself insoluble."

Indeed. Naomi closes the book. "History" is the problem. She twiddles her pen, wanting to write what she hears in the "silence" of Héloïse. A soul crying in the night in her nun's cell. You call this "silence"? Or, who knows, maybe what she's hearing is the song of a satisfied woman who found her own way. Like that woman in the park. Mona Lisa in a beret.

And yet. Who knows. History does have its methods. She opens Gilson again, to the part where he chews over the word "conversio," and expounds on the long line of (lesser) scholars who fell into a misreading that undermined the authenticity of the famous letters. Gilson defends the view he's committed to, half in love with Héloïse himself it sometimes seems. He's fascinated by her silence, excited by the breaking of it. How dare those scholars claim it was Abélard alone who wrote both sides of the correspondence? *Heretici!*

The story goes that after his mutilation, Abélard found refuge in a monastery. Fifteen years passed, leaving no written evidence of any contact. Then Héloïse begins the well-known correspondence by accusing Abélard of abandonment: "In the precarious early days of our conversion long ago, I was not a little surprised and troubled…when neither reverence for God nor our mutual love nor the example of the holy Fathers made you think of trying to comfort me, wavering and exhausted as I was by prolonged grief."

The words swell Naomi's heart! But sympathy is not a scholarly response. A scholar studies the record. A scholar uses facts, events, to construct a story which guides the search for further evidence. Abélard had possession of some land in Champagne, near Troyes, where he retreated after the scandal. Paraclete, he called it, "place of Holy Comfort." His disciples followed him. Later they convinced him to return to Paris. When Héloïse and her new Sisters were evicted from their convent at Argenteuil, he gave them the Paraclete. He made frequent trips there to help his "wife in Christ" establish a convent in the wilderness, so frequent that the bishop forbade further visits. Gilson's opponents wonder why, given these trips, Héloïse would accuse Abélard of abandoning her. These scholars assert her letters and his response must have been written by Abélard himself, filled with remorse in his later years. Such fictional correspondence was, in fact, a genre of the time.

Outrageous. Gilson will not tolerate this threat to his fantasy of obedient silence, impassioned accusation. He fortifies his dearly-held view with a new argument: her words, "our conversion," do not refer to their initial celibacy vows. "Our" refers instead to Héloïse and her Sisters, left at the Paraclete to live by the Benedictine Rule, a rubric not suited to nuns. Why else, Gilson argues, would she refer to "the example of the holy Fathers"?

Why else. Why else. Gilson leaves no room for why else. "Tedious as such discussions are," he concludes, the controversy is a simple matter of "the wrong shade of meaning taken by Oddoul, repeated by Lalanne, then by Gréard, taken again by Schmeidler and meekly accepted by Miss Charrier." Meekly! *Miss* Charrier! With that final thrust, he puts "the text thus re-established back into its context, from which it ought never to have been taken."

Naomi slams Gilson shut, then sits tapping her pen on the yellow base of the lamp. Ought. Ought. *The mystery of Héloïse*, she writes in her notebook. *The mystery of Héloïse*, she presses down hard, refusing the image that comes to her of this "Miss" Charrier "meekly" accepting her predecessors' idea. Damn. Why does that bug her so? Because Gilson discredits the why else, the unknown. What she hopes to discover. *Men relish the unknowable in women. They don't want to know. They want to contain us within the walls of their desire. Heaven forbid we should speak their language. Or worse, a language of our own! Gilson's demand for text mutes Héloïse forever. There's nothing mute about her, Etienne baby. Read between the lines.*

Naomi scratches her pen lightly in the margin, making hatch-marks diagonal to the pale red lines. She opens a folder, and runs her finger down a dense block of calligraphy, a photocopy of Peter the Venerable's letter to Héloïse upon Abélard's death in 1142. He reminds the middle-aged abbess that her learning "surpassed all women and most men." He portrays her in youth: "Men were speaking of this wonder—a woman, still in the world, giving herself entirely to the study of literature and philosophy, nor permitting anything, neither the desires of the world, nor its vanities, nor its pleasure to turn her from the laudable ambition of learning the liberal arts."

Hmm. But then she met her Great Man. And then desire did determine her disastrous choices. Still, she stayed with her work. She spent her life adapting the Benedictine Rule to the needs of monastic women. She educated girls. She admitted it was the love of Abélard and not God that led her to the spiritual life. But couldn't her silence mean what Gilson writes off as unthinkable, that she "had found in the cloister the calm, the peace, and the consolations of divine love"—or at least, some self-knowledge, some satisfaction? *Why is it such a mystery for Gilson to imagine that a woman can have a life apart from men?* she scrawls. *Meek is how they want us. But not how we are.*

Well, maybe. She gets up to cool her face against the glass. Maybe I am meek. She opens the doors and steps out onto the balcony. It's late, and so quiet she hears the bread rising. Across the little park, a woman in a trenchcoat with the collar turned up walks briskly along Rue Monge. Some women aren't meek. She steps back into the room and closes the doors.

What is it that makes her so meek, when inside she burns? She raises her sweet face to her mentors, loving them, only to be crushed by their cold rationality. If "the love of learning" is really "the desire for God," in LeClercq's phrase, then she sees God in them, and yearns for their light. *Desire, that's the problem. For a learned woman, desire is a passion for knowledge. It fuels her. But when the mentor looks at her, he sees a body, and desires that body. She becomes a calamity in the making. And a danger to herself. She has to hide her body, and follow her desire for knowledge through the back alleys where he won't see her, where she can be a mind walking in the dark. But then, when she gets lost, who will be there to help her?*

The chair creaks as she leans back, thinking of her first encounter with Abélard's *Story of My Calamities* in Grappone's seminar on confessional literature. Basking in the glorious light of her first Great Man, she found a warning in Héloïse's fall from grace. They read Augustine's *Confessions* in seminar, too. He confessed his sins, and grew and changed, and went on to become a bishop, a saint. A fallen woman, though, will not survive to tell her tale.

No wonder Naomi went right out and found herself a safe old mentor like Kurtzmann. When she left the outskirts of Grappone's "group," she could have gone over to Bart Petersen, the young medievalist from Berkeley who had no following yet, and probably needed a graduate student to boost his chances for tenure. She clicks her pen point in and out, remembering coffee with him at the student union. Her heart wouldn't stop racing, as if he were a blind date and not a professor giving her a bibliography. She couldn't help studying his classic profile, the way he held his adorable chin in thought, and then with a spasm of erudition splashed names and dates across a yellow pad. He did more than answer her. He amplified her. And respected her. As if he could learn from her, too. Rare teacher! Naomi loved the excitement, but there was danger. Petersen was married. Desire for *learning*, remember, girl? She didn't want to end up as someone's calamity. Funny how they never called Héloïse's story a calamity. She gave up a life, for him. She gave up a child, for him. None of this is "called" anything by her own quill. She is just the "mystery" behind Abélard's ruin. *What the hell would she call it? And how can I find out?*

She pictures Kurtzmann rocking back in his chair with a smile as she delivers a stack of old volumes. And Petersen reaching across the table in the student union, sloshing coffee into his saucer to scribble one more thing on her reading list. She'll wend her way between safety and danger, keeping to herself, thinking what she thinks. And because of her young face, her innocent blue eyes, her scholarly skills, they'll support her. When she commits her knowledge to words…who knows where it will lead, and what her teachers will say. For now all she has to do is live with the loneliness, and desire *learning*, and…darn it, save enough money next week for a pastry!

The notebook was worth the no éclair, though. Finding a voice, instead of cramming her mouth with custard and cream. Well, chocolate might be better than voice. She slips her flannel nightgown on, snaps off the yellow lamp, and slides into bed. Sacrifice is part of the game, especially for women. What on earth is she talking about? Abélard sacrificed a body part! Yeah, but didn't he make the most of it? Oh, stop…he did suffer, of course he did! And Héloïse? Did she? Naomi lies with her eyes open in the dark. The cars passing on Rue Monge send slivers of light between the balcony rails. The sheets feel clammy, the nightgown damp. There's another thud from beyond the faded pink wall. She is already asleep.

⪼ iv ⪻

Naomi stares into a mug of bouillon. Paris is mean, and walking back to her room in gloomy twilight rain, she got soaked to the skin. In the foyer, the mail cubby contained nothing but the feel of splintered wood, no check from Cornell, late again. On the fifth floor, a cold radiator greeted her. She filled a mug with water and plugged in the forbidden heating coil. One cube of Deux Magots to warm her hands and nose, though it won't do much to stave off hunger. She lowers her face into the steam, and studies the sad eyes reflected in a circle of gossamer grease and salt.

Then she hears, "Mademoiselle! Mademoiselle Weiss!" from downstairs, and opens her door. The smell of beef and bay leaf drifts up from the private quarters below. The landlady raises a thin face to watch Naomi spin down the spiral stairs, then hands her an air-mail envelope from her apron pocket. "Pour vous," she says, fiddling with a hairpin. The girl looks so wan in the dim light that the woman considers offering her a bowl of broth as well. Naomi takes the letter, gives the light timer another twist, and disappears again.

The devastating aroma of beef lingers at the top of the stairs, and Naomi's stomach growls angrily. Two more hours till the restaurants open. She steps across the faded grey rug, back to her Deux Magots, and rips open the letter. A clipping flutters to the floor, a mild old face, "WERNER KURTZMANN, RARE BOOKS HEAD, DEAD AT 81."

12 November 1969

Dear Miss Weiss:

I am sorry to tell you that Professor Kurtzmann has died. He
died in his sleep of heart failure last week. His secretary passed
your request on to me. Enclosed is a letter of introduction, hoping you will have better luck with the Sorbonne. I studied with
Mauriet myself, back in the early fifties. Perhaps this will help.
I will be in Paris in January, to check some manuscripts at the
B.N. Let's meet for lunch one day. Until then, good luck.

Sincerely,
Françoise LaTour
Professor of French

She reads it over twice, sipping lukewarm bouillon, and stares out
at the slick streets and dripping lamp posts. Kurtzmann gone.
Mademoiselle LaTour—hardly a substitute. Still, she is French. And a
member of her dissertation committee. And a woman. Sort of.

The next day, she zips Mademoiselle LaTour's letter safely in her
briefcase pocket, and climbs the broad staircase to the second floor
of the Ecole des Chartes. To calm herself, she slides one hand along the
cool brass banister, clutching the briefcase handle in the other. Why
is she so afraid? Mauriet can't kill her or anything. Scholarly power is
only a matter of ink. At the top of the stairs, fear grabs the back of her
neck at the smell of chalk dust in the empty classroom. She can't believe
her friends were chanting "On strike! Shut it down!" at Cornell, with
its carpeted lecture halls, upholstered seats, recessed lighting and all!
Boy, the young sure have the old running scared back home. Their
demands can topple college presidents. The *New York Times* devotes
whole sections to them. Even governors pay attention. Look at this
awful room, hard wooden benches, a raised pulpit where the Professor

is God—no wonder all hell broke loose here last spring! Naomi feels like throwing a book through the window. She'd love the sound of shattering glass on Rue St. Jacques this very moment!

"Qu'est-ce que tu veux?"

She whirls around, startled by the rude what-do-you-want, in the familiar form no less. Emile Mauriet fills the doorway, this world-renowned authority on twelfth-century manuscript production, the man she came to Paris for. Maybe this King of Ink can't kill her, but he can certainly erase her. She opens her mouth, and French syntax fails her once again.

"Je…je…viens vous voir."

"Speak English," he commands.

"Oui, Monsieur, merci. I…I have a letter of introduction from one of my professors in the United States. I am an auditor in your medieval paleography class, you know."

"I know no such thing."

"Oh, I, er, I sit about halfway back on the left. I came here on the recommendation of Professor Werner Kurtzmann."

"Hmph. Kurtzmann. I knew him at Cologne in the '20s. He went to America?"

"Yes, he was head of Rare Books at Cornell University."

"Corneille? Où est ça?"

"In New York State, Monsieur. But he just died." Naomi fights down a lump in her throat. Kurtzmann's grin, lost forever. Unmoved, Mauriet continues his inquisition.

"You were his student?"

"Yes, I studied paleography with him, and worked as his assistant. I…I'm researching Pierre Abélard, and Kurtzmann thought that…"

"Abélard, eh?" One of Mauriet's nostrils flares, twitches, settles back into place. "Abélard. Hmph." He glares at her. "What about him?"

"Well, Monsieur, I'm not sure yet. I…I'm only a second-year graduate student. Maybe his letters. Or, or, his ethical philosophy. I need your permission, though, to use the libr..."

"Hrmph," he interrupts. As if she were a small bug crawling up his pantleg, the effort not to flick her off produces a disgusted grimace on his chalk-white face. "What did Kurtzmann tell you to study?"

"He told me to study with you."

"Hmmpf." Mauriet considers whether or not this is flattery, decides it is not. "Your name?"

"Naomi Weiss, Monsieur."

"Weiss, eh?" Mauriet studies her surreptitiously from under his coarse white eyebrows. He sees another one of these, these...oh, these gullible young women, these Jews from America who know nothing, nothing. His forehead furrows with the effort not to look in her eyes. "Hmph," he concludes, the matter of her name closed, though he clearly disapproves of it.

"Well, Monsieur," she swallows, studying his fleur-de-lis tie, "the reason I came with this letter..."

"Let me see it." He grabs the letter. Françoise LaTour! So *she's* behind this. He re-folds it and slaps it into Naomi's shaking hand.

"Je regrette, Mademoiselle. Auditors are not permitted to use the library."

"But, Monsieur, how can I learn? I can't even identify the scripts you lecture about, except looking on with the student next to me. Mademoiselle LaTour thought you'd..."

"Don't talk to me of her."

"But...well, Kurtzmann, then...Kurtzmann would have wanted..."

"Kurtzmann is dead. It doesn't matter what he wanted. We have our rules. We are not concerned with what you Americans want. Go back to Corneille if you want to do what you want. Our students do what we say."

"Yes, they do—and that is a real problem." Mauriet's jaw goes slack at the strength of this girl's voice, and his eyebrows plunge to guard against the urge to look right at her. "Why do you think your students rally every night?" she goes on. "Times are changing, and not just in America! Where were you in '68? Pardon me, sir, but students have rights, too!"

His face turns the color of raw meat. No, she's not one of those gullible Americans. Worse! The new breed. No respect for authority. Brrrmpph! He raises his brows and pins her at last with his hateful eyes.

Naomi hears her voice from afar. What in hell is she doing? She's never talked back to a teacher, let alone this one! And where does she think *she* was in '68 when Cornell burst into flames after Martin Luther King was assassinated? Arsonists threatened to spell out A-T-L-A-N-T-A with fires. Annabel Taylor Hall, A-T, burned first. Would L be her beloved Library? She hoped they would target the Law school next, anything but the books! Then, shame of shames, she found herself crossing the street to avoid the student union where black students guarded the door—with guns! Ducked her head and kept walking. Went up to her library carrel. Grabbed her books and notes. Evaded the tumultuous 1960s by monkish devotion to the past.

Yes, she was a sell-out, just as Sharon said. She even stopped reading the *Cornell Daily Sun*, not to mention the *New York Times*. Ashamed now she didn't picket or attend teach-ins or boycott classes or hand out leaflets. Sorry now, too late, and frightened by the rush of her rage, she holds her tongue and turns away from Mauriet. She bounds down the marble stairway and out into the mauve afternoon.

Revived by the chilly air, she skips down the front steps to the sidewalk. Tomorrow when they arrive for lecture, they'll find Mauriet frozen in shock. They'll poke at his eminence with their fountain pens to make sure he is dead. And then they'll shout with triumph, Naomi included for once in her generation. They'll tack slogans all over his body like a kiosk. It's not too late for her to rebel!

She giggles as she hurries along Rue St. Jacques. But the memory of his hateful stare renews her terror, and she begins to run, as if chased, toward the market at Place Painlevé. It *is* too late for her, she's still chicken, and of *course* she hasn't killed Mauriet off! Nothing of the kind! It's Kurtzmann who's dead, and she is mentorless, alone, lost. My God, she doesn't dare show up at lecture, after the way she talked to him. She finally got him to notice her, and now he *hates* her. She wants to hide among the vegetable stands, or maybe slip into a café and never be seen again. Radical slogans—sticks and stones—can't break his bones. He's made of stone, just like Paris, damp stone that's stood since the Middle Ages. And even if they topple all the Mauriets, another Jacques will pop out of the pulpit. Nothing ever changes in this old city.

Reaching the marketplace, out of breath, terrified, she buys three yellow apples wrapped in newspaper from a stout farm woman with no teeth. "Merci, Madame." She hugs the fruits to her heart as if they were the only truth. She heads past shops that will soon close for the night with an iron shutter pulled down over every window and a locked gate over every door. Past the café where a woman writing at a table watches with interest as Naomi turns on Rue des Bernardins and heads for her safe, though chilly, haven.

She races up the stairs, not fast enough to beat the timer, and gropes her way up the last two spirals in the dark, fumbling for the key. "My dear, you simply must go to Paris and see Mont Ste. Geneviève, where he taught." Yes, Kurtzmann said that, didn't he. But she forgot all about it. There is a steep, narrow street off Rue des Ecoles. Rue de la Montagne Ste. Geneviève. Yes, that must be the way Abélard fled when they kicked him out. His students followed their master outside the walls of the Latin Quarter. And so will I! He's no deader than Kurtzmann. Anyway, dead mentors are better than old ones.

She unlocks the door and throws her briefcase onto the bed, juggles the three apples till one falls and rolls across the rug toward the bidet. What will I find in the old neighborhood? Maybe a rebellious trace of young Abélard, before his fall from grace. Go tomorrow, girl! She tosses one of the apples too hard and it hits the ceiling and comes falling down onto the bed, its skin bruised, its pleasant aroma tantalizing her.

$\backsim v \backsim$

In the dawn-hour café, two young men lean over a book until their berets nearly touch. They argue whether words have substance, or whether they simply stand for an idea. An old argument. We sat like that ourselves, before time drifted over the face of this *quartier*. He and I—it is strange to say *I* after so long—having the old debate. Realism and nominalism. Now they call it structuralism, post-structuralism. Nothing has changed except the name, which is proof enough, you see. One side insists there's a presence behind words, a truth, and the other calls it an absence. All they really know is what I, too, believe: words leave a trace of something never finally found in words. I taste the residue, and what comes to me is a garden. And so I begin with what I see.

The row of cabbages stretches from one stone wall to the other. Born from a small black seed, now each pale green head is fully formed. Layer upon layer, tightly folded around a white heart. The knife cuts the stem, and juice spurts out like blood. The head rolls off. I trim the outer leaves, dew dripping down my sleeve, mud on the blade.

I look up from writing. The two young men have ceased their debate and set out along Rue des Ecoles for morning lecture at the Sorbonne. The girl, coming out of Chez Montreux across the street, will she go toward the Sorbonne, too? Or where something peeks out of thawing ground? It's not up to me. There's nothing for a planted seed to do but swell and burst. Patience mingles with a cautious hope as I watch a life unfolding.

Up the path from the garden, the heavy cabbage bumps against the sides

*of the basket. All this from a frail seedling with a wispy root, lowered into a hole
I dug with three fingers. Firm the dirt. Pour water around the stem. Sun, rain,
time. I push open the kitchen door.*

She's standing by her café. Monsieur Montreux watches from
inside as he polishes the already shining bar, wondering at the way she
ate today with a new kind of hunger, as if it were the first morsel, and
certainly not the finest, as if a feast of wine and meat awaited her. He
watched her finish the *chocolat* and croissant as if she might blossom
before his very eyes, but only if he looked away. He tried it, rubbing
the brass faucet to a shine, and when he did look back she was gone.
There's no telling now what she will do, looking left and right, holding
her briefcase in front of her with both hands. Finally she sets off with a
decisive turn of the heel. Montreux returns to his polishing, and I to
writing the visions behind my eyes. Vegetables carry my hope, as always,
that something remains.

*Inside the kitchen it is dark. The stone floor is cool. I put the cabbage on
the chopping block, and sharpen the cleaver. The head sits, silent and still,
on the marred wood. Yet the cabbage is not dead. It waits, furled around the
secret of earth. A secret anyone knows, who listens to cabbages.*

Naomi bucks the stream of black berets that flows against the
chill wind. She heads the other way, wind at her back, toward a thin
slant of November sun rising over the chimneypots of Mont Ste.
Geneviève. Her first few steps falter, but as she crunches over fallen
leaves where leaflets usually blow against the gated bookshops, as she
gains distance from the iron bars of the Ecole, the bowed heads, the
droning professor half-dead at his lectern, she lengthens her stride and
swings her briefcase, whistling a tuneless song. Rue de la Montagne Ste.
Geneviève rises past crumbling stucco houses with crooked shutters.
Cats in the recessed doorways. One door, propped ajar, smells deli-
ciously of broth. She pictures a woman inside, peeling carrots and
onions with strong, patient hands.

At the top of the hill, the pale sun peeks over a rooftop, lighting up the plaza inch by inch. So! She stops to catch her breath and survey the classical Panthéon from the rear. Over there, the sooty back of the Sorbonne. She looks down the hill she just climbed, at the Seine draped across the city, a blue-grey net. So! She opens her coat to cool off. This is it, the "Mont" Kurtzmann sent her here to see. Abélard must have looked down at the Ile de la Cité from here. There was no magnificent cathedral yet. The guildsmen were just laying the foundation stones of Notre Dame. Did he think the island looked like a barge pointing downriver, going nowhere once he was banished? Did he feel bitterness, seeing this lofty vision of the Latin Quarter? Or triumph?

Naomi crosses the Place du Panthéon. From a wooden bench, she enjoys the early sun spotlighting a small green-domed building. The same light fell on Abélard and his pupils, over eight hundred years ago. Arc of sun, shape of hill never change. Did they meet out here in the open? She imagines Abélard slicing the air with a pointed finger, running his palms through tousled hair. He paces, head down, thinking. When he looks up, his forehead shines. He sees the angle of argument, and now he goes in. There's no turning Pierre Abélard back once he perceives the logical pathway. There's no dissuading him, no interrupting him. He penetrates to the heart, while his students sit spellbound at his feet in their hooded robes. They know their master's quick syllogisms will never stop at the Q.E.D. He turns on his heel to pace the other way, proving the very opposite.

Never a resting place, mumbles Naomi, spellbound herself on a bench at the top of this hill centuries later. His mind slices truth in half, and each half in half again. She doesn't want his syllogisms. She just wants to know him, to cut through his brilliance and not be seduced by it. She stands up from her bench, now in the shadow of the massive Panthéon, tomb of dead poets. Long hair brushes her collar like a brown hood slipping off. She walks back into the sun, toward the building across the plaza. A brass plaque reads, "Bibliothèque Ste. Geneviève, 10h-16h," and she smiles. She has, without even trying, found the place Kurtzmann meant for her. She jiggles the latch, though it's not yet 10 o'clock. The door creaks open.

Inside, a compact rotunda with a marble floor. To the right, the rare books, locked up behind a filagree gate. To the left, the reading room. Naomi hesitates to show the attendant her pink card, wishing it were blue. "Passez, passez, Mademoiselle," he says with a smile, waving her toward the sunlit room. Surprised and relieved, she heads for the card catalogue. There's no point looking up Héloïse. She won't be listed. Naomi pulls open the first drawer and flips to "Abélard, Pierre (1079-1142). *Oeuvres.* 10 tomes." At Cornell, she could go into the stacks to browse through all ten volumes. In Paris, she'll have to know what she wants. What does she want? The *Sic et non?* No, she's sick of logic. *Theologia christiana*, condemned as heretical? Or perhaps the *Ethica?* The *Letters*, Kurtzmann says in her ear. Yes, go for the man himself, agrees Petersen with a mischievous grin. And through the man, perhaps the woman, too. Okay. The letters it is. She's read them already, but this time she's looking for something. She wants to see if Gilson is right, if there really is only one way to read them—his way. She hands a call slip to the librarian and flashes him a gleaming American smile. Bleary eyes look at the slip over the top of his glasses, and he shuffles into the stacks.

Naomi settles down at a broad, shiny table and takes out some paper. Letters to a fictional "friend" were a ruse for telling your own story. Abélard's calamitous tale was meant to console a "friend's" woes by comparison to his. But as it turned out, an actual friend received this long letter: Héloïse. And she was not consoled, but alarmed by his mental state. As he told it, he endured the castration in 1119 with "more shame than pain." He was a crass seducer who deserved the mutilation. And he claimed his intellectual arrogance far surpassed his sexual shame. After he left Héloïse, vindictive monks drove him from one monastery to another. Finally, in 1126, he took refuge in his native Brittany. He became the abbot of St. Gildas de Rhuys. But his reforming zeal turned the monks against him, and they tried to murder him. During this time of paranoia and isolation on the rocky coast of Brittany, when "every day I imagine a sword hanging over my head," he wrote the *Historia calamitatum*.

Naomi, still waiting for the putty-faced librarian, thinks of Etienne Gilson's scholarly certainty that it was a devastated Héloïse who responded to this troubled story. Gilson swears the ensuing letters are authentic. See how they're bound together in the surviving manuscripts, see how the tone of her letters implores, pleads, and finally subsides into wisdom under Abélard's firm guidance. Clearly, he insists, this is a dialogue of two distinct voices. The allusions to events, places, and shared intellectual concerns can only serve to convince one of...what? Can't there be other ways to hear these voices? But like Gilson, she admits her own reluctance to let go of the romantic duet. She's repelled by the idea that Abélard, out of his own need to console himself, would create both voices as a fiction.

The first time she read the *Letters*, at Cornell, Naomi found the linguistic wrestling compelling. The learned abbess tries out different rhetoric to fit their transformed relationship. She begins, "to her master or rather her father, husband or rather brother." She calls herself "his handmaid or rather his daughter, wife or rather sister." By the third try, she addresses her letter simply "to Abélard, Héloïse." Abélard responds to her as "his dearly beloved sister in Christ." Please! How much, really, can language hold at bay?

"Mademoiselle," a gravelly voice startles Naomi, "voilà les tomes." The sallow librarian slides the volumes across the counter.

If she's to pursue this research, it's the man she's looking for in all this language, the man locked behind his own words. Petersen, whom she supposes will direct her research now that Kurtzmann is dead, says "go for the man." But does he recognize the risk involved? The risk to his own reputation, which is green yet? He needs a graduate student who can sling unequivocal revelations about some manuscript or other. What can she possibly offer to verify the man known in this way, as a man? The only evidence is imagination and heart. She thinks of the seasoned medievalist Helen Waddell, whose historical novel, *Peter Abelard*, is called "Miss Waddell's little book." Is hers to be a "little" book, too? Naomi carries the heavy tomes to her table and pulls the chair in close. She taps her pen and stares out the window toward the Panthéon.

The librarian watches the young American's every move. She opens a dusty volume. She gathers her long brown hair into one fist behind her head, then lets it go, and adjusts her sweater. She looks at her watch and straightens the edges of her paper. She leans toward the book, breasts pressing upon her folded arms. Elle est jeune, très jeune, he concludes. Moi, I was young once, too. He inspects his veiny hands, his lavender nails, bony wrists. He gives his white cuffs a nervous tug, straightens the tie that bumps over his Adam's apple when he swallows. Elle est la première, the first to ask for the master Pierre, the first in years. Perhaps she is the one, oui? Her eyes say so, blue as the sky, that she is the one who will...Allons, I shall watch for a while, I shall wait before I offer to her the...perhaps she is not the one?

Naomi turns the musty pages. The volume begins with the *Historia*, and she finds the place where Abélard flees to his wilderness retreat and then returns to Paris with his students. He deeds the Paraclete to Héloïse, leaving the nuns to cultivate a women's community, and condemning himself as "the man who started to build and could not finish." In the *Letters*, Héloïse calls the nuns "plants which are still very tender and need watering if they are to thrive." What if, as

Gilson's opponents contend, he did write both sides of this correspondence? Could "Héloïse's" poignant plea express his own guilt at not tending the garden well? He excuses himself by claiming he trusted her "good sense, in which I have always had such confidence that I did not think anything was needed."

Nothing needed! Imagine putting the woman you love in the wilderness to fend for herself! Only the Latin law of Paris would condone that. What if, instead, he had followed the law of nature, learned the mother tongue? He could have openly married her, left Paris and lived as husband and father in Brittany, watching his child run naked in the sun. But he was a man who needed controversy, needed war. And so he planted the women in Troyes, and, by "Héloïse's" account, he left them there to wither.

"Of all the wretched women I am the most wretched, and amongst the unhappy I am unhappiest." What better way for a guilty man to heap blame upon himself than to write in his wife's voice? Abélard dubs these lines "your old perpetual complaint against God." Yet it could be the sorrowful Abélard uttering these unrepentant words to "God, whom I always accuse of the greatest cruelty in regard to this outrage...How can it be called repentance for sins...if the mind still retains the will to sin and is on fire with its old desires?"

Naomi runs her eyes down column after column, the weight of the woman's anguish finally exhausting her. Or the weight of the man's anguish, carried into text on a woman's words. Because maybe Héloïse found her own consolation? Did not wither, but flourished? And it was Abélard who got stuck with his grief? This is the very thing she wants to find out!

At four o'clock the librarian clears his throat and raps his knuckles on the counter. Oui, she is the one, not cold of mind like the French. This one has heart. Peut-être elle...will keep my secret? Perhaps I shall try. He watches the girl slide the volume over the counter. She steps back to brush the dust off her breasts, her sleeves. Oui, cette jeune fille-çà…tomorrow she will come again, non?

"A bientôt," she says, turning to go.

"Nous avons aussi des manuscrits," he murmurs.

"You have manuscripts? Oh! Well."

"Would you like to see…a manuscript, alors, next time? One I have been saving?

"Saving? It hasn't been seen?"

The man shakes his head. His sagging cheeks glimmer weirdly. She rubs her strained eyes. So much in one day. The open library, the books at last available, this strange guy offering…no, better stick to business.

"Oh. Well. Thank you. But first I have more reading to do." The librarian's face turns to ash again. "Soon," she assures him. "Yes. Thank you. I will take a look. I'm not used to being offered…but yes. Merci."

She staggers out of the library, dizzy from concentration and no lunch. She descends the Mont in the dusk, passing the narrow doorways, smelling again the rich aroma of soup, only now the smell has meat in it, and garlic and cabbage. She is suddenly hungrier than she has ever been in Paris, with three long hours to wait before the restaurants open their steamy doors. The last franc of her November stipend jingles against a chestnut in her pocket.

Hungrier still for the private voices swallowed by history. She suspects it is Abélard's anguish, Héloïse's strength she will hear, the very opposite of what the written record shows. At the bottom of the Mont, she pulls up the collar of her nut-brown London Fog. Damp river air follows her up the spiral stairs of the Hôtel Plaisant where she opens the door and sprawls across her bed, coat still on, exhausted and famished, and falls asleep.

I balance the head so it won't roll. I say a few kind words of praise. The blade of the cleaver glints. I bring it down once, with a gentle violence. The cabbage squirts, splits open. The cleaver meets up with the wooden block. The cabbage, not dead, reveals its inner folds, its smooth half-core wet with juice. I and the cabbage understand the cleaving of a heart. With a smaller knife I cut away the core. I set the kettle to boil. Even now, the cabbage is not dead.

⟨ vi ⟩

Naomi tosses in half-sleep, tangling her damp brown coat. Letters swirl on the red screen inside her eyelids, but she can't read the script. She squeezes her eyes tighter and the screen goes black. In place of letters, she sees a pair of strong hands chopping onions on a worn wooden board, thump, thump, and then the thump is footsteps on a cobbled way, and she is walking down the steep Rue de la Montagne Ste. Geneviève wearing a brown hooded robe with a rope belt. Beside her, another robed scholar walks, head down, talking with his hands. They turn into a recessed doorway, scattering cats. A woman is ladling soup into wooden bowls. Other students, sitting along both sides of the long trestle table, fall silent when they enter the room. Her companion throws back his hood, and it is Pierre Abélard. He sits at the head of the table and dunks bread into his soup. The students eat quietly, for soon he will speak. These candlelit hours with their master give them a better chance to ask their questions than in the wind at the top of the Mont.

"Quaestiones, discipuli mei!" he commands, waving his spoon. "Questions, not answers. Don't listen to what the theologians tell you. Answers are the death of thought. We live in a new time. Aristotle's logic has come to expand our understanding. What good is the human mind if it cannot reason? We may be 'dwarfs on giants' shoulders,' as our brother Bernard of Chartres claims. But thanks to their shoulders, we dwarfs can see farther than those giants. We can see the whole of Paris from up on our Mont. We can see the very walls of the old quarter, which constrain the mind of those who dwell within. And what we see will change us. We are not dumb oxen, to plough the same field over and over, responding to the master's whip. We are men! The new giants! And we must never believe without first understanding through reason. We must never accept a truth we have not derived ourselves through logic. Even God!"

He thumps the table, and an uneasy silence falls in the dim room as the disciples stop spooning their soup. The matron stands in the doorway with arms folded over her thick waist. "Yes," the master repeats, meeting every pair of dubious eyes along the length of the table and holding longest the blue gaze of the student sitting by his side, "yes, even the truth of God." He wipes out his bowl with a heel of bread.

"You know, my pupils," he continues, mouth full of bread, "that I have incurred the wrath of those who were my teachers. Their fame rests on tradition. They swallow but they don't chew, and so I say Adieu." He laughs, and wipes his mouth with one long sleeve. "You and I will shun no question. We will apply the rules of logic to any perplexity—even the problem of the Trinity—the most compelling *quaestio* of all! Why should we stop when we get to that wall? Just because the authorities say we must? They want us chained to their books, just as they chain books to the lecterns at the cathedral school. We need no books!" He thumps his fist on the table. "We will write our *own* books, and just let them try to stop us!" Thump!

A siren bleating on Rue Monge wakes Naomi to hunger pangs and skin cold as stone. She jerks her head up and rubs her eyes. Six o'clock. *He* certainly had no doubts, even about the need to question.

She starts to get up, then sits back down on the edge of the bed. The top of her head feels like a tonsure of light. She's the one with doubts. She's the one who stops at the wall every time. Thump.

She holds her breath. Thump. Something beyond her pink wall, in that other building. She gets up and curls her knuckles, about to knock, but then a chair scrapes and she backs away. If she is not safe here, alone with her notebook, alone with her thoughts, where can she hide? This faded pink wall is her protective shell. She doesn't want to know what's on the other side. It's nothing. "Don't worry your pretty little head about it," a voice soothes, the voice of pampering men who look at her nubile face, her innocent eyes, her full breasts, and fail to answer, or even hear, her questions. That would mean admitting a woman into their world on her own terms.

She wants in, but her ambition to scale their wall frightens her. What if she falls off? She hears them taunting, Can you pass our test, girl? Can you climb this high? What part of yourself will you cut off to get over the wall? Will you sacrifice your best thing? Your curious mind, your imagination? Your love? Perhaps your body will do. Hand it over. Then we'll let you in. Maybe.

Cut off. Mutilate. Castrate. She sits down at the table and switches on the lamp. She can barely hold the wobbling pen, for hunger. *At least castration handles the problem of desire! But a man can prevail even thus reduced. Abélard's castration made him more potent than a woman who never possessed what he now lacked. How ironic—a eunuch has more status than a woman! The phantom limb, by its very absence, gives him authority in the world of men.*

Naomi leans back, enveloped in the quiet lamplight, the blue of her words on the page. *Was it loss that gave rise to "conceptualism," the middle ground he came up with, between realism and nominalism? Words don't refer to real things, he said, nor to a perfect Idea. He rejected both Aristotle and Plato! And substituted a psychological approach: words correspond to mental concepts. Mentally, he still possessed the phantom limb, and could draw potency from it, though it was missing as a real thing...*

She can entertain this thought here in her safe room. But she could never defend it. "Gone But Not Forgotten: Abélard's Missing Member and the Development of Conceptualism." Uh-huh. Anyway, where's the evidence? Could she cite her own notebook—"Pensées de la Nuit"—to prove it? She stands up, pivots on her heel and flops down on the hard bed. She can't unknow what she knows. Trouble is, she can't prove it either. And men demand proof, even Kurtzmann and Petersen. IF this…THEN that. But logic demonstrates the very thing it tries to deny—ambiguity. The great big IF on which that wall is built. IF this, THEN that. But—what if NOT?

Heresy! To question logic itself! She rubs her eyes. Didn't she just dream…something about "question even God"? Something about "write our own books"? Yeah, her own book where she won't stop at the question of language, logic, the word as "God."

Of course, if she's so interested in what's missing, maybe the School of Chartres would have been a better choice for her research than the Ecole des Chartes. Only one letter difference in name— Chartres, Chartes—but a vastly different medieval world, the one Petersen studies. He would prefer her to choose not the schools of Paris, the minutiae of handwriting, the sterility of logic, but that other famous cathedral school. Twelfth-century poets like Alain de Lille, Bernard of Chartres, and Bernardus Silvestris gathered in the town of Chartres. Nature, to them, was *speculum mundi*, the mirror of the world. Study nature to learn about man.

Her choice to study Abélard, master of logic, "to whom all that is knowable is known," is a funny one, really. She reconsiders the pink wall, and softly raps on it, but the thumping has stopped. It's the unknowable she's after. So if not the Chartrian poets, why not study the mystics, someone like Bernard of Clairvaux? Bernard of the clear valley, whose ascetic monks rejected the dialectics of the Paris schools. Bernard preached knowledge through love, and the discipline of kneeling and fasting. He offered vision. And, after all, here she is living on Rue des Bernardins, where Bernard's followers once gathered. Here she is, seeking the unknown through hunger like one of his monks. Waiting for some kind of vision. On her knees, ready to believe.

A shattering crash, like a whole box of lightbulbs thrown at the other side of her wall! She stumbles to the desk, clasps her hands under the circle of lamplight to keep them still, holds her breath. Nothing.

Behind the wall, he stifles a scream at the oblong of light intersected by the iron bars of her balcony. The bars on his window are a cage. He peers between them, and sees through the stripes all the way to the lighted café at the end of the Street of Bernardines. Forget these bars! It's the black ink of words that imprisons me. And the men—oh oh oh the men with hoods—who burned my book! Bernard, she says! Love? What does she know? History calls him Saint! Just because he helped end Pope Innocent's exile in Avignon. Back in Rome, Innocent and his drunken bishops couldn't stay awake long enough to read my book. They burned the *Theologia christiana*—and I wrote it again—and that coward Bernard refused to debate me—ME, a eunuch before God! That "Saint" persuaded them to excommunicate me. They burned my words again, condemned me to perpetual silence. If only I could erase these bars!

My old friend Peter the Venerable took me in, at Cluny. Brought food to my cell. Implored the Pope to lift his judgment. They agreed to let me die a Christian. The abbess was the one to hear my confession. "Logic has made me hated by the world," I told her. "They proclaim the brilliance of my intellect but detract from the purity of my Christian faith. I do not wish to be a philosopher if it means conflicting with Paul, nor to be an Aristotle if it cuts me off from Christ"—oh oh—! Nothing can release me from my own sentences. Cut off my tongue instead! Gouge my brain! Let me out!

Naomi jumps at the sound of a window rattling open. She snaps off the lamp and creeps to the French doors. Pulling back the gauze curtain an inch, she thinks she sees a face in the dark of the next building. A desolate, dissolute face staring straight ahead as if without hope. She holds her breath. She stares. Maybe not. The reflection from a street lamp. She moves her head back and forth. Does it move? Is that a pale hand feeling along a jawbone, like a man checking to see if he needs a shave? No, probably not. She returns to her desk, flicks on the lamp.

Now her head really aches, worse than before. She puts a hand over the part in her hair, to keep her famished soul from flying out. She scrapes the chair back and digs a franc out of her pocket, ravenous now, but for some reason not afraid. Hopeful, in fact, remembering the little library, the strange librarian. Remembering that he said something about a manuscript—or was that a dream? No more knocking on all the usual locked gates, getting *non* for an answer. *Ne pas revenir! Je regrette, Mademoiselle. Pas possible. La porte est fermée.* The winding streets of the Latin Quarter have led her from one such gate to the next, until today. That whiff of broth on Mont Ste. Geneviève seemed to jar something open, a door someone forgot to lock. Now, mysteriously, a *sic* and not a *non*. A sense of direction, a Yes. What destination? Who cares. I'm off to buy a loaf. She curls her knuckles and raps hard on the pink wall, thump, thump, and waits. A moment later, thump, thump, someone raps back.

⇜ vii ⇝

The December stipend finally came. It weights the bottom of Naomi's pocket. She thrusts her hands deep inside, away from the night mist falling now as freezing rain. She pauses under the café's icicled awning and inhales the rich espresso smell as three young men push open the door. Elegant jazz and laughter beckon, not like those rowdy Goliardic taverns that once thrived in the nest of streets down by the river. The old names are gone now, The Swan, Two Swords, the Sign of Our Lady, places where medieval students from England, Germany, France, Italy, Flanders, would gather to brawl and sing drinking songs and love lyrics like those Abélard was famous for. He certainly lived in a time of contradictions! Asceticism, study, prayer, and a burst of bawdy song. They say he destroyed all copies of his love songs. Punished himself by deleting a record of his delights. Punished the future with that loss. The melodies linger in the stinging river air, she supposes, sniffing the coffee aroma that trails off the young men's coats as they pass into the mist.

She sighs, lonely, looking in the window at this milieu of modern student life. She is a spectator. But at least she has her work now, even if her landlady and the librarian LeFrère are the only ones in all of Paris who know her by name. LeFrère. How odd he is, with that face the color of eggplant flesh, that ill-fitting suit, and the way he watches her with haunted hunger. It's not like he's never seen a scholar work. One or two besides Naomi come in for a short spell, old men mostly. Only she arrives at 10 and stays till 4. He acts as if he wants to tell her something, but barely works up the nerve to stammer "Oui, Mademoiselle," running a hand over his greased-down black hair as he disappears into the stacks with her call slips. He brings her the tomes, currently the *Letters of Direction* in which Abélard sends pastoral guidance to the Abbess Héloïse and the nuns of the Paraclete. Then he smoothes his thin hair again, breathless. LeFrère handles the volumes with impoverished longing, the way the ragged man near the Métro stirs the chestnuts over his bin of fire and sells them, wrapped in newspaper cones, to passing students, never himself eating one of the rich, sweet, soft nuts, never warming his hands around a clutch of them.

"Nous avons aussi des manuscrits," LeFrère murmured that first day. He appeared desperate for her to take a look. But today, when she finally asked about the manuscripts, ready to get beyond the edited volumes and sink her paleographical teeth into something unpublished, he yanked his tie as if his Adam's apple were caught under it. He glanced at the guard by the door, and cast her a silent "non" from the pits of his olive eyes. Maybe she offended him by waiting so long to take up his offer? Anyway, she has plenty to do. Already mid-December, and she's due back in Ithaca the first of February, for Petersen's seminar. But she wants to test her skills on whatever LeFrère might be offering.

She sighs again, watching steam drip down the inside of the window with its arc of lettering, "Café des Etoiles." Students sit in two's and three's over their wine. She pinches the unaccustomed wad of francs in her pocket. Wonder how much for a glass of wine. It's that, or an éclair from across the street. It's been so long since her last pastry. Cornell's habit of sending the monthly check late shows no regard for the true staff of life! She's about to cross Rue des Ecoles to the corner pâtisserie, and an evening with her notebook back at the Hôtel Plaisant, when she notices a woman in the café window, the one she saw feeding the pigeons in the park that first day. She sits alone, twirling the stem of her wine glass as she gazes into the candle on her table. She looks up and smiles at Naomi, the smile of one who knows her own soul. Naomi ducks away from the window, embarrassed. Knows my soul, too?

The woman's ageless face invites her in, but Naomi hesitates, half under the awning and half out in the freezing rain. The woman purses her lips and bends to her writing. She pretends to move her pen, watching the girl through downcast eyelashes. Nothing blooms when watched. Avert your gaze, and wait, and hope. She must enter on her own, just as I must speak my own words. All this practice, trying out my voice as if I'm addressing her, will bear fruit. There is a story to unearth, though my vision so far only marks the place. But look. She comes, entering my story as I have entered hers, two flavors marrying over a slow flame.

Naomi pulls open the door with one hand, the other squeezing the francs inside her pocket. Cigarette smoke hovers over the well-lit bar, and a daunting sea of berets bobs all around her. She feels so frumpy with a wet scarf sticking to her damp hair, raincoat clinging to her shoulders. Perhaps she should leave. An éclair, in its frill of pink, is calling to her from across the street. She holds tighter to the francs in her pocket. Then someone touches her elbow.

"Venez, asseyez-vous avec nous." Come sit with us. Naomi hesitates, then plunges between the crowded tables in the wake of a tall young woman carrying a full carafe. The woman's friend, plain and blocky, sits on one side of the booth facing two young men. The tall woman shoves the blocky one over until their hips touch, then Naomi slides in. The table is littered with plates and tumblers, candle wax dripping into a saucer, an ashtray filled with butts. They chatter away in Parisian slang, a language Naomi has all but given up on. She hasn't said much more than "merci" in several months. She opens her mouth. Nothing comes out. They wait, the men eyeing her across the table with faint amusement. Finally, lamely, she turns to the women beside her and utters, "Vous êtes étudiantes?"

"Oui," they laugh indulgently, "à la Sorbonne. Le Collège de France, vraiment. Et toi?"

Oh, no, the dreaded *toi*, *tu*, the familiar form of address. She had dropped Conversational French to take the Dante seminar with Grappone, so the more formal *vous* is as far as she'd gotten comfortable with, if you can call her stammering comfort. She knows enough to recognize *tu* means solidarity, and they will be offended if she responds with the formal *vous*. Mauriet had called her *tu* to signal her inferiority, and expected *vous* in response. But these, her peers, four of them! What the heck is the plural familiar? She pictures the page in her grammar book, *je tu il/elle nous vous ils/elles*, then waves her hands in linguistic distress.

"Il n'y a rien à faire!" the tall woman next to her declares. "English it is!" She pats Naomi on the shoulder, and pushes the carafe and an empty tumbler toward her. The larger of the two men across from her, curly black hair and dark eyes, pours her a full glass, splashing some on the table.

"Tiens," he says, and gives the glass a little nudge.

"Okay," she says, and they all laugh, and then she remembers, "Salut!" and they raise their glasses.

"Are you a member of Hess-D-Hess?" the curly-haired man asks her, leaning his elbows on the table.

"'Hesty-hess'? Oh, SDS! Oui, uh, I mean, non." She sips her wine. "But my friends are."

"Your friends? And not you? Do you not, how do you say, support the révolution?"

She scans his handsome, wry face, and the thin, serious face of the other man, whose wire-rim glasses reflect two candles. What can she tell them, how she left Cornell fed up with the protests, the unending stream of leaflets every time you crossed the Arts Quad? How she put no stock in "the movement"—and believed if it weren't for the draft, they'd still be the silent generation? How the "radicals," the men, wanted sex, drugs, and rock 'n' roll, but nothing had changed for the women? She saw Sharon spending more and more time at off-campus apartments, running the mimeograph, making coffee, and she never came back to the dorm until morning, her eyes bloodshot and unhappy. Could she tell these earnest French students, with their black turtlenecks—no patched Army fatigues here, no long India-print skirts—that she came to Paris to get away from all that SDS stuff?

The curly man fills the awkward silence with a stream of rhetoric. "We French were in Southeast Hasia for years, you know, before les Américains, and we know hit's juste a capitalist plot to hexploit the peasants! At least they never made us go to fight there, and they wouldn't dare either, les salauds!"

Naomi recognizes this all too familiar speech, Marxist in flavor, spiced with expletives. How those SDS men love their anti-capitalist speeches! Then they call the women "uppity" for voicing their own oppression, and accuse them of distracting from the important goal of ending the draft, ending the war. Ending what oppresses the men, that is. But "free love," that's a kind of compulsory draft notice for women. Women don't go to war, but they do get pregnant, risk their lives with illegal abortions, or give up their own ambitions to raise the child. These are bodily threats and sacrifices, too! But so far, from what Sharon has told her, the women at home haven't taken on "the movement" for what it is—a power shift from old men to young men, leaving the women in their usual place: "prone," Stokely Carmichael likes to say. Was that true here, too, even after "the events of May"?

"What are French women doing in…the revolution?" Naomi cautiously asks the plain woman next to the wall. She wonders if women even use this term, "revolution." Talking to women feels doubly foreign, more complex than the plural familiar she stumbled over a few minutes ago. The woman stubs out her cigarette.

"Oh, les femmes," the curly man breaks in, raising his wine, "they are the soul of the révolution!"

The quiet man lifts his tumbler. "I'll drink to that, Alain."

The woman in the middle shoots a knowing smile at the woman by the wall, an annoyed glare at the men. "We have a group, for women only," she tells Naomi with pride. "We read, we study."

"Hélène is our leader," the wall woman says, lighting another cigarette from the candle flame. Naomi looks at this Hélène, taking in the high forehead, light brown hair that forms a graceful curve along her cheeks and down to her shoulders, intelligent green eyes.

"What are you reading?"

"Simone de Beauvoir, of course, and other…"

"…lesbians! They study lesbians," Alain asserts, smirking as he refills Naomi's tumbler.

"And what if they do?" Naomi retorts, the wine going to her tongue. "They can read what they want. Men don't own women, I hope you know!"

"And women don't own men either, finalement," the quiet man says, his glasses glinting. "Though they have a special charm they know how to work on us."

"Special charm, you call it," mocks Hélène with a beautiful pout. "You men with your libido. Blame it on us, why don't you, Louis?"

Naomi thinks of how Abélard's pupils blamed Héloïse for their teacher's distraction from dialectics. They flocked to Paris for his *Sic et non*, and then he turned to writing love lyrics to praise his lady's beauty. When the scandal broke, his students blamed it on her feminine wiles. Hélène is right. Ever since Eve, women always take the rap.

"Allons, Louis, je m'en vais," Alain says to his friend, "let's go." The two men slide out of the booth. "Au'voir, mesdames," Alain bows to the women, pulling his beret over one eye, and Louis pushes his glasses up with a finger, and they are gone.

"Alors," says Hélène, relieved. She shakes her long hair over her shoulder with ennui, traces one eyebrow with her little finger. "Et toi? What are you studying à Paris?" she asks Naomi, who moves to the other side of the booth to face the two friends.

"I'm researching Pierre Abélard." She wishes she could offer a topic worthy of their women's study group. But really, Abélard wasn't that bad, for a man. He taught women, after all, and even thought them closer to God. "I've been noticing how scholars treat Héloïse so marginally. Just because she didn't battle it out in the schools with the men, and didn't write any books."

"Just because she got pregnant!" sputters the blocky woman by the wall. "A fatal mistake, where history is concerned."

"Ah oui, c'est justement ça," sighs Hélène. "The woman, she is effaced from history without a name. We have only what the men say of her, and the fruit of her womb. Abélard was not the only one in that couple who suffered. Tous les deux, how do you say, they both were castrated!" She flashes a defiant look toward the door where the men had disappeared into the night mist.

Tous les deux, the woman writing at the next table overhears, and repeats to herself. Castrated. A body dies in the midst of its own story. But something lives. She dips a finger into the pool of wax dripping from her candle, peeling the dried pieces off her fingertip and flicking them into a white saucer with her thumbnail. And yet what name is there but bitterness for that which will not die? How can words resurrect the nexus of time and space which was, once, a life? She draws a swirl in the hot wax. She picks up her pen, shrugs her shoulders, and begins where she can.

Horseradish root you cannot kill, no matter how many times you dig it up or even burn it. A root hair, a peel of skin, a flake of ash survives. My shovel wrenches a crooked root from the thawing ground. The bare branches above me will bend with the weight of pears by autumn. And I will remember what this work makes me forget. My harvest of bitterness will wait for me here, just where I buried it centuries ago, it seems.

"Oh, Hélène, there you go again with your 'castration.' You see," the dark-haired woman interprets for Naomi, "that's what she calls women's silence, their loss of tongue. She thinks men silence women by blaming us for their anxiety. They act as if the whole culture hangs between their legs! Ah, bpf! We don't even know our little American's name and already we speak of castration! Moi, I am Marie."

"Naomi. Naomi Weiss."

"Weiss? And you come from…"

"Upstate New York. Cornell University. I am, I was, an auditor at the Ecole des Chartes."

"Mon dieu, not the Ecole!" exclaims Marie. "You study with Mauriet?"

"Yes. That's why I…"

"He hates Americans," adds Hélène.

"No kidding!" snorts Naomi.

"And he hates Jews. 'Weiss' is Jewish, non?" Marie asks.

"Yes. Yes, it is. But how do you know he hates Americans…and Jews?"

"That old man, he was a Nazi sympathizer, don't you know? My parents, during the war, they…" Marie gulps her wine. "They were killed, you see. For the Résistance. They were trying to save children by hiding them at the convent in Argenteuil, just north of Paris, where I come from. Mauriet, all he cared about was his little arrangement with the Nazis."

"What arrangement?"

"They gave him the manuscripts they found when they sacked convents and monasteries in all France. He was an informer, Naomi! I hope he got a good manuscript from betraying my parents, is all I say." Marie's lips coil as she swallows the rest of her wine.

"My God. I'm so sorry." Naomi shakes her head. "What a paleographer won't do for a bit of parchment." She swirls her wine and watches it glow in the candlelight.

"Oui," says Hélène, "they lust for it as if it were flesh. They did make parchment out of Jew flesh, of course you must know."

Naomi shivers and pushes her cold hands up under her sleeves. She can almost feel, in the way her fingers glide over her skin how, yes, how animal a manuscript is, covered with words instead of hair, how brittle it gets, like dead skin, if not cared for in a proper archive. And how the pores fill up with dust, unreadable to a passing finger.

She looks into Marie's brown eyes behind thick glasses. "And you...?"

"Moi, I was hidden in the convent, too. And survived. Obviously."

Naomi squirms. She came here to escape. What a joke. Escape her suburban American Jewish upbringing. She had relatives in Europe who disappeared, and an uncle who fled. But no one wanted to talk about what happened in the war. She really didn't know. "That was before you were born," her parents would say. "Things are different now." As if they could keep her unmarred by fear as long as no one raised the specter of prejudice. Even the rabbi only talked about Israel. The kids gave money to buy trees. No one said why Israel was such a big deal. Why being Jewish was anything but a demand, a limit to her teen-age life. Bland, empty, their assimilated life reflected her parents' caution. She wanted to be free.

She practically ran off to Cornell, to study languages, poetry, history. Not her own history, which she did not know, or even want to know. Her professors acted as if no one but Christians lived in the Middle Ages. The gorgeous cathedrals. The glorious crusades against the infidel, giving rise to epic poetry. Just by chance she read about the expulsion of Jews from Spain and England, but that had nothing to do with her. A footnote in her philosophy text gave a passing nod to the blossoming of Jewish mysticism. Arabic mathematics crossed the Mediterranean to enrich the Catholic world. Why would Naomi not want to study Latin poetry, Gothic architecture, sacred music, monasticism—just because the rabbi, under pressure from her parents, tried to talk her out of that choice? Just because they warned her she'd be on her own?

She wanted to escape. The decades of her life held no appeal. The turbulent '60s, the quiet '50s, the patriotic late '40s when she was born to live as an all-American girl in spite of Jewish roots. Her Christian choices meant to bury those roots even deeper. But maybe you can't do that. Maybe you have to dig them up before choosing to throw them out. You have to know your own history. There is no escape.

"I am so sorry," Naomi says to Marie. "About your parents. That's terrible."

"The past is over. Il n'y a rien à faire. Can't be helped."

No, thinks the woman, writing, overhearing them. The past is never over, told or untold. Traces remain. Clues lead you back. And you must go back, if you are ever to learn anything worth teaching. She leans into her pen.

Horseradish keeps insects from the pear tree, but even a stone wall cannot stop it from invading the carrot patch. I've tried to dig it up for good, for my own good, this bitter root that makes me weep. My spade can do nothing against this fiercely rooted thing.

"So." The silence is awkward, and Naomi doesn't want to think about the Jewish thing. "You're from Argenteuil? That's where Héloïse was raised. And where Abélard hid her after their marriage."

"C'est ça. The nuns raised me, too. We ate our meals in the same refectory…bpf, but of course you know this story!"

Hélène snickers into her glass. "Even the nuns could not suppress such a story!"

Marie smiles with one side of her mouth up, the other down.

"Non, we all knew. In fact we even knew the very corner, and we always fought to sit in that one!"

Oh, yes, everyone knows the story, recounted in the *Letters*. Abélard came to visit his hidden bride. Right there, on the stone floor of the refectory, swallowing their sighs and moans so the nuns wouldn't hear, they lifted the robes of their mock celibacy and entered into the joy that should legally have been theirs as husband and wife. Later, the nuns and girls would eat their soup while the abbess preached from a lectern only a few feet from stones warmed by the lovers. Héloïse kept her head down to disguise the roses in her cheeks, the tears in her eyes.

"Oh, well," giggles Naomi, "a little sex never hurt anything!"

"Au contraire, Naomi," Hélène's eyes flare green in the candlelight, "sex changes everything, for a woman! Sex with a man is what buries her deep in the ground, what destroys her political power, enfin."

"Sex is...political?" stammers Naomi.

"Bien sûr, my little one. This can hardly be news to you, in your American women's movement!"

"I, um, haven't paid much attention. Or, that is, I wondered why the women..."

"Well, it will take we two Frenchwomen to teach you then!" asserts Marie with a chop of her square chin. "Heterosexual sex, you see, is the most political act there is."

"Help!" Naomi covers her ears. "You're robbing me of my innocence!"

"Non, ma chérie. We are saving you from your innocence. Listen!" Hélène puts her hand over Naomi's on the table. "In the act of sex, the woman is the submissive lower class, the man is the imperialist. She is the resource, he the conqueror. She is the root of his power. Source of his life! And worse, she agrees to it, this oppression, because of course she feels pleasure. C'est une situation impossible!" She pats Naomi's hand.

"Wow." Naomi picks up her glass and rolls it between her palms. The swirling wine glints red across the woman at the little table.

"'Wow,'" mimics the sardonic Marie, and the woman next to them turns her face, as one who is just awakening from a doze will turn toward a sound she's been dreaming. "Nothing is simple, you know, Naomi," declares Marie, "least of all, l'amour."

"I thought you French invented the very word, love."

"Oui, we know what it means, to love," says Hélène. "But love is not a word only. Love is a body that risks everything. Just look at your Abélard and Héloïse!"

The writing woman jerks her head away from the three young women, a flush rising under her beret.

"Do you think they knew the risks, at first?" asks Naomi. "Or was it just, kind of like food? They were hungry, they took, they ate."

"He took. She gave. The apple story all over." Hélène flares green again.

"He wants. She provides. Is hunger to blame? Or is she?" asks Marie.

"There is a lesson here. Listen, Naomi: Sex. Is. Political. The consequences go way beyond nature." Hélène picks a wad of warm wax off the candleholder, forms it into a cube with her fingers, and passes it across to Naomi. "Got it?"

And so I take what I can wrest from the darkness, spring after spring. I carry it in, to scrub and scrape as fumes fill the kitchen with a bitterness that holds firm in the earth, season after season, and won't let go for all my weeping.

Naomi studies the cube on her palm. "I'm starved. Do they have anything to eat here? Or is eating a dangerous political act, too!"

Hélène laughs and takes the wax from Naomi's hand like an indulgent teacher releasing her restless pupil. "Oui, par là, go, take what you want."

The woman puts down her pen and watches. Naomi walks shyly through the smoky crowd. She brushes the edges of tables with her hips, and does not meet the eyes raised in greeting and curiosity, the men's eyes searching for some life in the night. She is chaste and lovely and round. Her hair, grown longer now, softly frames her breasts. Hair, sweater, skirt, all shades of brown, with a pink knee peeking over the top of brown boots. See how she is changing, as a ripening yellow apple will change to gold adorned with a blushing cheek. Everything changes, first by falling toward the center and then away. No ripeness stays. The blushing cheek signals a beginning, the fall from the tree, the contact with earth, the process of decay, which is another beginning.

Naomi reaches for a Napoléon, delicately decadent in its frill of paper, flaky layers with custard in between, topped by a white glaze with jagged chocolate lines. She puts it on a plate. The woman gets up from the little table, clearing her throat to speak for the first time in ages. She makes her way toward the pastries, toward the girl at last.

"Good choice," she confirms. Naomi turns, startled, holding her Napoléon. "I like these, moi." She reaches for a flaky pastry shaped like a butterfly and covered with a sticky glaze. "Oreilles."

"'Hurray'?" the girl repeats.

"Oreilles. Ears. I like them."

The girl smiles nervously. She studies the woman's eyes, astounding in their intensity, a deep blue-green, nearly turquoise or jade. She finds it hard to look away from these eyes that seem a concordance to the history of time itself. Finally she looks down to her plate, examining the custardy Napoléon. Then she looks up, trying to speak.

"Vous écrivez?" she asks feebly, then tries again in English just in case. "You write?"

The woman nods, a single emphatic nod. "Toi?" she asks in return.

"I don't know. I mean, I think so, I, um…I'm a student."

"Then you do."

She smiles brilliantly at Naomi, and turns toward the table holding her plate up high before her like a holy monstrance. Naomi follows, bearing the luscious Napoléon and three forks. They both sit down again, the woman to the serene contemplation of her candle, and Naomi to the excitement of new friends in the night. She feels suddenly drunk, flushed, enormously young, like a corked bottle waiting in the dark for time to put her sugars to the best possible use.

second
folio

viii

Naomi sleeps till sunlight bathes the ice-coated city. She skips her morning croissant. Instead of going right to the Bibliothèque, she follows the path of ice from last night's freezing rain as it melts off the slate rooftop and iron balconies of the Hôtel Plaisant and flows down narrow streets to the Seine. At the quai, she wanders among the stalls of art dealers and *bouquinistes*, sniffing the yellowed pages of old books as if they were food. Ice slips from bare branches high overhead and tinkles festively to the cobbled street. Across the river, Notre Dame Cathedral gleams like flesh in the morning sun.

The flesh of Our Lady. Virgin and mother. Maybe Hélène is right about sex. Maybe it is...p...something with a p...a parable? Was that what she said? For men to worship a woman, she has to be a virgin, untouched by what they hate about themselves. And there she is, Notre Dame floating on a green velvet pedestal in the middle of the river, yet moored to the banks by bridges so men can reach her. The scholars of the Middle Ages crossed the Petit Pont from the Latin Quarter to approach the front of the cathedral, the imposing west façade draped in morning shadow. Two flat towers, a Yes and a No, implacable as the Law of Dialectics they studied. Gnawed by hunger, shivering under patched robes, they were made small by the Biblical figures carved in the timpanum over three huge portals.

Naomi is not a robed scholar but a raincoated one, a knee-socked one. She prefers the Pont de l'Archevêque, which crosses the river behind the cathedral. She sits on a bench at the cathedral's east end:

rounded apse tied down by flying buttresses, the single lacy wrought-iron spire reaching for the blue sky. Grotesque gargoyles spit melted ice from their wretching tongues. The rose window is black in the sunlight, its stone tracery white as bleached bone.

She is hungry, too, without her usual croissant, and chilly despite the December sun glaring off the massive structure. What was it her new friends had said? Sex is...polemical? paradoxical? Political! Yes. That was it. Nothing she's ever considered before. She's interested in sex, of course, how it infiltrates everything without being addressed. But not now. She can't afford sex. Not if she wants to be a scholar, a professor. Is that what makes it political? The fact that she has to choose—scholar or sexual being—like Abélard's vow of celibacy? Damn, Bart Petersen's handsome face would spring to mind at the very thought of celibacy! If only he were safely unattractive. He's the only one who takes her seriously, and she needs someone like that who loves her mind. She can't afford sex, and most especially not with him. A married man, and her teacher. No. Definitely not. "Galeotto fu il libro," remember? "A Galahad was the book" that seduced Paolo and Francesca, for which Dante put them in hell. And Abélard and Héloïse had their Ovid, don't forget. They're in a kind of hell, too, history's fixed circle.

The fifteenth-century poet François Villon wondered, "Où est la très sage Hellois, pour qui fut chastré et puis moyne Pierre Esbaillart à Saint Denis?...Où sont les neiges d'antan? Where is the very wise Héloïse, for whom Pierre Abélard was chastized/castrated...and where are the snows of yesteryear?" Naomi's sure the lovers have not melted away, but slip in and out of doorways along the ancient streets, Abélard to meet with students, Héloïse to do her Uncle Fulbert's bidding, carrying messages, or bottles of wine and baskets of vegetables for her guardian's supper. Héloïse returns to the tall house on Rue des Marmousets, her room on the third floor with its books, its bed. Fulbert's scholarly boarder had the fourth floor, the young Pierre of Le

Pallet, a short Breton with broad shoulders and aristocratic manners, a firebrand in the schools. In lieu of rent, he became Héloïse's tutor. Yes, Naomi old girl, don't forget how the book was their Galahad, too. No matter where they are now, the books still live that did them in. Sex is political. Books are political. Therefore books are sex? That will have to do, for now.

Naomi gets up from her bench to walk around to the front, facing the Préfecture de Police across the plaza. What a stroke of city planning genius to house the heavenly and earthly law together on an island! She looks up at the balanced square towers, and passes through the center portal like a speck of dust drawn by a draft into the vaulted interior. Light descends from tiers of stained-glass windows, the colored rays merging to white shafts that swarm with incense smoke.

Naomi can barely see the living people in dark coats who pray in the nave on folding chairs. She can only see stained-glass people in every arched window, stone people in every carved capital along the aisle. She leans against a pier and strains to read the images, but she is more accustomed to reading close-up, magnifying glass in hand. Abandon the desire for detail, the windows seem to say. Give up analysis. Forget about proof. These stories are not for you. This everlasting intricacy is a gift to God. Become a dust mote, a particle of light, the spice of incense rising. Naomi presses her spine into the stone column and squeezes her eyes shut. Is this a hangover? She should have stopped for a croissant.

The warm smell of candle wax wafts past on a cold draft. She opens her eyes and rubs her chilly hands together. The candlelit alcoves flicker with Mary's presence, the Lady who inspired this masculine structure. It's odd how these places of comfort are not central but pushed off to the side. The warmth of a living woman's womb is not marginal but essential to all this immensity, don't they get it? The fruit of her womb started all of this Christianity!

Not that Mary chose the role. Who would choose to be the *mater dolorosa*, the martyred mother? She did the hardest thing. She bore the son, only to see him go about "his father's business," leaving her bereft. The cathedral spells out, in stone, two answers to a mother's pain: find comfort in the low-ceilinged chapels that perpetuate, candle to candle, earthly weeping; or step out into the high aisle, transcend, let the tall columns bear the weight. Let the Church stand triumphant. Follow Me. I am the Law. I am the Lord.

But what about the Lady, namesake of this place? "Stabat Mater." The mother stood there. She did not follow. She stayed put. Enclosed, as Hélène said last night, in this structure called "patriarchy," a new word for Naomi. Encased at the core of the structure, its source and its sacrifice. Marie called Mary the zero that holds open an empty center. Mother of the word-made-flesh, she has no words. She seeks comfort in his word. Which doesn't mention her. Except to call her blessed.

Is blessing enough to pay for pain? Naomi steps into a chapel and warms her hands over a bank of candles. Héloïse didn't think so. "Cease praising me, I beg you, lest you acquire the base stigma of being a flatterer or the charge of telling lies." My pain is real, she kept repeating in her letters, my holiness a pretext. I am a hypocrite—she used that word—stuck here under a nun's habit, childless, alone on this hard pallet without another body for comfort. Naomi shivers, and pulls her raincoat closer around her. Even the "very wise Héloïse," flesh and blood and…and mind, darn it, had no choice how to put herself to best use. What is the best use of a learned woman? She's caught in a structure of stone, of dust, her flesh like a parchment peeled from her body and covered with someone else's language, locked away in a vault—

—of course, think of him, too. Pierre. A man, yet cut off from that structure, unmanned by men—

—but still, what is a woman's own use, outside that structure? Naomi walks out from the low chapel and cranes her neck at the crossed rib vaults. To teach. Other women. That is the highest use.

Hélène spoke last night about her parents' farm near Chartres, and how they promised her the barn and some land to start a school for women. "She's a real visionary, cette femme-ci," Marie had said, admiring her beautiful friend. "Have you been to Chartres yet, Naomi?" she'd asked.

"No, but my teacher—no, not Mauriet, don't worry!—a young one, back at Cornell—yes, a man!—his field is the twelfth-century School of Chartres—"

"His 'field'!" snorted Marie, amused by how the English idiom perfectly described the School where nature was the source of knowledge. "If only your Abélard could have ploughed that field—he would have saved himself from the sterile maze of dialectic!" she laughed.

"Oui, la campagne, she is a good influence," affirmed Hélène. "Paris breeds argument. Too many buildings, too many men—"

"Too much sewage floating in the Seine," Naomi rhymed, chuckling at how the history books never mention the stink those scholars had to cross over on their way to the Cathedral School. The denied stink of their denied bodies!

"Hélène's school will borrow the name of your Héloïse's convent, you see. The new Paraclete. We French women find our models, even when they live in servitude as nuns! Hélène will start a 'place of holy comfort' in Chartres for women to come, study, make a life on the land. Myself not among them."

"Marie, why not? I'd like to live in the country myself someday. If I could think of what to do once I got there. All I can picture is baking bread and staring at trees."

"Moi, I am a city person. I don't like my hands in soil. Give me newspapers and cafés and the sound of sirens. Paris will be my political arena."

"Will your school be…political, Hélène?"

"Naomi, I'm trying to tell you, everything is political! Because everything is either with or against the structure. And it's a structure that does not have your signature upon it, you see. Do you think you chose how to live?"

"Well, sure. I could have finished school by now. I could be out earning a living, or married! Instead I chose to pursue…"

"Or did they choose you? Do you suppose, if you told the truth as you see it, or even if you questioned theirs, they would fund you? Naomi, you either live their way, or you start a revolution! Even if you bake bread and stare at trees—that's a revolution, ma petite Américaine, especially if you do it in a community shared with women, without men!"

"But the convent tradition has always put women together in communities. What's so revolutionary?"

"Naomi, think about it," interjected Marie. "Nuns serve men—even if they don't sleep with them."

"True," she had to admit. "And nuns are supervised by men. Héloïse always conferred with Abélard about her management of the Paraclete. She revised the Benedictine Rule to suit women, but she had to start from a male directive. Actually, she believed women were morally weak."

"Oui, and where do you suppose she got that idea?" teased Hélène.

"Not from Abélard. He thought women were stronger. He always pointed out how much Jesus relied on women."

"Bpf! Don't listen to that horse shit," said Marie.

"Hey, what ever happened to the old Paraclete, anyway? Is there still a convent there in Troyes?"

"Non," said Marie, shaking her head as she contemplated what remained of their candle. The hour grew late. Even the woman with the jade-green eyes had pulled down her beret and walked off into the icy night. "Non. The convent was sold at the time of the French Révolution, ma chérie, and the buildings demolished. All except for the abbess' residence, where Héloïse lived. But the Nazis destroyed the last of it, after so many centuries. It became a great mother-house under your Héloïse, you know. With many sister-houses throughout France. She was a leader of women. But then the nuns—her spiritual grand-daughters—were caught hiding Jews. The Nazis put them all to death, nuns and Jews alike."

"Nuns and Jews are alike," commented Hélène, "outside the out-side, on the margins of marginality in this Christian, male structure."

"Eh bien, they're both excluded from the center. But separated by a skin," Marie corrected, "that is to say, nuns on the inside of the outside, being Christian at least. They both serve the needs of the struc-ture, though. Someone's got to live on the margins to maintain a center. It's a simple matter of physics, of geometry!"

Naomi looked from one to the other, not understanding all this talk about structure, skin, center. Geometry? People just live where they live. They do what they do. Don't they?

"So what happened to the buildings and everything?"

"All burned, Naomi. The chapterhouse, the gardens and orchards, tous finis," Hélène said, "and the library," the word a glancing blow to Marie, "the…the manuscripts, all destroyed."

"Or ransomed. Like kidnapped children," added Marie. They sat looking at each other over the low candle.

"So," Naomi finally said, "your community in Chartres will be a new Paraclete?"

"Oui, but this time we'll live by our own book and not the Father's Law, as your poor Héloïse did. We will bind ourselves to each other and the land. Our Paraclete will be a refuge for women who are isolated from each other within the lives of men."

Remembering this late-night conversation as if in a dream, Naomi, dizzy with hunger, stares up at the sun now piercing the heart of the rose window. As my poor Héloïse was pierced. "My" Héloïse? And what about "my" Pierre? I came here to study him, didn't I? He was a man, but wasn't he isolated, too? His first step "outside" this structure Hélène keeps talking about was to give up his rights as eldest son, to break the rule of primogeniture. Then to exclude himself from the comforts of faith to live by logic instead. Then to suffer the censure of faculty who chased him from Paris, and the dictates of celibacy whether kept or broken. Secrecy, punishment, treachery, even a Papal decree of heresy. How much farther "outside" can you get than excommunication?

She imagines Abélard locked in a monastery, condemned to silence, the parchment before him tracked with his ink. He had writing, but no audience except history. Which is also a kind of structure. Her head spins. Abélard's grizzled face shimmers behind the stained glass. Yes, he seems to say, and No. It's all structure, inside or out. It's all circumference, there is no center. She lowers her gaze from the glaring rose window and covers her eyes. I should have had breakfast. Ugh, that incense. Let me out of here.

Sliding her hand down over her mouth and nose, she rushes toward the three huge doors, the pool of sunlight and fresh air that fills the Parvis, the bridge to the Left Bank, and her life there, where the Bibliothèque on the Mont is already open and LeFrère is wondering where she is. She's eager to begin what feels like a new chapter of her project, now that she knows these two women who listen and talk back, and not just dead mentors who give advice and then disappear, or some half-dead librarian. She hurries across the Petit Pont. That older woman in the café had assured her, "Then you do write." Yes, yes, I do. But eating comes first. Let's keep our priorities straight! She ducks into the first boulangerie on the other side of the bridge and buys a crusty baguette to eat on her walk up the Mont.

"Et voilà, Mademoiselle." Monsieur LeFrère sets a volume of Abélard's mature work, *Ethica: scito te ipsum (Know Thyself)*, before Naomi as if it were an elegant dinner on a white plate, as if he knew a magnificent pastry awaited his customer, later, after she pats her satisfied lips with a linen napkin. He never removes his dust-brown eyes from her as she polishes a magnifying glass with her scarf. He admires the delicate rose clinging to her cheeks from the chilly winter sun outside, and the curled ends of her wavy brown hair. He lifts her raincoat off the chair, and hangs it carefully on a coat-tree in the corner of the reading room.

Naomi pushes her hair behind her right ear with a finger, then pretends to look for the place in the *Ethica* as she watches LeFrère from the corner of her eye. Should she try again for the manuscripts? He acted so strange yesterday when she asked, like something dead was walled up behind his eyes. She looks at his head tilted forward obsequiously, leaving a gap around the stiff white collar that encircles his scrawny neck. She notes his dark brown suit sagging in the rear, the jacket too short, the pants too long, the middle buttonhole frayed and mended. He bows slightly, bringing his liver-spotted hands together as if in prayer, then clasps them at his waist to hide the buttonhole.

"Est-ce que vous voudriez autre chose, Mademoiselle?" He brings the heels of his worn black shoes together and awaits his customer's command, for anything, the finest wine in the cellar, a ripe pear, some chocolates peut-être, whatever she wants.

"Non, merci." She picks up her new fountain pen and tries to ignore him standing there. His belt, at her eye level, is on the tightest notch, with the leather tongue sticking out. He looks as though he hasn't eaten for centuries. Or if he did eat, it would be mashed eggplant to match the color of his face, his hair the color of eggplant skin, the stubble of his beard like the spikes on an eggplant stem. Mon petit aubergine, she wants to croon, pitying him.

"Uh, oui, there is something," she says to her eggplant. "Les manuscrits? You have manuscripts, non?"

"Oui, Mademoiselle." LeFrère casts a glance around the room, then reaches with a trembling hand to assist her out of her chair. His skin, cold as stone, comes alive as it grazes the ink-stained middle finger of her right hand. "Il y en a par ici," he whispers, and leads her through the empty reading room out into the foyer. He assesses the guard pacing back and forth on the marble floor, his footsteps echoing in the small rotunda. He will not notice anything.

But what if she is not the one? LeFrère stops, turns on his heel, and looks right into Naomi's eyes. She gazes back, unblinking. Elle est la première, the first to ask, and her eyes, oui, her eyes say she is the one who will. French eyes, they know too much, but her eyes, they tell me she is of the heart, cette jeune fille, a heart come a long way to return. Alors donc, I shall try her.

"Vous avez une carte d'étudiant?" he asks, testing her one more time to be sure. He sees a nervous look in her eyes as she swings her hair over one shoulder and turns back to get her card. I must be careful. I mustn't frighten her.

"Peu importe," he calls, beckoning with a wave, and she slips a pink card back into her briefcase pocket. "Venez avec moi." Her blushing face fills his eyes as she walks toward him, pulling her brown sweater down over her hips. Oui, she can be trusted, celle-ci.

She follows him into the rotunda and across the marble hallway to the rare books area, caged in with an ornate wrought-iron gate. An ancient key unlocks the creaky latch. He pulls the chain on a hanging lightbulb. The room is in disarray, with manuscripts piled everywhere. Some are just sheaves tied together, some pressed between cardboard, some huge folios lying on their side. At the back are boxes of uncatalogued material. Naomi's eyes widen at the sight of a scholar's treasure trove, as yet undiscovered, or why else had she never heard of a Ste. Geneviève collection? Surely Kurtzmann would have mentioned it. Or did he? "My dear you simply must go to Paris and see Mont Ste. Geneviève, where he taught." The site of Abélard's school, that was the reason he sent her here. He said nothing about a library. This building couldn't be the twelfth-century school. The architecture is pure neo-classical. A miniature panthéon. Abélard's school, if there were a building at all, would have been rough stone, one room, thatched roof, no dome.

LeFrère leads her around to the back range of shelves. He reaches up for a slim, unbound folio on the top shelf. Fine particles of decay cascade down on them as he lowers the manuscript and caresses its cardboard cover. Dust sticks to his shiny hair, and to the shoulderpads under which he appears to have no shoulders, and to his long, lavender fingers. Dust coats Naomi's hair, and her breasts, and she brushes it off her sweater, embarrassed. But he keeps his eyes down as he turns toward the gate, and she follows him out and waits while he locks up again and hangs the key from his belt. They cross the marble hall in silence. He brings the volume to her seat.

"Voilà," he says with the satisfaction of a pastry chef placing his triumph before a favored patron. He bows, and stands beside her chair as she unties the string that holds the folio together. He takes a pair of glasses out, slips them on his narrow, crooked nose, and leans over her shoulder.

"Très bien, alors," Naomi looks up at him, waiting for him to leave her alone with this treasure, her first real manuscript at last, and all the skills that Kurtzmann bequeathed upon her, including his faith in her.

"Ah oui, bon, ben, Mademoiselle, excusez-moi." He walks too quickly to his desk, looking back at her once with something akin to hunger, or awe, mixed with a little fear.

She will believe it, non? Or will she dismiss it, as that…other scholar…so many years ago? Non. She is the one who will hear at last our suffering teacher. Too long he has been buried dans la cave silencieuse de l'histoire. Celle-là, she is warm, she will give him life. Her schooling has only tempered, not destroyed, her trust. I see it in the eyes. Celle-là, she is the one we've been waiting for.

He commences to whistle to himself, thin lips puckered, hollow cheeks moving to a rhythm only he can hear. He can relax now, and wait, for she has stopped watching him. The peculiar manuscript, so real under her palms, her fingertips, absorbs her attention. It's *sui generis* all right, she notes, one of a kind. Not bound with other items, as was the usual practice. She glances up at LeFrère and he seems to suppress a smile, if an eggplant can smile. How long has it been since anyone requested this manuscript, if ever, or any other from that jumbled cage? Of course she knows of the three manuscript copies of the *Letters* at the Bibliothèque Nationale. And yet, it would make sense for Abélard's writings to be here. Abélard himself was once here on this hill. Could the manuscript indeed be his? Remember to doubt, Naomi. A doubter looks for all the evidence. This could be anything. A fake, a bad copy, a remnant of some nineteenth-century monastic collection, who knows. It could be something LeFrère cooked up. Why else would he give it to her without even checking her identification, an American, an unknown scholar, a girl really.

She turns a quizzical look toward the librarian again. He stops his breathy whistling. Open, open it, he gestures. Most librarians protect their manuscripts like guard dogs, wanting to keep them from the salt of human fingerprints, the chance scholarly sneeze or careless ink blot, the covetous knife that might slice a page out. But this one, he offers the manuscript as if it were a gift, or something he wants to get rid of. Weird. What does he want with her? Is she just a tool in some scheme to raise the prestige of his little library? She shakes her head and lays open the brittle folio along its center crease, where the three small leaves folded in half are stitched together with a gut thread.

The handwriting is certainly a twelfth-century hand, or a very good copy. Look at the simple abbreviations that conform to the minuscule used in the Paris schools. The straight downstrokes of the m's and n's, the diagonal hairlines to dot the i's. No curlicues obscure the letters, none of the Gothic diamond-shaped o's or elaborate capitals. This was before the noble Italian style streamed into France on the parchments of traveling scholars. Then the spare legibility was flooded with Mediterranean curves, pregnant a's, complicated and inconsistent abbreviations. No influence here of the curial scripts from the Papal scriptorium either, which strove for the look of authority not simplicity. Yes, this could very well be an autograph manuscript, straight from the hand of its author, whoever that might be. Let's have a look at the salutation.

Naomi turns back the leaves, written *recto* and *verso* in a brownish ink that was probaby once black, on lightly scored guide lines, until she arrives at the first page. She jots "folio 1-r" in her notebook. The beginning is a good place to look for evidence of authorship and provenance, and—she sees Roman numerals in the first line—a date. Sometimes a title, or a salutation if it's a letter.

"Anno mcxxxvii." In the year 1137? Naomi's heart quickens. This would be about five years after Abélard wrote the *Historia calamitatum*, eighteen years after his separation from Héloïse. After he'd spent five years at his refuge, and then abandoned that place. After he'd been an abbot in Brittany, where he feared for his life. After he gave the Paraclete over to Héloïse and the Sisters of Argenteuil. He'd returned to teach here again, at this school on Ste. Geneviève. But wait…are there three x's or only two? Is this 1137, or 27? Naomi picks up her magnifying glass. Three x's: 1137 then. Okay. He's back here on the Mont. Maybe this is one of those lost works, or a hidden version of *Sic et non* which the bishops warned him to disown after they burned his books the first time. Maybe, could these be the popular love lyrics he's said to have destroyed after his castration? Maybe he stashed them here, maybe this library is built on the old cellar of Ste. Geneviève? Whoa, Naomi, you're getting ahead of yourself, girl. Just slow down and read. She runs her finger over the first line of text, feeling the parchment glowing like skin under the ink and dust.

"…in monte sancto geneveso…" Here. Whoever wrote it, wrote it here, in 1137. Naomi peers through her magnifying glass at the strokes well-seated on the guide lines, only the p's dropping below the line. There is no skimming, when it comes to these old scripts. No speed-reading. Word by word, line by line she will have to transcribe this into her notebook and translate the Latin, attempting to bring together the "then" with the "now," 1137 to 1969. The "here" they share in common: writer and reader both sitting on Mont Ste. Geneviève. An occasional word stands out as Naomi moves her eye quickly over folio 1-r, the right side of the first page. She catches "ethica" and a few lines down "gratia." Already she begins to formulate a context. She can't help herself. Eyes are one thing, mind and knowledge another. Even as she tries to stick to transcription, she finds herself unable simply to observe. These words evoke the lifelong dialogue between Abélard and Héloïse, carried on in their later letters, about the "ethics of intention." They write of "love freely chosen" (gratia), and seek to atone for their life choices by asking what God really judges. They conclude that God judges not what one does (deeds), but the mind with which one does it (intention). This concept provided Abélard with a justification for his mistakes. He could excuse his lust because he truly loved God, as the rest of his life proved. Héloïse used it for self-condemnation. She committed herself to the religious life for the love of Abélard and not God. She wrote, over and over, that her intention to love only Abélard negated the outward piety of her deeds.

Naomi opens the heavy volume LeFrère brought her before they went and got the manuscript. The *Ethica*, written around this same time, in the late 1130's. She's always admired how, without talking about himself, Abélard manages to explain away the sinfulness of his choices, especially what he calls his "lust." Naomi runs her finger down the columns. "There are people," yes, here's the place, "who are wholly ashamed to be drawn into consent to lust...and are forced out of the weakness of the flesh to want what they by no means want to want."

Wanting what you don't want to want. Only a philosopher could come up with that one. Look, here: "For example, if someone compels a religious man who is bound in chains to lie between women and if he is brought to pleasure, not by his own consent, but by the softness of the bed and through the contact of the women beside him, who may presume to call this pleasure a fault, made necessary by nature?"

Smacks of group sex to her, with chains no less! But, hey, who can blame the guy if his imagination takes him into soft beds? Here's a man whose celibacy was forced upon him by mutilation. No wonder he's worried about intention more than deed. He couldn't do the deed if he wanted to. But he'd better not even want to, because the wanting to is what counts in God's eye.

Naomi closes the *Ethica*, curious to find if the manuscript is perhaps an early version of it. She turns to the last folio and finds it almost completely illegible, so damaged by exposure to moisture and dirt. Where was this manuscript retrieved from? Several large worm holes obscure the concluding passage, and she can discern no signature, even with a 2.5-power magnifying glass. The worm holes go all the way through, mercifully landing in margins on the preceding pages, so she knows the three folios came down from 1137 folded together.

Somewhere very moist, she concludes, sniffing the mildewy parchment. And it was resting on this unprotected back page, since this one bears the most severe damage. Indeed, it is nearly destroyed. Was that purposeful, to destroy the conclusion, the signature? But why would a valuable commodity like parchment be left to rot? More commonly an unwanted manuscript would be rubbed out with pumice, the parchment used again. Kurtzmann taught her to recognize evidence of this process, where the original text would still show up under the imposed one, though faintly: a palimpsest, it was called.

She turns the six leaves back to the beginning. "Anno mcxxxvii." That xxx still looks a little like xx, perhaps a haplographic error, where the scribe failed to complete the correct number of repetitions. Abélard would be at St. Gildas in Brittany in 1127, and Héloïse outside Paris at Argenteuil, not at the Paraclete until 1129. That would make a difference. Naomi rubs her forehead and jots a brief physical description of the manuscript itself.

LeFrère looks with regret at the clock on the wall. The hands say four o'clock. He raps his knuckles on the counter. She looks up at the clock, her eyes swimming with visions of wormy letters, her fingers coated with fine dust. Four o'clock on December 19, 1969, as dark as it would have been on December 19, 1127, 1137. No place for Naomi to go but her room. What cold December rooms has this manuscript seen in those 842 years, or 832? Ten years hardly seems to matter in such a long context. But it does, it surely does. Naomi shuts her eyes and sees an after-image of the clock hands, black on white. She squeezes them tighter, and the white background reverses to become dark, with hands pale and strong, the same hands she'd imagined chopping onions after her first afternoon here at the library. This time, one hand grips a fat green pepper, the other a sharp knife. From the knife's edge, slowly falling to the chopping block, one emerald pepper ring after another, each with a pulpy center, holding seeds. She rubs her eyelids and shakes her head. It would be better if those hands were writing out the answers hidden in the dusty lines of text. Better, but who would believe that kind of evidence?

LeFrère watches the beautiful girl open her eyes. She gathers her notes, pen, magnifying glass. It was enough, alors? He watches her tie back her hair with the scarf. She will come again, she will transcribe? He rubs his hands together to warm them in case she should chance to touch him.

The sun has long ago sunk behind the Panthéon, just across the square from the little library. Naomi fetches her coat from the hook, and brings the *Ethica* to the desk. She returns to her table to tie up the cardboard around the manuscript. What does he know about the manuscript, where it was found, if there were others? LeFrère stands there rubbing his hands like a lonely miser. She passes the folio over the counter and he grasps it to his chest without taking his eyes off hers.

"Je vais revenir demain," she says, slipping her coat on. He tilts his head. "Tomorrow," she repeats, thinking he has not understood.

He smiles with small, yellow teeth, relieved. Enough, alors, to whet her appétit. He watches her move toward the door, and sighs. She turns!

"Est-ce qu'il y a d'autres manuscrits comme ça?" she asks. "Are there others?"

"Non, Mademoiselle. Ceci c'est le seul."

"Très bien, alors, Monsieur," she shrugs. "Till tomorrow."

"Oui. À demain." He watches her leave, running his hands over the dusty cardboard, untying and re-tying the string.

X

Naomi sits down on the bedspread holding Petersen's blue aero-gramme. She's told him too much. How much can she expect him to believe? How much does he really need to know? It was a mistake to tell him about the cellar.

At the time, she just had to tell someone about this LeFrère, stand-ing like a sentinel behind his counter day after day watching her exam-ine the manuscript—was it a fragment?—that damaged leaf was a prob-lem—trying to determine, if only she could, the date: 1137 or 1127. She knew Abélard was back teaching at Mont Ste. Geneviève by 1137, and dating the text for sure might make a difference in deciphering that last page. She needed more clues. Feeling LeFrère's gaze burning her with a slow fire, she shifted in her seat, crossed her legs one way and then the other, and finally approached him. His face turned ashen, as if she'd deprived him of oxygen. She asked him, "Où était l'école de Ste. Geneviève, Monsieur, where exactly did he teach?" and watched the lavender-green color return to his cheeks. He smiled his yellow smile, and pulled his cuffs over bony wrists.

"Dans la cave, Mademoiselle, on peut voir les pierres originelles, the original stones. Venez avec moi. Come. The cellar, par là."

She leapt at the chance to follow him into the stacks. That familiar odor of paper, leather, glue, ink, and dust filled her nose like perfume, call it "essence of history," unless history has nothing to do with books after all. Stones…he'd said the original stones. The original Pierre. Nothing to do with books, the dynamism of this powerful teacher. We'll

write our own books! Where had she heard that phrase? She shook
her head to clear away the excitement and fatigue, to restore herself to
objectivity, to open the requisite space for doubt. She needed some
extratextual clues, that was why she followed Monsieur LeFrère through
the narrow door, where he stopped to snap on a bare lightbulb.
Cobwebs maybe hundreds of years old rose and fell with their footsteps
as they descended a steep stairway that hugged a cold, crumbling stone
wall. Les pierres originelles. They stepped down onto a packed dirt
floor. The walls were crudely cut, irregularly placed grey and beige
stones with plaster in between. Next to the stairway, a missing chink
formed a recessed shelf where a broken lightbulb lay in the dust. In one
corner of the small cellar, a wooden crate filled with moldy bottles. A
broken chair in a heap. Otherwise the cellar was empty.

"Ici," Monsieur LeFrère indicated with a sweep of his hand. Here.

"Ici?" Now she couldn't remember her question. Where was the
manuscript found? No, that she hadn't asked. Not yet. Where did he
teach? Yes, that was her question, where did he teach.

"Oui, Mademoiselle, c'était ici."

Naomi had no trouble conjuring Pierre Abélard in this cellar surrounded by pupils. Here he paced, first *sic*, then *non*. Kurtzmann whis-
pered, Here of course, this is what you came to Paris for, isn't it, my
dear? The cellar, once at ground level, now sunk in eight hundred years
of soil, a square structure with only a doorway for light, a steep roof
to shelter these fervent minds. Ici, ici. Here. So this is history: not proof
or evidence, not books, but a joining of experience with imagination.
Here, here. She stood next to LeFrère, breathing the dust of time as they
seemed to wait for the master in the damp chill of descending night,
century after century.

She shouldn't have told Petersen anything. She should have told
Hélène and Marie, if she couldn't stay bottled up any longer. "Hie thee
to Chartres, get thee hence!" was Petersen's only response, scrawled

across the back of the aerogramme like an afterthought. Naomi tosses his envelope onto her little table. Are you listening, Bart Petersen, you easy-going, handsome, confident American male, you? Doubt never strikes you down, does it, not mine, not yours, certainly not Pierre Abélard's! With a start, Naomi realizes her picture of Abélard looks like an older Bart Petersen, whose blond curls haven't yet turned grey and whose face begins to show lines of happiness, not pain. How different the two men are, one forging a new way of thinking, stuck in a time when the learned man was a celibate man, denying the body; the other a brilliant young academic with a long career ahead of him, grants and fellowships staring him in the face, and then tenure, and a carpeted office in a tall glass library. And a wife, of course, Petersen has a wife and a young son, while the other man faced painful choices: to devote himself to love or to God, to be a husband or a cleric, a father or *magister*. Petersen will never face those cruel choices. He is young, well-bred, educated, well-fed, and sexy as hell.

Mind. Body. Stupid of philosophers to insist on this choice. Professors don't insist on it, when it comes to attractive women students—the hand on the knee, the wanton glance, the adroit move from textual to sexual during an office conference. Naomi was on the alert, ever since she read the story of Abélard and Héloïse her freshman year. To hear Abélard tell it—because one would certainly never hear Héloïse tell it, with parchment so hard to come by—it didn't take long for body to usurp mind as they bent over the huge tomes by the window overlooking the Seine at her Uncle Fulbert's tall house. And of course the tutor would choose Ovid as his text, the *Ars amandi* no less. Naomi can never forget that passage in the *Historia calamitatum*: "With our lessons as a pretext we abandoned ourselves entirely to love. Her studies allowed us to withdraw in private, as love desired, and then with our books open before us, more words of love than of our reading passed between us, and more kissing than teaching. My hands strayed oftener to her bosom than to the pages; love drew our eyes to look on each other more than reading kept them on our texts."

How that passage had turned her on, the spring of Grappone's autobiography seminar! She would tear herself away from the long question-and-answer period to meet her boyfriend on the sunny rocks in Cascadilla Gorge. When she tried to leave, to go back to her dorm and study, Phil would grab onto her waist and pull her back down again, teasing her for being "too brainy." Finally she would climb the path out of the gorge and cross the bridge, up the steep hill past the Law School, past the libraries, through the Arts Quad, across Triphammer Gorge, up another hill, until finally she would reach her dorm in a muggy spring-heat sweat, walk up the stairs to the stuffy corridor where no one else was studying and windows were wide open and music was blaring, to read Augustine's *Confessions*, and Abélard's *Calamities* with its terrible story of Héloïse's fall into the arms of her mentor.

So she was well defended against Petersen's considerable charms, which he graciously did not use on her. "Hie thee to Chartres" had the ring not of seduction but of command and warning, as if he knew she'd had enough magnified minuscule for now. As if he knew Chartres was a healing place where his nature poets had resolved the mind-body problem not with Biblical exegesis, but with laughter and praise. Paris was chilly in body, cut in half by the river, chilly in mind, cut in half by dialectic. Was it her story of LeFrère's cellar that made Petersen so quick to prescribe a trip to Chartres where perhaps she would find wholeness and warmth, an answer to the constant back-and-forth of the logical process, a resting place?

Anyway, it's funny, this "hie thee to Chartres," because Hélène had invited Naomi to spend Christmas in Chartres with her family and Marie. "We have to take care of our orphans and our Jews," she'd said, touching Naomi sweetly on the cheek. Naomi said no, though, not sure she had the money for a train ticket, not wanting to take time away from the manuscript, especially now that her curiosity was at full alert sitting in that reading room right over the old cellar. But she learned today that the Bibliothèque will close for *les vacances*, and if she stays away from the café and the pâtisserie until her January stipend arrives—she digs her wallet out of her briefcase pocket—one, two, three ten-franc bills left till the first of January, six dollars. Just enough for a ticket to the countryside, and a chance to see Chartres Cathedral.

She picks up the aerogramme again. Something about his flippant message bothers her. Is it Hamlet's "hie thee to the nunnery" that echoes in his scrawl, get thee back to where ye belong, woman? And the double meaning of nunnery, whore-house as well as convent? Probably he'd just prefer it if she chose a topic that sets the ground for his next book on the Chartrian poets! Or some safe little topic, some easy line of research, the kind Mademoiselle LaTour taught them to do in methodology seminar. Be a good little scholar, let the Great Men take the risks necessary to establish the texts, and then go do the background work, meticulously footnoting footnoting footnoting. And really, wasn't that what Kurtzmann trained her for? To be a glorified and extremely specialized secretary, running bibliographical errands in exchange for his approval? Oh, phooey, she's reading the whole history of academic women from a typical Petersen witticism. Stop. She'll take Petersen's advice, and accept Hélène's invitation. She'll go to Chartres, and come right back to the mysterious manuscript, and the cellar. Her head throbs with hunger. No supper tonight, to save money for the trip. She slips on her pink flannel nightgown, clicks off the lamp, and falls back onto the hard bed. Back and back into hungry sleep.

She is back in the cellar of Ste. Geneviève. She is naked, standing at the bottom of the stairs, waiting. She hears the creak of a wooden door on iron hinges. A thin silver-grey light enters the room, a dusky light with no warmth to it. The room is dark, but her body glows like a parchment lampshade. Footsteps on the stairs. A man, sort of Petersen, but thicker, older, sadder. Pierre. She floats up the stairs to meet him, rough frock against her tender skin, a moment of pure delight as her parchment body burns brighter, lighting the whole cellar. The heavy door slams. She falls, wakes, looks around in the semi-darkness of her room until she recognizes the French doors reflected in the silver mirror of the armoire. She rolls over and sleeps again.

This time LeFrère is there, too. They're all wearing brown robes with the hoods up. It is cold, and they huddle together near a tallow candle, drinking wine from clay cups, the three of them. Eyes gleam in the candlelight. Pierre reaches a hand out from inside his full sleeve to grab the wine bottle by the neck. He pours all around, sloshing wine on the dirt floor. It sinks right in. He raises his cup and toasts, "In nomine Domini," and Naomi starts to laugh, and can't stop laughing. She stands up and begins to dance around the cellar, pulling the rope tighter around her waist to keep the robe shut. She reaches down to LeFrère, and pulls him up. His hands are cold, cheeks sunk inside his hood. "Comme ça?" he asks, embarrassed that he can't dance. "Oui, oui," she laughs, and Pierre claps his hands, and the candle flickers and sputters out. Pitch-black. Naomi gropes for LeFrère, Pierre, the walls, but she touches nothing as she stumbles around, blind with the darkness closing in and the cold dirt floor under her bare feet. She screams, and wakes up to the sound of sirens on Rue Monge.

For the first time since September, she is actually hot in her room, even in the dead of this long December night. She gets up, shaking out the damp flannel and running her fingers through her hair. She opens the French doors and steps out onto the narrow balcony. The rain has stopped. She feels drops of water icing up on the railing, and coating the iron grate under her bare feet. Cold air climbs up under her nightgown and she takes a deep breath, watching the occasional late-night car passing on the street beyond the dark little park.

A dusty manuscript in an obscure library. A cellar that some strange librarian tells me is the ancient school. Sure, sure. A joke on me? Sharon would laugh, wouldn't she, my old friend. You're so gullible, she loved to say. Naomi flushes, embarrassed and then angry, recalling her dream and how Sharon always said, "It's all sex, everything is sex." How wrong she is. She just has to be wrong! And even Hélène, with her "sex is political, everything is political." Somehow these two dicta fit together, a neat syllogism.

Maybe her friends are suggesting an explanation for the cruel mistake that ruins so many women in the university. Naturally a mentor, a man, loves the willing mind of a woman pupil, the depth of her understanding. But how should he channel this attraction? With his men students, he knows what to do: he guides their work along accepted scholarly lines, he initiates them into the profession by taking them to conferences, helping them publish their papers in the right journals, lending them the force of his connections. He invests in them, his future colleagues. But a learned woman is so…delicious, so delightful, so extraordinary, so beguiling. And how could he take her to a conference but as his mistress, sneaking down hotel corridors late at night, tasting with her the secret joys of his most benign erudition? And besides, she isn't serious, she'll just get married and teach part-time, there's no great body of work within her. Some children, yes, but no opus in which he might see his own work cited, to which he can lay the claim of mentorship. And the woman goes along with this. She believes what they think of her, the lack of greatness, the body presenting its claims in her search for stature among those who will never be peers.

Just look at the dreams I have! I freeze and starve in Paris for the sake of a manuscript, giving my youth to Minerva, forsaking the joys of Bacchus and Venus, and then I have these dreams! For you, Sharon, "it's all sex" that calls you to the barricades, protesting a war, restructuring a university, fighting for relevance. Or Hélène and Marie with their "politique." But something else wills me along the streets of this *quartier* trying to discover for myself what lies behind the force called history. Some deeper attraction pulls me through layers of time. I know, Sharon, you say I sound just like a medievalist, reading exegetical levels into my sexy dreams! But how else can I understand my life if not as an allegory?

Naomi shivers, her sweat congealing in the cold night air. She turns to go back in, and notices a faint light glimmering through the barred windows of the adjacent building, as if an inside door were open and light shone through from another room. Before that thumping on the wall, which never recurred, she viewed the building as nothing more than a façade, like a stone curtain demarcating the end of her street, the limit of her daily life. Curious now, and a little scared, she leans over the railing and peers toward the light that comes from the depths of the interior, stepping from one bare foot to the other on the freezing wrought iron.

And there, just behind the barred window, the figure of a man looking out toward Rue Monge. Another sleepless human watching the lonesome Parisian night. Watching her watch the night? She skitters over the threshold, rattling the glass doors shut. She stands on the little square of rug with her arms wrapped around her flannel waist, trying to get her breath. What is that building? Some kind of mental hospital, with bars on all the windows? Or a prison?

She dives under the bedspread. A cowardly mouse. Like Mademoiselle LaTour, who parts her hair severely in the center and pins it back at the nape of her neck. Long sleeves, dark clothes, the incongruous gash of red lipstick. The woman I am to become, hiding from my own answers? Will I walk head down across the campus of some university or other, no long line of graduate students outside my office door awaiting guidance? Weekends will stretch before me, promising intimacy with a card catalogue, a carrel, a carefully documented article in which no earth is shattered. An evening alone in my apartment with Dubonnet and Débussy and, if I'm daring, my bare feet resting on a Danish footstool. And for adventure, a trip to Paris, ah Paris!, to check a manuscript at the Bibliothèque Nationale and sip a little wine at a Right Bank café, and rescue someone else's graduate student, in trouble on the Left Bank. No! This can't be the best I can hope for! But the worst is even worse, the fate of the mentorless woman: teaching high school Latin, wire-rim glasses propped on my nose, teenagers tittering at the tear in my stocking, my hanging hem, as I conjugate verbs until the bell mercifully rings.

Oh, forlorn future! Am I a fearful little brown mouse? A mouse doesn't choose. She can only run, tiny briefcase gripped between her clenched little teeth. Running from…oh, God, who is that man behind bars?

She sticks her head deeper under the covers, and sleeps fitfully for what's left of the night.

XI

While church bells ring all over Paris, the train lurches out of the station, passing domes and spires and towers, crossing bridges that look down on slick mansard rooftops, cobbled streets and broad avenues. Hardly a flower stall open anywhere, hardly a chestnut man this Christmas morning. Sleet cuts diagonally across Naomi's reflection in the train window. Fat snowflakes radiate into constellations of waterdrops. The snowy suburbs pass beyond her mirrored face. Bleak plane trees, high stone walls around each yard. Then quilted fields, ghostly hedgerows, low-roofed farmhouses.

Naomi imagines her way into the root cellars stocked with potatoes, carrots, turnips. Kettles simmering with a soup-bone, an onion studded with cloves, bay leaves. She can almost smell garlic wafting across the quiet land. She watches the distant windows from her passing one, the unseen women who repeat the gestures of cooking, century after century. Hypnotized by the swirling snow, the rocking train, she closes her eyes. Yes, no, yes, no, know, know, know, you know, you just know… she opens her eyes a slit, to streaks of white and blue, farmhouses blurred by snow and speed…you just know those kitchens you will never enter…

She reaches down to pull up her knee socks. Hélène had said, Come to the countryside and see the earth that the cobbles of Paris cover over. Earth exudes answers…exhumes…humus…human… Petersen, too, same advice. Was he steering her away from Abélard who chastised himself so bitterly for having a body? Did Petersen look at her, a round, fresh young woman, and think she'd be better off more in the body, less in the mind? Why does a person have to choose between them, yes or no? Petersen, athletic, healthy, sexy Petersen, of course he would choose to make his scholarly reputation through Alain de Lille's *De planctu Naturae*. Nature's lament, the loss of holy human body in the natural order. The awful split that led to Abélard's suffering. Is that what's real, then—nature? Is that what Petersen wants her to see on this journey, and Hélène, too? And yet she can't let go of her search for the artifacts she's trained to decipher. The written evidence of a man's life, his letters squirming under a magnifying glass, the rhythm of his mind displayed there in the strokes of ink, and his body, too, which propelled the quill. If that's not real, what is?

Real shmeal, her grandfather would say. Life is for living. But it isn't that simple. Sharon always laughs at Naomi's habit of allegory, which complicates life. But how is allegory any different from what Sharon calls "CR"? To Naomi, CR is a library call number. To Sharon, it's the call of a new doctrine—"consciousness-raising." The new women interpret their personal life from a political level, Sharon says. And the SDS men, they Marxify everything as a struggle of the masses against the elite. So why is Naomi's sense of another level shimmering behind her life dismissed as "medieval"?

The one charge she admits to, watching the pearly sky with its tenuous disk of sun, is fear. She runs to the past, it's true, away from unstudious students flashing the peace sign, away from drafted boys, napalmed peasants. It's easier to care about Pierre Abélard, though he was easily as disruptive as a Marxist in a medieval paleography seminar. She would have hated him. But from the safe distance of eight centuries she applauds his subversiveness. Yes, it's true, she can't hack radical absolutism in the present tense. You have to take sides, Sharon says. Naomi takes sides, all right—both sides—yes and no. Which is not the same as maybe.

…pale yellow farmhouses each with a kettle of simmering soup…

Chopping carrots is real. A few of her Cornell classmates had gone to live on communes, where she's sure they chop carrots in a big way. The women do. The men chop wood, and probably ask all the questions, as if carrots could provide no answers. Now there's a question women need to ask: why isn't soup central to history, and those who make it? A shift from scriptorium to refectory, that might be just the move she has to make. Manuscripts come and go, but soup remains. The hand that wields the spoon can stir the world—a new view of humanism she could hardly defend before her dissertation committee.

The train cuts across the last stretch of undulating fields and approaches Chartres. Twin spires appear out of the blur, rising from a quaint town capped with snow. Through every archway, above every sloping roof and chimney, at the end of every street, the cathedral delicately holds the center. Where Notre Dame dominates the island in the Seine with its geometric towers, Chartres tugs gently at buttresses anchored in village life. The rose window over the front portal is dark yet luminous, like moonstone set in carved bone.

Hélène and Marie had promised to meet her here in the plaza. Naomi stands in a veil of snow, admiring the *pointilliste* effect. Dots of stone, a mottled outline of spires. Vision and labor created this. Generations of guildsmen, farmers, scholars and teachers, cooks of steaming broth and crusty bread, all converged through tiers of time to shape this wordless song. Is this what's real in history, then?

Yes! Yes! She bends her neck back, snowflakes melting in her open mouth. The spires don't match. At Notre Dame, two identical square towers force the eye from one to the other and back again, the either-or of dialectic. She squints and superimposes two fingers over these pointed spires that say *yes* and *yes*, like two fir trees in a forest. "PEACE!" she shouts, flashing the V-sign, her first ever, at a medieval cathedral no less.

"Unh, excusez-moi!" She thuds against a thick wool coat. Someone laughs. It's Hélène and Marie, stumbling under the weight of a heavy basket carried between them.

"What are you doing," Marie asks her, stopping to straighten the crooked glasses on her nose, "toasting the sky?"

"The cathedral! Let's go in!"

Marie takes Naomi by the shoulders and turns her around. "The cathedral she is closed for renovations. You see the sign?"

DANGER! it warns. Naomi hasn't got time for disappointment as they sweep her away from the plaza, down a twisted street and out of the town. An old farmer stops his truck and lets them climb in back with the empty milk cans. As they bounce along the dirt road, past fields and farmhouses, Hélène's face shines. She points out the cluster of trees in the distance where her school will be. La ferme des femmes. The women's farm. They'll raise their own food, they'll work and study. Without men.

"Why no men?" asks Naomi.

"Pourquoi, she wants to know!" teases Marie, warming her hand on a fresh baguette sticking out of the basket. "Women have to educate themselves, ma chérie."

"We want to learn the b-bod-y," Hélène's voice bumps as the truck crosses a narrow bridge and takes the curve in the road. The basket slides to one side of the truck. The milk cans clang. "Our body yearns to bend and stretch, to sweat and ache. To be a useful tool, not the body men lust for, which is nothing more than an object."

"We want privacy, you see," adds Marie. "Only the nun is allowed her own body, yet she is owned. Even the Virgin Mary, she had to bear God's child."

"Our choices are so few! We must speak our own story."

"I don't see how growing radishes will do that!"

Hélène raps on the cab window. The old farmer's beret gives a quick nod. "C'est par là," points Hélène. They jump out of the truck and climb a long driveway lined with chestnut trees. A wisp of smoke rises from the chimney.

"Elle est belle, la ferme, non?" asks Marie. "I could almost quit Paris for this. If only they had newspapers and cafés out here!"

"Start your own newspaper," suggests Naomi. She stops to listen— the absolute quiet of the snowy land.

"Now you're getting the idea," pants Hélène, weary of the basket's weight. Two men appear at the head of the driveway, walking toward them in antic imitation of two women with a basket.

"Alain and Louis are already here, I see," says Marie without enthusiasm.

"Those men from the café?" Naomi can't cover her dismay. Hélène's vision of a farm without men has already begun to expand in her like a soaking bean seed.

"Les mêmes." Hélène tosses her head, swinging her hair back from snowy lapels. "Alain comes from this village, too. He is an orphan. My mother likes to feed the hungry, you see."

"Alain is a Jew, Naomi, like you," says Marie. "And an orphan like me." The men are falling over each other in the snow. "Of course they will not help us with the basket."

"Non, Marie. That much we've taught them!"

"Here, I'll help." Naomi takes Hélène's handle.

"Naomi! Allô! Did you finish from studying your cathedral?" shouts Alain.

"It's so beautiful," says Naomi, out of breath. "But it was closed."

"Closed for Christmas. Ha-ha! C'est mieux. You do not want to enter that monument to the bourgeoisie, that token of unpaid servitude. The hungry cannot eat stones, you know. Stones, enfin, crushed them. But do those glass windows commemorate their deaths? Mais non!"

"Oh, shush, Alain," says Hélène. "You don't want cathedrals, anyway, Naomi. Cathedrals are…"

"...the prison of Mary," continues Marie, "the tomb of thy womb."

"Tiens, ma chérie, what you came here for is cellars."

"Cellars?"

"Give her a taste of our French country wines," says Alain. "Get the poor girl drunk, why don't you? Then she will see the tragedy of this history of which she is part."

"Non, Alain, not the wine cellar. "

"Ah, the Jew cellar. Much better."

"Jew cellar?"

"Ah, oui, Naomi, we bottle and age them here in Chartres, you know," explains the dead-pan Louis.

"My parents wouldn't like it. Let's slip around to the barn before they see us. My father is napping, and Maman is roasting the goose."

"What won't they like?"

"All these old barns hold secrets."

Secrets. If she'd wanted secrets she'd have stayed in Paris. LeFrère's cellar of crumbling stone. She came to Chartres to lighten up, to experience the source of Petersen's amiable research, the joy of body and earth. To escape from Abélard's obsessive doubt, the solace he found in his secret wife—

—is this the prison Marie means? A woman made to serve a man's obsession? Kept outside his arena, to fortify him for battles she can't engage in—

"It is not fashionable even yet to admit you were, how shall I say, a Jew-lover?" adds Hélène, calling Naomi back from her thoughts.

"All right, then." Naomi raises her chin. "Show me this cellar."

"Not us," says Louis, and they stalk off toward the beech trees at the edge of the field.

"Just the women, then," Hélène smiles, "come!" They leave the basket on the back step, and cross the icy dooryard. Over the worn threshold, they enter a darkness warmed by cows steaming in their stalls. They walk between an aisle of switching tails to the frosty back wall, a window obscured by cobwebs and chaff.

"C'est ici," says Hélène, squatting to push the hay aside. Ici, ici. The word that speaks the missing trace, the "here" history books lack.

Hélène raises a hatch and they climb down a ladder into an earthen pit. Marie touches a match to a candle stub. Bins along the wall store turnips. "Cattle fodder," explains Hélène, lifting a gnarly globe and brushing it off, swinging it by the long taproot toward Naomi, who catches the cold thing. She grimaces at its bitter tang. "It makes them give good milk, these." Naomi tosses the huge root back to Hélène, and kneels to touch the dirt floor. A pile of old quilts lies molding against one wall, a few empty bottles, and…oh, what is that? She jerks to her feet, bumping into Marie. The candle flickers.

"A skeleton?"

Silence answers her shock.

"Alain's grand-père," Marie confirms. "The others went to Büchenwald, Alain's parents and brothers. Alain was an infant. The schoolmaster took him as his own."

"Oui, my parents agreed to hide the grandfather and grandmother. After he died, she stayed down here alone."

"With the body? They didn't remove it?"

"Suspicious activity could lead to discovery, you see," Hélène explains. "A fresh dug grave would never do."

"And Büchenwald is…?"

"Like Auschwitz? Of course you've heard of it!"

Naomi's stomach flips and rises. Her parents never spoke of what happened in Europe, wouldn't utter the word holocaust, never wanted to scare her. It couldn't happen in America, was all they said. It? All she knew was how mad they were when she bought a Volkswagen, which sat now in an Ithaca parking lot. She thought their anger was stupid, bigoted. How was she to know? Her German uncle would mention "Auschwitz," and how he'd clambered over barbed wire leaving scars she'd seen herself. But "Auschwitz," it sounded like a sneeze, something you would respond to with "God bless you." He'd wipe his nose on a rumpled handkerchief from his back pocket, then pat her on the head. God bless you. Why burden you? American Jews don't need to know. Now she feels ignorant. What is "Auschwitz"? And what else lies buried in Europe, hidden from her, holding the key?

Key to what? Her own history. A "here" that doesn't lie. That's not what she came for! She gags on the turnip smell. She doesn't want to know!

Marie blows out the candle. They climb the ladder and close the hatch. Following family custom, Hélène disguises the hinges with hay. Cows shift in their stanchions. Alain and Louis, backlit in the barn doorway by snowy daylight, kneel in pantomime, swinging their haunches. "Moo! Moo!" They're used to making jokes to cover the deep sadness Naomi struggles up out of for the first time.

They head inside for the Christmas goose. She's always loved Christmas, as only an American Jew can love it—with longing. Now she suspects her longing was not for a holiday she couldn't have, as her parents always thought, handing her a token candy-cane every Christmas Eve. There's something here in Europe she never knew she'd lost.

These good Christians risked their lives for Alain's grandparents, storing them like so many turnips. Old turnips get returned to the soil, but these bones they preserved from decay like a special manuscript. To bury is to deny, if not forget. So they keep the bones. To flavor the soup they live in. Her American soup, even in its Campbell's-chicken-noodle blandness, is made from this secret stock.

They open the back door to a flood of good smells. "Oo-là-là," says Alain, little Jewish orphan, little rebel pulling off his beret and shaking snow to hiss on the kitchen stove. Pain, unburied, fuels his passion. Naomi craves the fullness she's been protected from, the zest that pain has given him. Craves goose and gravy even more. She catches Alain's joy as he prances around the kitchen, "let's eat…let's eat…"

XII

Naomi tucks her damp raincoat around her legs for warmth, waiting with four companions for the night train back to Paris. The basket at their feet is heavy with fruit preserves and cider from the farm, leftover goose on thick trenchers wrapped in rough cloth. Never since leaving Ithaca has Naomi been so stuffed. And never have her feet been so sore and wet, after walking most of the slushy way back in the dusk before a truck with full milk cans finally stopped for them. It's one thing for a man to pick up three young women, an act of chivalry—or, Marie would say, lechery. Add two men to the group, and no farmer wants to stop.

The presence of men changes things, that's for sure. As they all climb into the second-class car, Alain and Louis create a commotion out in the narrow passageway. Marie pushes Naomi into a compartment with one bench already occupied by a father and mother, a little child with chocolate-smudged cheeks sleeping between them. She slides all the way to the cold window, and Marie next, while Hélène wrestles with Alain and Louis for the last seat. The train clunks into motion. The men admit defeat and move down to the next car. Naomi relaxes as Hélène takes the seat. Two hours trapped in this glass compartment with a radical young man would be a hell not even Dante could have thought up.

Arguing with those guys at Hélène's farm was hellish enough, even on a stomach full of delightful country food. No wonder she lived alone in her pink room at the Hôtel Plaisant, where she could hear herself think. All through college and graduate school, there'd been so many men—professors, classmates, boyfriends—with their subtle put-downs, their self-seriousness. There was never a conversation that wasn't an oral defense. She'd gone whole semesters without saying a word, after a while not even bothering to disagree in her head. Just letting them blot her out. Yet only today, leaning against an oak tree in Chartres, France, did she see through Alain's penetrating brilliance, Louis' sharp wit, to a habitual image of herself as a bit of a fluff. No more of that!

The train picks up speed. Naomi stares out the window at the cathedral spires against the navy-blue sky, the moon hung between them. She watches her reflection in the window against the soft out-lines of the darkening village and the blue countryside. Alain's adamance was just boring! Hélène had taken them out to a barn on the far side of the hill. The school would be here, in a ramshackle stone rectangle with roof beams exposed to the sky, which they would repair by their own labor.

"A pig sty!" Alain declared. "But then, c'est juste."

"We are not pigs!" Marie retorted.

"What else explains why you pen yourselves in here, and keep men out?" asked Louis quietly.

"Separatism, it is not the answer," insisted Alain. "We must rise up as a class. You women fall into the bourgeois belief in individual destiny. No such thing is possible in this Hegelian structure in which we are all cogs in a machine run by economic necessity..."

"Bpf!" Hélène swished her long hair. "I'll show you structure. Take a look at this barn!" She stomped across the threshold into the dank interior with snow drifting down through open rafters.

"Some structure!" mocked Alain. "You'll need men, if only to fix this mess."

"Is there a cellar?" asked Naomi, and the men hooted with laughter.

"Ah, bien sûr, they must have a cellar, Louis, non? And not to store their vegetables, or their wine. To hide from the enemy—men! You make yourselves the victim. You make us the Nazis."

"Shut up with your Nazi and Jew scheme, Alain. There are more than two sides to the world!"

"Hélène's right. There's more than men and not-men," added Marie. "Women are women. Can you conceive of a structure that doesn't include you?"

"Yes. This one. Stay here and freeze your buns off. We're going in for a smoke by the fire with Hélène's father."

With that, the men left them to stand sheltered from the wet snow by a large oak tree next to the barn. Leaning against the trunk, Naomi looked past a fence woven out of branches, toward an old orchard she hadn't noticed till the crunching of the men's feet on the snow subsided. The long, blanketed vista, pink in the fading afternoon, with the cathedral against the opal sky, made the pear trees in the orchard appear bigger than the spires at the horizon, the broken-down barn more perfectly formed than the distant Gothic master-work.

"Alors, ma chère Naomi," says Hélène, interrupting Naomi's memory of pear trees and bringing her focus back to her friends' reflection in the train window. Marie shakes out a wet beret and leans down for an orange and a small knife from the basket.

"Alain and Louis will never change, will they, Hélène?" Marie sighs. The pungent scent of orange peel, the exquisite curl that drops from the knife, stir the child on the opposite bench awake. It yawns and curls up again between the parents, rubs one eye with a fist, and sleeps again.

"They're just like men I know back home. What makes them so predictable?"

"Well, you know," Hélène smiles slowly, "with men it's all hanging on the outside."

"That Hélène, she likes to joke." Marie glances at the peaceful family on the opposite bench, her knife working the orange into sections. "She looks angelic, but she has a tongue of fire, celle-là!"

"A woman must have a tongue of fire—to burn through the barrier of her two closed lips."

"It's different for men," says Naomi. "Words spill from their mouth."

"But of course, Naomi!" Hélène reaches to touch her hand. "God told Adam to name everything!"

"That's what you get when you leave history up to the men," adds Marie.

"Mark Twain tells it another way," says Naomi. "His Eve always beats Adam to it in the naming game."

"Merde, another male joke," Marie asserts. She catches the falling orange peel with her leg, nearly knocking over the little family's satchel. She grabs the long loaf sticking out of their bundle to upright the load. Neither the man nor woman moves on their bench, watching her. "That type of humor just denies woman's oppressed position." She drops the peel into her basket. "Which is why, Alain be damned, we need to be alone. Men like to pretend women have all the power—she talks a lot—she dominates him—it's a script that mocks her lack of power."

"To silence her all the more," says Naomi. "Abélard tells Héloïse that women should be quiet. He quotes the Apostle James, 'Women are gossips and speak when they should not. To provide a remedy for so great a plague, let us subdue the tongue by perpetual silence.'"

"Women do not need to subdue the tongue. They have no tongue!"

"Attends, Hélène, don't start with your castration theory again." Marie hands them each a piece of orange.

"How else to explain? We're cut off. We don't own words, as men do."

"Own?" says Naomi. "Nobody owns language." She looks from one woman to the other. "Do we? Don't we...just use it?"

"Mais non! We are formed by it, n'est-ce pas, Marie? Alain insists that economics shapes us, but I say it is language. Look," she shakes her orange section as if it were just the piece of evidence she needs, "look at our catechism, we good little Catholic girls. Father, Son, and Holy Ghost. Where is She, enfin? The Mother that gives flesh to the Word? A ghost has more of a place in their trinity! The Son, sent to dwell among 'us'? Does that 'us' include us? Where is our body in all of that?" She pops the orange into her mouth, and watches Naomi's puzzled face.

"What does body have to do with language?"

Hélène smiles. "Her womb is empty, you see. She needs his seed. She is nothing, she has no voice, except through him."

"Do you suppose that's why the Apostle James says, 'I do not permit women to be teachers'? And Abélard passes that on to Héloïse, which is ridiculous because she already was a teacher, alone there with her sisters at the Paraclete."

"Oui, now you are getting it. They make her nothing but his property. They make nuns of us all!"

"It's almost as if her body doesn't belong to her, any more than you say language does."

"Oui, Naomi, 'almost'!" Hélène snorts.

"The woman must first know her body from within," Marie says, breaking up the rest of the orange, "without his language."

Naomi nods, recalling the rough bark of the oak tree against her back. No words for what the tree said to her as she leaned on it. A language of trunk and spine.

"Her body is the object of man's desire," Marie continues. "She bears the baby his seed gives her. She bears the name his power gives her, la femme, elle. What name does she call herself?"

"Where is She, enfin?"

"Her lips can only speak to themselves."

"But..." Naomi interrupts their duet.

"'But...'" Marie mimicks, smiling, and hands her the last section of fruit. "'But' is the distinguishing mark of their language, you see. Back and forth from one pole to the other in the struggle for dominance..."

"...the process of history itself, Naomi! You heard Alain with his Nazi and Jew. These words contain nothing but our mutual destruction. The way men define choices—either, or—makes change impossible!"

"But how can we speak without 'their' language? How can we speak to men?"

"Bpf! Men." Marie's mouth twists as if she'd eaten a lemon and not an orange. "Who wants to speak with them?"

"If we ignore them, how will we ever get anywhere?"

"She thinks she is going somewhere, Marie." The two women smile and shrug. Hélène leans across Marie and looks into Naomi's blue eyes. "Où es-tu, enfin? If you want to go somewhere, first tell me: where are you?"

"I'm...well, I'm...in academia, a scholar! I have no choice but to speak their language!"

"C'est un problème!" Marie declares with mock seriousness. "Naomi, listen. Draw upon what you know as a paleographer. You deal with parchment, which is really a skin, the body of an animal. Words are written upon it. And sometimes a scribe would rub those words off the skin and replace them with other words. And yet the first words peek through the imposed layer."

"A palimpsest."

"Oui, c'est ça. This is the situation with woman's language. Erased. Written over."

"And woman's body is the parchment under everything, before language even...right? Without her body, there is no writing."

"Right! And what does that mean for you in academia, do you think?" Marie coaxes.

"Body comes first and lasts longest? In order to speak 'their' language, in order to fit into 'their' world...what?...I have to erase myself and write over my body with their words?"

"Brava!" Hélène's green eyes light up, and across the aisle the man's head jerks up from where it had fallen to his chest in sleep. "You must sustain the body, the most obviously living part. Be a woman, speak as a woman. Not as a not-man!"

Naomi surges with triumph. Always before it was a test to see how much she could remember of what her teachers had said, as if their words were a monument to re-visit like a cathedral. But a cathedral is a body, created by bodies, and her words in this glass compartment speeding through the night are her own. "But...I mean, if I voice the voiceless voice within me, it's like...I'm...afraid. What if...everything topples?"

Hélène tosses her hair. "Naomi, believe me: if everything crashes, you still have...you! There's nothing to lose! This is why women are the true revolutionaries of our time!"

Naomi's stomach tightens. Revolutionaries. Alain, Louis, the SDS men, Pierre Abélard. But Hélène and Marie, laughing here with her as they hurtle toward Paris...the true revolutionaries? And as for Abélard, his teaching style, his use of logic to arrive at belief, revolutionary, yes. But look at him, quoting the Apostles at Héloïse. He never even listened to her! Was Héloïse the one who'd already lost everything but herself—the true revolutionary?

The child stirs in sleep, and pushes its feet against the father's thigh. The train whistles and begins to slow, approaching Paris. Outside the window, blackness presses against the glass, blurred by flocks of golden light.

≈ xiii ≈

Light-headed with hunger, her money all but gone until after the New Year, Naomi clings to the exuberant Yes! of Chartres. She takes the back way up to the Bibliothèque Ste. Geneviève, avoiding the scurrying scholars on Rue St. Jacques. History gives no answer, if there is an answer. The history contained in books is really only the history of history, a chain of scholarly perceptions. The first link is a presence, not a story. Something really happens. She can do no more than follow her shadow back to that moment. She climbs the morning-lit hill, away from the cafés. The woman writing in the window, her white cup empty, holds a pen above the half-filled page, and watches.

Naomi passes the doorway that always smells of cooking, this time the delicate simmer of applesauce. She licks her lips, and hopes the next stipend check will come in time for the meeting with Mademoiselle LaTour at a Right Bank restaurant on January 7. If it had been Kurtzmann coming, or even Petersen, she'd assume the lunch would be a "father's" treat. But Mademoiselle LaTour is no father, and not really her mentor, so what is the protocol? Naomi suspects that her choice to study Latin with the untenured Petersen, rather than LaTour's Provençal poets, means she will be paying for her own lunch. The courtly love lyric, with all that sublimated adulterous desire, all that precious glorification of the lady—she'll leave that to the little brown mouse. If LaTour holds it against her, well, no breakfast or lunch this week, and no evening pastry.

Abélard had no worries about food or money, with devoted stu-

dents to bring him bread, wine, *denarii*, in exchange for the questions
that nagged his soul. But he paid a price. Even now he pays. Naomi
rounds the last shadowy bend into a flood of sun at the top of the
Mont. Some passion hides in this manuscript of LeFrère's, and until
the author's—Abélard? or who else could have written it?—until his
words are released from the Latin, and moved beyond the stones of this
Bibliothèque, he will keep paying. Eight centuries is long enough to
stay in hiding. Bone and muscle held the quill, yet all we get are words
deemed worthy of precious parchment: his ethical philosophy, the
moral dilemma of a man who "wants what he by no means wants to
want." The flesh-and-blood outcry of a man mourning for a life he
could not have, this he does not set down in ink. The triumph is that
he survived his pain and turned it into philosophy. Written history
is created by survivors who only tell the clarity, not the blur. Anyone can
miss important clues, even about their own life, for how can you know
until it's over just how much each moment cost? A human life resides
in the silent gaps of told time. She reaches for the brass handle of the
library door. It's up to her to tell that tale.

Locked. Of course. How could she forget the library doesn't open
till ten. She kicks a small stone in front of her, heading for a sunny
bench in the middle of the plaza. There's old professor Mauriet shuffling toward the Ecole des Chartes, leaning a shoulder along the wall
of the Panthéon for balance. Ha! Perhaps she'd drop in on his lecture,
after six weeks' absence. "Propter!" she wants to shout through cupped
hands across the plaza, finally giving him the answer she knew all along
if only he hadn't waved his magnifying glass at her that day. How
stupid to be intimidated by him. Look at him! He's nothing but a
decrepit old man with a shabby briefcase.

Naomi decides against the bench, and crosses to the other side
of the plaza. Isn't that the front of the forbidding grey building that
abuts the Hôtel Plaisant? She shivers, remembering the eerie light shin-

ing through the bars, the man watching her in the dark. Or had she dreamed that? She approaches the façade. If any building fit the word *bâtiment*, this place was just such a bastion. Barred windows, an iron gate across the doorway. Big letters painted on the grimy stones, "Défense de stationner," No Parking. Down in the Métro station at Boul' Mich, some students had painted "Défense de défendre," No Prohibiting! This intimidating building illustrates what they're rebelling against. French history reeks of fear. Those who resist will be locked away in the Bastille; burned at the stake; beheaded by the guillotine; deported to the gas chambers; publicly stripped and flailed; shoved into paddy wagons; expelled from the university; sent to the army. Castrated, she's sure Hélène would say. A smaller sign on the building says "Défense d'entrer." Not that anyone would want to. And she's been living her little pink life right on the other side of the wall! A clock strikes ten. She hurries toward the Bibliothèque just as the guard opens the iron filagree gate with a huge key.

At the table in the reading room, Naomi rubs her hands together to warm them. Monsieur LeFrère appears like a genie, carrying the manuscript as if no holiday had interrupted the work. He bows stiffly and returns to his post. Magnifying glass, notebook, pen, she turns to the long task of transcribing the manuscript. Enough wondering, doubting. Enough side-trips to some lovely country place. Enough counting her francs and worrying about where her next meal is coming from. To work!

The manuscript is a pleasure to look at, in perfect Carolingian minuscule, but there's still no skimming it. Every word is abbreviated, a practice that bespeaks the value of parchment. She continually checks her faithful Cappelli. But even relying on this *Dizionario di abbreviature latine*, it's easy to confuse the letters f and s, both written as a straight down-stroke to the line. And, though p dips below the line, it too can look like an f or s. Add the complication of cross-strokes that stand for a wide range of abbreviations, depending on the length and angle of the stroke—per, pro, prae, post, and her old favorite, propter. A quill could become inexact with wear, blurring the loop of a "c" to look like an "e," the tail of an "a" to resemble the raised ^{9} that represents the Latin ending, -us. The photocopies they'd used in paleography seminar were easier to read than the textured, stained, smeared skin lying on the table before her.

Naomi rubs her eyes. She transcribes into her notebook, "Hic incipit [smudge] epistula[m?] [epistolii] in anno mcxx[x?]vii in monte sancto geneveso deposituram [deposui? deposuit?]." The grammar in this salutation seems all mixed up! How to match the case endings when she can't tell even what part of speech the abbreviations indicate? "Hic incipit [smudge] epistula...," here begins the epistle? Or here someone [name smudged] begins the epistle? Or is it "epistolii," notes, not an epistle at all? A few letters one way or the other never seemed to make much difference, sitting in Kurtzmann's seminar. But here, is the epistle "deposited" on this Mont? Or is it "to be deposited" in the future? One error could change the entire story.

Even the date is still not clear. One x more or less, 1127 or 1137, intercepts a different moment in the author's life. Biography itself is made of difficult documents like these, cobbled together by scholars who see with the bias of their own experience. Here she is, transcribing today through memories newly burnt onto her imagination: cellars with skeletons, pear trees, the roof of an old barn. She plunges in again, finding what she thinks are the words "peccatum malum nostrum puto," I think about our evil sin. Okay. That seems clear enough, and sounds like Abélard for sure. Or is it "putus"? She turns to her pocket-size Latin dictionary: adjective, "perfectly pure." Or, wait, is that "puter," rotten? Or is it a noun, "boy"? Or "puteus," a well or pit? She squeezes her eyebrows toward each other with thumb and finger.

What the hell am I doing? I can't read the stuff, and I can't figure out the meaning either. How can one word mean pure or rotten? And why does the word for boy—I thought boy was "puer"? But it says here, "putus, *m.* boy"—also mean "perfectly pure"? That hardly seems fair! Here, look in the dictionary how there's "pudor," meaning modesty and disgrace—is that a mixed message, or what?—and the very next word is "puella," girl or young wife. Vocabulary alone inscribes a message, just what Hélène said.

It's not so simple, this process of transcribing. It's not just a question of copying it down. There are decisions to make, with no sure grounds. If I knew who, what, when, why—or even one of these—I could work from that. You have to know the story before you can read the story! With all their documentary evidence, historians are writing fiction after all.

Naomi pulls her hair for awhile, until she notices it hurts. The cellar below the library. The odd chink in the stone foundation at the bottom of the stairs. She turns to the spoiled final leaf and inhales its mildewed scent. Could Pierre Abélard, this man constructed by history, have walled up his secrets behind a foundation stone, la pierre? Her question assumes the "who" under the smudge is Abélard. Careful, Naomi. She looks again at the smudge, moving her magnifying glass closer and then farther. A blurred capital, something with a curve to it, and then a straight stroke to the line. "Ab"? Or is that "E"? She looks up. LeFrère watches her.

"Monsieur," she motions to him. He comes, hanging his head. "Excusez-moi, mais, um, comment avez-vous découvert le manuscrit? How did you discover this?"

LeFrère opens his mouth, closes it again, and runs a hand over his shiny hair. "Moment, Mademoiselle." He slips away into the stacks, leaving Naomi to the blurred "Ab" or "E."

LeFrère stands at the barred window behind the stacks. He looks across at the somber grey building with similar bars. He rubs his chin.

After all these years, can he trust someone, this jeune fille, this Américaine so innocent, so gullible, and yet trained to doubt? He rubs his chin. *A woman, she is not to fear, not like that other one who ridiculed me. I will not be mocked! I may be a curator only, but I know some things, oui? I understand the mysteries, as only one who is locked out can understand. Et lui...! Because of him I am locked out! Alors, I shall tell her. Whatever she asks. And, peut-être, if she is sympathique, I shall tell her more.*

He straightens the tie that bumps over his Adam's apple, pulls frayed cuffs down over his wrists, smoothes his hair, and returns to the reading room with eager resolve, like a lover who longs to reveal the secret etched on the view from his window. A secret that topples the foundation he's built his solitary life upon, on which cobwebs and mold have grown, and which, enfin, is nothing but an escape from what has hurt him, and now will hurt him no more. Bravely, he approaches the young woman who, in profile, is round of cheek, of breast, of knee, shoulders rounded toward her work, arms encircling the precious manuscript, round magnifying glass in hand, her breath, he is sure, coming warm from her parted lips as she studies.

"Venez avec moi, Mademoiselle," he beckons, "come with me," and leads her again to the cellar door, pulls out a large key ring, unlocks the door, clicks on the light. They descend the shaky stairs. The broken chair in the corner, the crate of bottles just as moldy as it was two weeks ago. A smile curves Naomi's lips, remembering her dream, dancing with LeFrère, floating to meet Pierre. She blushes, but he can't know her private world, this eggplant man who is more pathetic than she will ever be. She looks down at his scrawny neck from two steps above him, his scalp showing through the purple-black hair, dust on his shoulderpads. They reach the dirt floor, and there to the right is the missing chink of stone, an old lightbulb resting in the recessed area.

"Monsieur?" she asks, pointing at the niche.

"Oui, ici je l'ai trouvé, vraiment." He hangs his head. Here I found it. Here I lay myself bare to you. Laugh if you must.

Naomi shivers. Weird how she knew. "Continuez," she waves him on.

LeFrère releases his tale one stammered phrase at a time. "It is ten years since...I...came down these steps, for no reason. I slipped, you see, on the last step. I reached out for balance. A stone, là, was loose. I pulled it out, comme ça, to see, you know, what it was. A shower of plaster, and there, behind the stone, the manuscript."

He stops abruptly, waiting for her mockery. But Naomi does not laugh.

"I took it out, carefully. The outer folios were covered with mold. Inside, the parchment was clean, except the last folio, which you saw is nearly illegible. I studied paleography, like you, but I was not sure. After the guard went home, I brought it up and cleaned it with a soft brush, and put it in the vault until..."

"Until...?"

"Waiting for the right person. A long time waiting." He flashes Naomi a complicit look, if olive pits can shine with fleshless joy, if such joy can mean a kind of desire.

"Has no one else seen it?"

"Oui, il y avait un autre..." He brushes a cobweb from his brow. "Mademoiselle, ascendez s'il vous plaît," he points a lavender fingernail up the stairs.

His fists, hanging at her eye level as she follows him, are clenched at the end of two limp arms. He motions her to sit down in the corner of the stacks where two wooden chairs are pushed against a dirty window. On a crate is a glass tumbler and a chipped plate with crumbs on it. Suddenly famished and dizzy, she tries to look him in the eye, to keep from passing out.

"It is fifteen years," he begins, looking out the window and rubbing his chin. "I was a student at the Ecole des Chartes, like you, oui? Professeur Mauriet was my mentor." Naomi straightens her spine against the hard chair.

"I'd been sent to him for training. My teacher at Caen thought I had promise as a paleographer. My one flaw was…the imagination. My teacher, he always said let the evidence speak its own story, not to embroider with your imagination. I learned to quiet my visions. I became Mauriet's assistant. My future was assured. I was 24, and already transcribing for him at the Bibliothèque Nationale, accompanying him on research trips. He seemed to favor me. Even, you could say, to love me? You must understand, he was a man très très distingué."

Sad, sad, to admire that awful man. And how LeFrère had tried to overcome a handicap—his imagination!

"Then he hired another assistant. A woman. That was rare, you see, in 1955. And…Mademoiselle, to say true, I loved her. But so did he. Who. was I to compete with a man of power, knowledge, money? I had…a tiny room on Rue Racine."

LeFrère stares at his limp hands.

"They pushed me aside like a scrap of paper. What else could I do but catalogue the manuscripts he assigned me? One day, I was working in his office. 'Qu'est-ce que c'est?' he grabbed the paper. It was her work. I was correcting it. He had given her a manuscript to transcribe, which used to be my job. She should have been doing the menial cataloguing. 'She has misread it, this is all wrong!' I protested. 'I'm the one who says what's right!' Mauriet shouted, and threw the paper across the room. He slammed the door, and shut me out—" LeFrère turns from the window, his sallow face dark with shame, to see if Naomi is still listening. "He used to love me."

She might faint if she doesn't eat soon. But his story could be her story. For hadn't she, too, seen doors rattle shut in her face, those dark wood doors with frosted glass in Goldwin Smith, those brass latches clicking shut behind her at the Sorbonne? His story, though, has an edge of tragedy tinged with sex, which she has worked to keep out. And anyway, she can't assess her own story on an empty stomach.

"When I went up for my exams, they were oral exams taken before the whole *faculté des lettres* at the Sorbonne, Mauriet gave me an unfamiliar script. The professors sat up on the dais. I could see their black shoes in a row from over the top of my glasses. The letters squirmed like maggots before my eyes. I guessed at the salutation, formulaic, you know. Mauriet paced in front of my desk. I gave a wrong word. He rapped my hand with his magnifying glass. I failed. I was expelled. And yet, Mademoiselle, he threw me this bone! I catalogue books in this library now, books no one ever requests. You, Mademoiselle," he looks right into her eyes, "you were the first to ask for Abélard. Except for…"

"Mauriet? Was he the other one who saw it?" She remembers how the old professor had grunted, feigning disinterest—"Abélard, eh? What aspect of him?"—as his eyes struggled to avoid hers.

LeFrère nods, as if it didn't really matter anymore who wounded him. Castrated him. Yes, here was a man severed from his power. She puts her hand to her mouth. She feels like throwing up.

"I am sorry." She touches his cold hand. He meets her eyes with an ancient hunger, then looks out the window again. Naomi wants to know more. Did Mauriet see this manuscript? Did he think it was Abélard's? LeFrère averts his face, cut off from the rest of his story.

The clock strikes four. She leaves the stacks and gathers her things. Closing the decayed folio, here, near the end, a clear "Eloyssa" stands out on the last legible leaf—Héloïse. She turns back to the "incipit," looks closer, yes, that is "Ab" under the smudge. Looks like "Abd^9," Abailardus. But wait, could it be… "Abt^a," Abbatissa? Abbess. Naomi's head spins with hunger. She has to get out of here before she really does throw up. She lays the manuscript on the counter and hurries down the Mont trying not to smell the food she can't afford to eat.

Back in her room, she stands in front of the armoire and sees, instead of her pale face in the streaked mirror, the face of LeFrère, darkening the way cut eggplant flesh will darken in the air. So this is what mentors do to men. Over knowledge, and who holds the key to it. Will they do it to me, too? Or don't I count as a threat?

She falls backward onto her bed, so dizzy now it feels like death spinning down over her body from the cracked ceiling, her bones eight centuries old, eyes two sockets of pain, skull an empty shell rolling off a stone wall, falling into a yard that has no gate, landing in a garden face up in freshly tilled soil, clover for lips, grass for hair. La clé, la clé, a woman's voice sings, the key, the key, or is she saying the clay, the clay? Naomi tries to sing it, too, but has no tongue. Someone stoops to pull a weed from the bones of her mouth. A wooden cross on a chain swings across her skeleton, hanging from the white-wimpled neck of a bending nun. The clay, the clay, sings the nun, la clé, la clé.

~ xiv ~

Men, tor, mentor, men, tormentor…Naomi moves her lips in sleep, her head rocking back and forth on the grey bed. Her hand grasps for a string of rosary beads, but touches instead a chestnut and a paperclip in her raincoat pocket. Her eyes flutter open in the dark. A loud thump and scrape from the other side of the wall. She jumps off the bed and rushes to the French doors, but a wave of nausea overcomes her. She leans her forehead against the cold draft seeping in the crack between the doors.

"He-RE-ti-cus!" she hears a voice say, deliberating over each syllable. A stream of bitter laughter. "Ha, who gave THEM the keys to the kingdom? Even bishops burn in hell."

Naomi holds her forehead against the crack, barely breathing. She half wants to find out whose voice it is, but her arms hang limp at her sides, her will diminished to the size of a breadcrumb. She sways like the gauze curtain, until the voice yells, "WILL GOD CONFIRM THIS SENTENCE OF HIS?"

Where has she heard that before? She snaps on the yellow lamp and opens her briefcase. The notes from Abélard's *Ethica*. Yes. Oh, my God, here are those very words: "If a bishop, through the anger or hatred which he may have against someone, has resolved to extend his punishment for ever, or never to relax it for him however long he does penance, *will God confirm this sentence of his?*"

Naomi yanks open the French doors. There, behind the barred window, a man in a white T-shirt sits gripping a large book. "They made me throw my own book into the fire. Did you know that?" he babbles to himself, not seeing her there in the dark of her balcony. He stares ahead without blinking. A lunatic? But how did he…oh, it could be chance, not Abélard's words but those of any paranoid calling on God in his wrath at what's been done to him. Poor guy. Naomi leans toward his bars and sees his mouth twist into a bitter scowl. He heaves a sigh, and squeezes his eyes with the thumb and forefinger of his left hand.

"I'm—sometimes I—my losses—," he stammers, about to weep, and then, suddenly, his eyes pop open, still not seeing Naomi. "WHAT PROOF WAS I WAITING FOR?" She runs back into her room and clatters the doors shut. She is not alone here. Now she's sure. She spins on the worn rug, not pinkly safe anymore, trying to decide what to do. Digging deep into her briefcase, she comes up with a single franc. She looks at her watch. It's late. She runs a brush through her matted hair and sails down the spiral stairs for the Café des Etoiles, hoping to find Hélène and Marie.

Her little street, five buildings long, is dark and quiet. Only a few lights up on the top floors shine, hers one of them. She stops walking and turns around. No light at all coming from the building with bars. And no shouting. What seems obvious up close is doubtful from a distance. She doesn't know anymore what she really sees. Rue des Ecoles is still busy, with people walking from the cinéma on St. Jacques toward the two or three open cafés, or heading for the river where she's sure taverns teem with life. She crosses at the darkened pâtisserie on the corner. An awning flaps. "What proof was I waiting for?" How very odd. This could be her own question. She pulls open the door to the café, and jazz pours out.

And there they are. Hélène and Marie deep in discussion. They wave her over, and pour her a glass of wine. She puts her franc on the table. Marie pushes the money back at her and starts to peel an apple.

Naomi's head feels funny, probably hunger. She doesn't notice the writing woman at the next table with her beret pulled all the way down to one side, hiding her profile.

"Do you know that grey building at the end of Rue des Bernardins, either of you?"

"'That grey building'!" teases Marie. "Naomi, ma chérie, all the buildings in Paris are grey!"

"The one that faces the Place du Panthéon? It has bars on the windows, and seems abandoned. Do you know the one?" They do not. The woman at the next table slides her beret over her other ear, and Naomi recognizes her. They both smile.

"You look pale, Naomi. Are you sick?" Hélène asks, taking her hand. "Cold hands, too. What's wrong? Working too hard on that manuscript?"

"It isn't going easy, that's for sure. The script is tiny, and all I have is a two-and-a-half power magnifying glass. The abbreviations are confusing!" She rubs her forehead, feeling fuzzy. "But really it's the librarian who's getting to me. Such a sad man. He told me how he was excluded from his métier by none other than Mauriet. Because he had the nerve to see what he saw!" She takes a sip of wine, not mentioning that man behind bars—judged a heretic, hadn't he said? For seeing what he saw? "Hearing LeFrère's story makes me think about mine. Other ways of being excluded. Invisibility, for example. I keep thinking of last year's Medieval Academy of America convention."

"Do tell!" giggles Hélène.

"I spent the entire cocktail hour studying my colleagues' elbows, and the bottoms of their martini glasses. On the way in to dinner, I got lost in the tweed understory and missed my chance to sit with Petersen and the 'someone important' he promised to introduce me to." Hélène and Marie can't stop laughing, so she continues.

"But no matter! I'd already been dubbed a nobody by the Graduate

School dean, who predicted I'd marry after the master's degree and never get my doctorate. That was his reason for cutting my stipend and awarding more to my colleagues with wives and children to support. Marriage, of course, would never keep *them* from finishing the degree. It would not be a mark of *their* lascivious nature!"

"You see?" interjects Hélène. "They hold your body against you. A handicap to be overcome."

"If you'd want to," mutters Marie.

"But LeFrère's lot seems more tragic, somehow. I guess it's that a marginal man has no place to go. A marginal woman…can always go home."

"C'est vrai, Naomi," says Hélène. "Because at home she is not marginal. Which is why to start my farm. At home, she is central."

"So where can a man go?"

"To hell!" laughs Marie. Hélène slaps her hand.

"But what makes me sickest of all is realizing that, as a woman, I could get away with writing the dissertation any way I want and no one will even look down from the high lectern long enough to sneer. No one will stoop to argue with me, or rise to honor me, or outright banish me. I'm not a threat, way down here at the level of their tie-clips. They'll humor me, give me the damn doctorate, and write me off into a footnote!"

"That is just as well, ma chère Naomi," says Marie. "If you insist on speaking their language, your only place will be the margin—or worse. Concentrate on the palimpsest, if you know what's good for you. Decipher what has been erased."

"You with your palimpsest imagery!"

"I was a paleography student once, too. Briefly." A story clouds Marie's eyes, then clears off like wisps of smoke. She regrets having spoken.

"What happened?"

"I left. I chose history instead—the new history, which considers social context."

"That idea hasn't reached Cornell yet. We're strictly text in the Medieval Studies Program. But context, yes, I mean, how can you detach a manuscript from the actual moment that produced it? And all the intervening moments until you yourself encounter it."

At the next table, the woman inspects her hands in the candle's glow. She has lost interest in her writing. How long will it take to write her way from what she sees to what she's looking for? She picks up her pen, sets it down, twice, and yawns.

"So you were at the Ecole des Chartes?" asks Naomi.

Marie's eyes get that look again. She glances at Hélène. "Merde, why beat around the bush? He tried to kill me, Naomi!"

"Who?"

"You know who! Mauriet, c'était lui."

"What! That shabby old man?"

"He wasn't always old, you know," Hélène reminds her.

"I didn't want to tell you. What you don't know…how do you say en anglais?…can't hurt you."

The woman looking at her hands overhears, and disagrees. Can hurt you. To know is to heal.

"Tell her, Marie," Hélène commands, and turns to Naomi. "You want context. But context is not always pretty, Naomi. In fact, never."

"You already know about his Nazi connection."

"Yes, you told me. But why didn't he lose his post at the Ecole, if people knew?"

Marie gulps the last of her wine and pours another tumbler. "We may think resisters are heroes, but academics are shrewd, you know. Why risk everything? They keep their eyes on their own work."

"And a woman who resists," warns Hélène, "watch out."

"Throw her to the dogs." Marie's mouth forms a thin line, her jaw tight and square.

"Did you…?" Naomi tries not to look into the candle, which stabs her eyes like a dagger.

"Expose him? Hardly. I was only Mauriet's assistant. I was lucky to get the job, being an orphan. My convent school could not spend much on me. Argenteuil has not much *argent!*" She coughs a brittle laugh.

"When was this?"

"Nine years ago—1960. I was your age, barely 21. He had a list of manuscripts acquired from monasteries all over France between 1942 and 1944. He had them stashed somewhere, except for one or two he was working on. Those he kept in a metal file cabinet. When I saw the list, those dates, 1942, 1943—I was a baby then, already an orphan—I wondered: how would a French scholar obtain manuscripts from occupied territory?"

"And? So?"

"And. So." Marie picks up her wine, then sets it down hard. "Though I was a paleographer, I did not imagine parchment as a commodity to trade for human life. Until I saw an exposé in *L'Humanité*. He made a deal, you see. Manuscripts in exchange for Jews. He wasn't named in the article, but I suspected. So I asked Mother Superior, at Argenteuil. She told me a Monsieur Mauriet had coordinated the hiding of orphans during that time period. Good cover. The acquisition dates on the list matched the death dates of all our parents! I had no choice but to confront him. And when I did, he dragged me down the stairway and threw me and my books out onto Rue St. Jacques!"

"Free at last from his domination."

"Non, Hélène, non! Because later a reckless Citroën drove onto the sidewalk as I walked toward the Métro! Narrowly missing me! Not knowing how he might strike made his absence more threatening than his presence. But stuck into my books that he tossed out into the street—was the list!"

"Do you still have it?"

"She has lost it."

"Oui, c'est vrai." Marie presses her lips closed, end of story.

Hélène empties the carafe into their three glasses and they sit in silence. Chilled by Marie's story, nauseated by LeFrère's, Naomi shudders then flushes. When she thinks of her own stupid story about the convention—the pink and the black!—she folds her head into her arms on the table, and wishes she hadn't come to the café. Or to Paris.

"You are sick, Naomi?" Hélène feels her forehead with cool fingers. "Oo-là, you are hot! Go home to bed, Naomi!"

Home. Bed. Ithaca? She pulls her coat around her and starts to say good-night, when the woman at the next table leans over.

"Excusez-moi, I am sorry, but I could not help overhearing...about the building on Rue des Bernardins...?"

"Oui, do you know what it is?"

"I don't know what it is now. It was once part of the wall that enclosed Paris. Medieval Paris consisted of the Latin Quarter only, which went from the Seine to the base of Mont Ste. Geneviève. They locked the gates at night, to keep the rowdy students in. You live there, non? I see you come around the corner almost every day."

"Oh!" Who else watches her? She's got LeFrère from his stacks, Monsieur Montreux where she eats her croissant, that man behind bars—or did she imagine him?—, and now this woman. She fumbles with her coat buttons, unnerved. The woman presses something cold into her hand. She takes a cautious look in the dim candlelight. A large magnifying glass, a ten-power. "Pour toi," the woman says, smiling deep into Naomi's eyes. "To borrow. So you can see your manuscript better."

"Merci!" Naomi smiles nervously. "For this. And for telling me about the wall." The woman smiles and picks up her pen with a joy she hasn't known in all these months.

I climb the cellar stairs with a celeriac root in my basket, tough, gnarled. Something ugly that should never have been unearthed. I scrub the pimpled root whose bitter greens once told where it lay in dark communion with the earth. I peel to reach the creamy flesh. I drop my cleaver down. The severed mass turns brown in the air, resisting its own beauty. A pungent scent of celery and soil rises from the work of my hands.

Outside, snow on snow as high as the garden wall, withered grape vine gnawed with frost. Inside, I hang the kettle from a hook over flames. Celeriac white, window white, sky white. I slice the root in strips as thin as parchment. These I simmer, not ugly now in their bath of white wine from the withered vine that scratches on the window as I stir. Not ugly now, what might never have been taken from earth. Not ugly now, scrubbed white root as pure as parchment bringing words to light.

"Peccatum malum nostrum puto." I think about our evil sin. That's clear enough, but maybe too easy? Isn't this just what one would expect, if one considered this manuscript an autograph Abélard, a lost work discovered, one thought, behind a rock in the cellar that, one believed, was the original site of the Ste. Geneviève school founded by a teacher banished beyond the walls of the Latin Quarter? Knowing his story, as constructed by historians obsessed since the twelfth century with the tragic tale of an arrogant and brilliant man's fall from grace, wouldn't one look at these letters, abbreviated and smudged as they are, and naturally want to read "our evil sin"?

Naomi pushes her hair back from her feverish brow and leafs through the Latin dictionary. What is easy may not penetrate. She's wearing the habit of doubt. After all, it seemed obvious that a man shouted from his window, and yet how can she believe it when the window remains dark and quiet? Anyway, never believe a fevered brain, especially at night. Still sick today, she should have stayed in bed. But there's not much time left to transcribe this manuscript. The Bibliothèque closes today for the New Year, and next week Mademoiselle LaTour is coming. Naomi wants to be sure.

As sure as eyes can be, which isn't all that sure since the mind makes choices for the eyes. Okay, then, if not eyes and mind, both of which throb today despite the aspirin, then heart? Can heart track a quill better than eye or mind? Come on, Naomi. The heart can't read Latin. Your brain is your only hope. She scans the "put-" column in her dictionary, following the intertwined stems: little boy, perfectly pure, stench, well.

Here it is: "puto, putare, putavi, putatum, *v.t.*" To think, transitive verb. To think about something. "I think about our evil sin." Surely these could be the words of one who "wants what he by no means wants to want." It would not be Héloïse calling their love, their sexual union, the birth of their child, or even their secret marriage *a sin*, because sin requires repentance, which she lacked so wonderfully. To Héloïse, who defined grace as "love freely chosen," her greatest sin was taking the veil, because she did not choose for herself. Naomi recalls Héloïse's defiance in the *Letters*: "I can win praise in the eyes of men but deserve none before God, who searches our hearts and loins and sees in our darkness." Loins! Oh, yes.

Naomi squeezes her eyes shut, and sees those hands behind her eyelids again, the competent white hands holding a knife over a worn butcher block. Of course, she still has to consider the theory that Abélard wrote both sides of that correspondence. Gave Héloïse all the honesty he was unable to express. And if he did write it all, then Where is She, as Hélène would ask. Mute? Mutilated? Naomi returns to the dictionary, seeking the common root to all those slippery words.

What about this: "puto, to prune *[a tree]*..." How interesting! A verb that can mean to think about, or to prune? Something clicks inside her pained head. "Malum." Doesn't that mean "apple" as well as "evil"? Another moralistic double-entendre in the chain of woman's bondage, apple becoming evil in her hand. She turns the thin pages, looking for the m's. Yes. Here: "malus, -a, -um *adj.*, bad, evil" and "malum, -i, *n.*, apple."

She polishes the heavy ten-power magnifying glass with her scarf. How that woman in the café knew exactly what she needed is a mystery. She raises and lowers the glass to find the right distance. Letters jump, blurred, huge, then tiny, clear. Here, steady. Big and dark, the letters she's been struggling with, "Abt^a." Abbatissa, definitely not Abailardus. "Hic incipit Abbatissa epist[ulam?]": here the abbess begins her letter. And then—so clear she can see the pores in the parchment holding the ink—the word is not "peccatum" (pct$_3$) at all, but "fecundum" (fcd$_3$)—or "fecundam," since apple-tree is feminine. "Fecundam maluam [?] nostram puto," I prune our fecund apple tree! Under the heavy glass, the words gleam with innocence against the creamy skin. Could any be called sinner who lops off dead wood to help a tree bear fruit?

I think about our evil sin. I prune our fecund apple tree. Two readings of a single text. The subtle submerged under the obvious. This is another kind of palimpsest, not a physical erasure covered by a newly scribed text. No, this was erasure by way of expectation, tradition, assumption—a far more serious error, as it implicates historical study itself. Because here—these words—all along was *she* here, redeeming sin by the act of pruning an apple tree, to cleanse and restore a life gone wrong? These words—hers?—tell of a new life without him, in the convent, tending the earth. He found a way of life without her, too, but it was a return to his old way, following the rules that nearly killed him, that literally emasculated him, that finally betrayed him as "magister hereticus." He needed to believe in her grief. But couldn't she, living into old age, a respected abbess, a teacher of women and girls, cut off the dead wood to find productive strength?

All right. This is starting to make sense. Must be 1137, then, when he was back here on the Mont, and she was building a self-sufficient women's community at the Paraclete, apple trees and all. Naomi holds the large magnifying glass over the date until the x's fill the round window, "mc...X X...vii." The first x is clear and single, the second x with a double cross-hatch—1137. Now her eyes and mind are sure about the date. If Héloïse indeed wrote it to Abélard, and he deposited it here "in monte sancto geneveso"—was LeFrère right, that it had been hidden behind a rock for eight centuries?—what does her heart say to the question, why had Abélard hidden it?

She looks up. LeFrère is watching her. And why had LeFrère hidden it? She wants her story to trace the manuscript from hand to hand, back to the scene of writing. She grips the thick handle of the large magnifying glass. She fancies peering through it at LeFrère. She'd see sharp spikes on his neck, like the stem of an eggplant, fierce under ten-power. But LeFrère is under no power, is not fierce, and close inspection would scatter him like dust. She tries to smile at him. She gets up from the table. Her head spins and she grabs the edge for balance.

"Mademoiselle?" He comes out from behind the counter with concern. The reading room is empty, and outside the sky is already dark at three-fifteen on the last afternoon of the decade. Will 1970 bring this manuscript to light? LeFrère has his hopes and Naomi has hers. She lowers her head. Closes her eyes. Tries not to faint. LeFrère glances at her open notebook, the folio, the glass resting on the wooden table. He puts his hand lightly on her back to steady her.

"Mademoiselle...?"

She raises her eyes to him. "How do you know, Monsieur, how are you so sure this manuscript was written by Abélard?"

LeFrère pulls his hand away as if burned. Ah, bon, alors, she doubts. She, too, will mock and betray me. I had not thought to defend myself. When he grasped me by the tie and pulled me close, so close I could see a crumb in the crease of his cheek, I thought peut-être he would love me again? But instead he locked eyes with me. He let go with a shove. From her, though, this jeune Américaine, I had not thought to defend myself. Her eyes, I can trust? I must hold to my vow, to tell her all, or die.

"Mademoiselle, I know what I know. Mauriet chose me as the one to carry out his fraud. When I learned what his work was, when I saw the work of the woman I could have loved, her terrible document, then I was, how you say, in a dreadful position, with no one to tell." He tugs on his tie and looks away. Naomi slides back down in her chair, pale face turned up to listen.

"His work, Mademoiselle, was…the Nazis gave him manuscripts as they went around France burning monasteries. You must understand, the discovery of manuscripts is très très importante here where our history is so old. We rely on scholarship from the nineteenth or eighteenth century. To maintain a reputation, a scholar must, bon, alors, must do what he has to."

Naomi's temples throb watching his face contort with the effort to break his silence. "What did Mauriet have to do?"

"He had to tell a new story, to give medieval French thought a new root—a Germanic root. To falsify! To attribute the greatness of the French mind to—I cannot speak the blasphemy aloud, Mademoiselle. And he could do this, you see, because with a name like Emile Mauriet, who would question? Who would check? He could pre-date his edition to 1940, 1939, and say his source was 'regrettably' lost in the war. He needed an assistant to do the false transcription—and that she did. And he needed someone to cover up, you see, to keep other scholars from seeking the original. This job as curator that he gave me? Do not be fooled, Mademoiselle. I am given this post because it is here that he hid all his Nazi prizes, and I am not to reveal, I am never to tell."

"How can he keep you from telling? Once you are working here, in the stacks, how can he keep you from seeing what you see?"

LeFrère sits down, pinching the edge of the table nervously. He looks over his shoulder at the guard standing in the hallway. At such a time, before closing, after dark, Mauriet would sometimes come. And tear up something, anything, a newspaper, a receipt, and wave it in his face. And pick up a pen, sniff it like a cigar, put it in his inside jacket pocket, eyeing him snidely, knowing he could do whatever he wanted. Walk by him without looking in his eyes, bump him into the mesh that separates the stacks from the reading room, snatch the key right off the librarian's belt to unlock the manuscript room and take what he wanted and leave with the key. At just such a time…or any time at all…he might…

"And this manuscript, Monsieur? This one you found in the cellar?" she asks, looking down at her hands folded in her lap. "Didn't you tell me it was here from the original time?"

"C'est vrai, Mademoiselle! Of this I am sure! I found it just as I told you, behind the stone at the bottom of the cellar stairs."

"And Mauriet saw it?"

LeFrère's face goes sallow and he lets go of the table edge. The clock strikes two soft bells, half-past three. At just such a time…any time he wants… "He found where I had placed it, on the top shelf, to dry it out after eight hundred years in the cellar. He took the key from me and found where I'd laid it…"

Naomi studies LeFrère's olive-green profile, trying to believe him, but doubting as she watches his eyes dart around the reading room, from the clock to the guard to the stacks. Complicated. Sad. The story is so unlikely that, somehow, she is moved to believe it. She reaches over to touch his shoulder, but he shrinks from the fingers that brush his shoulderpad.

"And what did he think, when he found it? He did look at it, didn't he?"

"He threw it in my face! He told me I was a fool, and he was a fool for giving me the curator's post. He backed me against the shelves and warned me never to touch the manuscript again or he would…"

"He would what? What? What can he do to you?"

"Take it! Take it even though he called it a worthless nothing. Take it, if he ever finds me fooling with it again."

"But that's ridiculous! If he thinks it's nothing, what's the harm? Are you sure it wasn't something he had hidden, and you found?"

"Mademoiselle," he asserts, desperate for her trust, "it is impossible that the manuscript should have been in that cellar any less than eight hundred years. It was practically growing there, the cobwebs, the dust. On this I swear! I stake my career—"

And on this she stakes hers, too. The image of Hélène's roofless barn flashes through her mind, and comforts her. The clock strikes three bells, three-forty-five on this last day of the year. She wants to believe him. What else would explain the worm holes? She closes the manuscript. The back, mottled with stains where he must have brushed or sponged off the mold. The edges, chewed by mice. Eight hundred years of damage. Or, could it be one of Mauriet's "Nazi prizes"? Then why would he have hidden it, separately, in such a damp place, this parchment so dearly bought? And why would he not have simply removed it from LeFrère, since he was so free with the key? She opens to the final folio. "El-yssa," clearly written on the second to last line, not abbreviated, with a worm hole right through the o.

"Monsieur, pardonnez-moi, but could this have been written not by him but by her?"

"Sacre dieu!" His face turns dark purple. To think, if after all, he found someone to take this writing out into the world, to sanctify the name of his blessed teacher, Petrus Abailardus, who has accompanied him in his isolation, whose story is sadder than his own, yes, and far more noble, for he defended himself before bishops, and loved a worthy woman who would never betray his ideas, to think that this girl with eyes so blue, oh, it is unthinkable to have released this parchment to her, mon dieu, if she reads here "Eloyssa" and believes even for an instant that... The clock strikes four loud gongs.

"Mademoiselle, je regrette, we close at sixteen hours."

He sweeps her manuscript off the table. His manuscript. Their manuscript.

"Monsieur! Attendez! Isn't the point to decipher some truth in the words? And to release it from captivity?"

"Some truth? Non! It is *the* truth I want for this manuscript. I thought you had the right heart. It takes heart, to read a manuscript like this."

"Don't I know it!"

"Peut-être, Mademoiselle, your heart finds a different truth from my heart. Is this not possible, to each find what we need to find?"

"Of course! And that's the struggle, that's why history is so messed up, don't you see?"

"Mademoiselle, I am a lost Frenchman. For years I have, so to speak, shared a cell with Petrus Abailardus, one of the great minds of our nation…"

"…though, of course he was a Breton…"

"…and it is through him, through his final justification, that I seek to atone for my failings. He will speak for me, c'est-à-dire, for all who have been mutilated by the men in power."

"Exactly! That's what I want to find, too. A voice that sings in the face of those who silence. But I am not a lost Frenchman. I am a woman."

His eyes flicker from her flushed face to her round breasts. "Bien sûr, Mademoiselle. You are a woman. An American woman."

He turns toward the stacks, carrying the manuscript. Naomi twists the end of her scarf as he disappears down the cellar stairs. Hiding it again? Taking it back to its grave? She feels sick, really sick, too sick to follow him, suddenly too sick even to care. She grabs her briefcase and stumbles out into the marble foyer, where the guard holds the door open for her, then locks it behind her. Outside, she stands in the dark looking one way and the other. Has she made a mistake, skin flushed with excitement, eyes bright, knowing what she knows with her body and not just her mind, knowing that her judgment belongs to her body as undeniably as to her mind, despite what her education has taught her? No! Even sick, she knows. But who will believe the voice of Eloyssa? What evidence can Naomi provide?

An old man hobbles across the other side of the dark plaza, leaning against the Panthéon for balance. Is it Mauriet? She wants to shout, something, she doesn't know what, across the plaza, if only she can gather some strength into her lungs. Even sick, she is stronger than that old man. "WILL ANYONE CONFIRM THIS SENTENCE OF YOURS?" she yells hoarsely, and laughs at the echo, "...of yours, yours?" bouncing off the Panthéon. She walks past the corner of the Bibliothèque and stands directly across from the grey *bâtiment* with bars on its windows which, if she could fly straight through, would land her right on her own cold balcony.

"WHAT PROOF ARE YOU WAITING FOR?" she shouts with the last of her strength.

"...ting for, or?"

The plaza falls silent. A hacking cough doubles her over and propels her down the hill toward bed.

At Argenteuil, it was my chore to lower the wooden bucket down into the well, a hole in the stone courtyard encircled with moss. Had I only learned the lesson of that well! When I left the nuns who raised me and went to Paris to serve my uncle, when he made you my tutor, I learned from books a false lesson. I learned how much I did not know. I learned my lack [inopia]. A well is filled with water. Though it is a hole, it is complete.

From stone, my Peter, formerly mine though never truly mine, I learned to hold love within myself, as the well holds water that springs from the earth.

Naomi, leaning over her desk in long underwear and bare feet, laughs to think she'd read "puteus" as "young boy." It's a well, of course, and drawing water was a young girl's chore. She can just picture Héloïse, dressed in a heavy brown frock, a bucket hanging from each thin arm as she crosses the courtyard. She enters the fragrant kitchen, garlic hanging in braided bunches from the beams, crocks of cabbage fermenting in the corner. An elderly nun smiles at the girl as she puts down her buckets, not spilling a single drop, and returns to the rough table by the window to practice her letters with a goose quill dipped in vegetable ink. How could she have known, this girl with sun shining on her hair, what life awaited her, what consequence of these literate hours?

Indeed, how can Naomi know what life awaits her—what consequence of this moment, now, warming one bare foot against the other as she stands over her notes, re-reading the words she's spent the first week of 1970 culling from a moldy manuscript? Ever since New Year's

Day, when she lay so sick in her grey sheets staring at the cracked ceiling with no one to bring her tea, listening to bells ringing all over Paris, she's known there would be some clear path drawn from this horrible bed to her future. These pink walls are watching her become…someone. She hates how dumb and silly her hopes seem, her work in Paris nothing she can defend. That day, she knew she'd have to win LeFrère back into her confidence, or else see no more of the manuscript. Without it, she'd have nothing to show for all her work, nothing to pay herself back for all her freezing and starving in Paris, and no recompense to LeFrère for his wounds.

Poor hurt man. He did finally believe her the next day when she showed him, under the ten-power glass, the *you* writ so clear here, the *my Peter.* And the difference between "pcto" and "Ptro" which meant the difference between "peccato," sin, or Peter. LeFrère hadn't wanted to believe Naomi, preferring to read *sin*, which requires absolution. Naomi understood why the librarian's shoulders disappeared under the cloth of his suit, why his sallow face sank as he said, "Oui, Mademoiselle, you are right." *My Peter* was that much less his Peter. Once again, it seemed, LeFrère had lost a man he loved, to a woman.

She also began to understand, this first week of 1970, why Abélard might have pushed the letter behind a stone in 1137. In the *Letters,* known to the world for so long, he deflected Héloïse's anguish by invoking the wisdom of the Church Fathers. He forced her to address him on his own terms, and she responded "to her only one after Christ, she who is his alone in Christ." But in this manuscript she finds her own words to quell the pain.

Here at the Paraclete, the stone is flecked with iron. When it rains, the stone weeps blood. This, my Peter, brother not in Christ but in God's whole creation, instructs me to replace my mistaken desire with the strength of iron, which does bleed. As I draw water for washing clothes upon the rocks, I mourn a memory left unspoken, the price still owing for my lost blood, our son

Astralabe. A woman's living heart must pour rain upon iron. Her voice must speak of loss, as water must fill a well. Drawing a bucket from that well, I bring life to the surface, and I drink, and give you to drink.

Could it be the mention of Astralabe, "our son," that made Abélard push the letter behind a rock? Or the way she addresses him in terms so foreign to his life—blood, heart, tears? Or the earthly concerns of washing, drawing water, giving to drink? "Brother in God's whole creation"—how this flattens the hierarchy of Abélard's accustomed world! Naomi shivers at her reflection in the armoire mirror, trying to decide what to wear for her lunch today with Mademoiselle LaTour.

LaTour had written Naomi to meet her at the Café Richelieu on Rue des Petits Champs, by the side of the Bibliothèque Nationale. The usual brown turtleneck seems too Left Bank. She chooses a black wool skirt and a creamy silk blouse, and peels off the long underwear. Her nipples stiffen at the touch of cold silk. Her feet are ice as she eases stockings up over her calves instead of the usual knee socks. She coughs so hard she's thrown back onto the bed. Probably she should still be in bed. But she can't. This is her one chance to confer with someone from Cornell before she leaves Paris at the end of the month. LaTour is the next best thing to—well, of course Kurtzmann is out of the picture— who, then? Petersen? She rubs her forehead. Anyway, it's cold and damp in bed. Maybe it will be warmer on the Right Bank. Maybe Paris is warmer where people have money and a good meal laid on a white tablecloth.

Listening to the church bells of Paris ring in the first new decade of her adult life, she had resolved to ask Mademoiselle LaTour to look at the manuscript, assuming she could get LeFrère to give it to her again, which she did. Now she's got most of it transcribed, all except that ruined last folio, and the voice rings out as clear as those bells. She can't decide if Mademoiselle LaTour will…she runs a comb through her hair and inspects her red-rimmed eyes…what is it she's worried about? LaTour won't believe her? Doesn't like her, is that it? Or that she'll be jealous? The kind of research she taught them in methodology seminar stayed on the safe side. She never made any finds, and now her young student has a strange manuscript that might (or might not) be career-making. Naomi parts her hair in the middle and combs it down on either side of her pale face, then pulls back the waves with a clip behind each ear.

LaTour does have a few books to her name, and tenure. Nothing to sniff at. Say Hélène and Marie are right, that women should speak their own language. A woman like Mademoiselle LaTour, fluent in men's language, still serves a purpose, even if she is a bell without a clapper. Doesn't it count that she translates for other women, perhaps at the sacrifice of her mother tongue? Doesn't she deserve some credit for that? Naomi sticks out her white tongue at the gargoyle woman in the mirror, slips her coat on and zips her boots. Together they descend the spiral stairs.

She walks quickly in the raw cold toward the Métro at Place Maubert. Her mind converses with her body about how costly women's choices are. But how do you know the price? It's not like there's a menu telling how much each entrée costs so you can count under the table to make sure you have enough before you order. Even safe women like Mademoiselle LaTour have paid a price: they've denied the body, which also reins in the erotic mind—to explore passionately, take risks, embrace unconditionally. To go all the way!

Héloïse did not play it safe. She owned her body and her mind, as Abélard's intellectual companion and lover. She did not want to marry. He chose the secret marriage. Her body became his property. Then he forced her to renounce her body, once his was disabled.

What a dismal outline of woman's choice these two women offer up—to give away her body, to deny her mind, damned if she does, damned if she doesn't. Damn, she's crossed to the wrong side of St. Germain. Her mind doesn't know what her body's doing! She crosses back, descending from the light of day to the underground Métro track, and back to her thoughts.

Why was the manuscript hidden in the cellar? The salutation was curious: "epistolam in monte sancto geneveso deposituram," she thinks it says. And she thinks it means the abbess wants the letter kept there on the Mont, like a will. But if, as she says, to speak of loss is a drink of water, bringing life, then why store it underground? Why not drink, and let plants flourish?

Maybe Abélard just hid the thing. She stands in the arc of light under the blue sign, "Maubert-Mutualité," studying the two sets of rails that ribbon through the dark tunnel. He didn't want to drink from the well of sorrow, didn't want the memory of his castration to flower. Héloïse speaks of giving up her baby, giving up her body as fully as he lost his. She took the veil not by her choice, any more than castration was his choice. The train screeches around a curve, sparks hellishly flashing. That's it. If castration is the loss of choice, theirs was a double castration. When Abélard chose his wife's new vocation, he...it's hard to make this accusation...well, let Hélène say it then: he castrated her, he cut off her tongue. His loss can never be assuaged, but she can retrieve her own voice, by speaking.

The Métro clatters into the dark, dirty station. She sees a repeated image of herself, small on the platform, in the passing glass doorways, flash and flash and flash as the train slows. The door opens, erasing her image, leaving her standing there surrounded by blank-faced men heading for the Right Bank. She takes a seat and wraps her coat around her against the cold draft. Is this the erasure that Hélène and Marie mean—to be reflected over and over and over again by men, until some door opens like a throat, breath pours through, a tongue moves, and there she really is, telling her story at last in her own voice? She leans her head against the cool glass, and feels herself falling, gracefully, to the rhythm of the moving train.

Falling, falling, Héloïse's fall from grace as she defined it—love freely given, love freely chosen. So choosing the path of mind would be her state of grace, not body which was expected of her. And Abélard's grace? He is expected to be learned. To reach his state of grace, he'd choose to be a lover, a father, to live in Brittany and raise his son. He'd sacrifice the brilliant career expected of him in the schools.

Naomi's head knocks against the glass. She straightens up on her bench, surrounded by opened newspapers on all sides. In the end he did just what was expected, didn't he, by denying love? He sacrificed his body, and achieved success in the academic world, fame, a place in history. While Héloïse forsook learning to follow her expected destiny, but lost the fruit of her sacrifice. Astralabe.

The train screeches to a halt at Châtelet. Naomi staggers to the Métro map on the wall and pushes the button for her destination. "Bourse" lights up. Follow the purse. Follow the men with folded newspapers under their arm.

Her thoughts carry her along the tile passageway. Who says Héloïse's sacrifice was fruitless? There might have been more children in Brittany, but there would be no textual record of them, as husband and wife. The "magister hereticus" and the abbess of the Paraclete would be lost to history.

Pneumatic doors roll open and she takes a seat in a sleek train that moves on silent rubber wheels under the Right Bank, toward the stock exchange, the theaters, the Bibliothèque Nationale. She watches her image in the window against the speeding dark tunnel. Let's face it, they both fell, each in a different way, down the same deep well. And from the bottom of that well they both sent up work that lives after them, as fruitful as a family tree.

Is it the fall, then, the very fall which is the state of grace, as in

Dante's geography, where his journey takes him down to the deepest pit, only to find it is a mountaintop? You go down and down, expecting to hit bottom, but there is no bottom, no state of damnation or grace, no end to the pilgrimage. Only the journey, like this one from Left Bank to Right, toward a shining Paradiso...the Café Richelieu, and a good lunch!

She grins at her face in the glass, and rubs her burning eyelids. Behind her eyes, those familiar hands again, peeling garlic held between strong fingers, one, two, three, four cloves, and bruising them against the inside of a brown crock. She opens her eyes and flashes the V-sign at her reflection, then closes them again, overcome by a dizzy fever as the pneumatic doors hiss open at Bourse and a forest of suits springs up around her. She looks again at her reflection, alone, as men swirl away from her. Get up, girl. Your brioche awaits. She pulls her aching eyes from the eyes in the window, hoping the pallor that stares back is just from hunger after all.

Françoise LaTour sips her second Dubonnet. Through downcast lashes, she scrutinizes this young student, weighing the commitment of her own precious time. She's traveled here to check a certain manuscript at the Bibliothèque Nationale, one morning's work already accomplished, so much still to do. It would be different if she were the mentor, if this girl's field lay more to the south, in Languedoc, among the troubadours, and not in the infected streets of the Latin Quarter. But to sit here listening to her Petersen-influenced talk about twelfth-century humanism, of all things. She sets her glass down and inspects Miss Weiss' tired face. Perhaps she can be reclaimed. Kurtzmann would have wanted his protégée to develop the meticulousness only she can teach her now. She owes that much to the old gentleman, and to their profession.

"Miss Weiss, do you not like your Dubonnet?" She nudges the glass closer to the girl's silky sleeve which, she notes, is missing one pearl button.

"Oh, oui, Mademoiselle LaTour," she answers, dutifully taking a sip. The awful, sweet taste recalls the reception Mademoiselle LaTour held for their Old French seminar last spring at her apartment. One of her classmates poured his Dubonnet down the drain when the professor had her back turned. The rest of them had forced down a glass apiece before saying goodnight. "And can you please call me Naomi? I'm tired of being 'Miss Weiss'!"

"Bien sûr—Naomi. As for me, I tire of being 'Mademoiselle,' the lady professor. Call me Françoise if you will."

The way her look shoots straight across the narrow table makes Naomi squirm. She's never been this close to her teacher before, always at least a cluttered desk between them, if not a row or two of seats. She can smell her face powder, which is applied much thicker than it needs to be, her skin still young up close like this, with just the beginning of lines around her eyes and one side of her mouth.

"Françoise…" Naomi tries out the name. From their corner booth with leather backrests, Naomi scans the Café Richelieu, the oil paintings, dark wainscot, half-moon marble bar with a brass footrail, the mirror behind the liquor bottles, waiters in white aprons, patrons in dark suits. "Françoise, do you think–," she hesitates, not wanting to offend her, but who else does she have to talk to about her hopes for an academic future? "Do you think 'lady professors' get the same respect as the men?"

"A kind of respect, oui. But not the same," smiles Françoise with the left side of her mouth, revealing a smear of red lipstick on her eyetooth. The right side stays immobile, her cheek smooth. "A type of Mary-worship, vraiment."

Naomi gulps her Dubonnet, shocked to hear Hélène and Marie's favorite metaphor. Must be those convent schools they all went to. "We worshipped Grappone as God," Naomi remarks. "The heavenly chorus! I remember in seminar, our heads would move in unison following his pacing. When he put his cigarette to his lips, we all inhaled with him."

"What happened between you two?" Françoise asks. Naomi's rising blush makes Françoise want to push her to reconsider what to specialize in, whom to study with. These things matter. In France one has no choice. "You used to be a budding Dantista, I seem to remember, but then you left Grappone, the 'great man' who could help you. And you chose…well, Kurtzmann was one thing, but Petersen has no reputation, you see."

Naomi sips her Dubonnet. Blood red, thick. Horrible, really. She swallows with a shudder. Stupid to have mentioned Grappone. She thought she'd handled the break with him so subtly, shifting her major to Latin and never seeing him again. It didn't occur to her that anyone in the department took notice. She watches Françoise's hands grip her empty glass, the very image of the little brown mouse, except for those piercing eyes, not mousy at all without the glasses. What would a mouse know of Grappone's brilliance, or the risks his passionate intellect subjected him to?

"I did worship Grappone. I'd never seen a man so desperate for answers. Pounding on Dante's door, if you know what I mean."

"Bpf," Françoise puffs her red lips in disdain. "He hangs his identity on this anguished search of his, and the never finding. One tires of existential crises year after year. There is work to be done."

"But Mademoiselle La…, Françoise, that is his work. He searches. What happened between us was—I didn't understand then, but now I think I do—I actually believed what he said! And this threatened his life's project, which was perhaps as you've said, never to find the answer. And yet he's got the answer. The never finding is…the answer?"

"Naomi, you are young." Françoise circles the rim of her glass with one finger. Naomi, embarrassed, slides back on the slippery leather seat until cold silk presses against her spine, and she throws the last of the Dubonnet down her sore throat. "Naturally you are attracted to another's confusion," Françoise adds, pushing a long loaf of bread across the small table. Naomi tears a piece off. She shivers, wishing she'd left the thermal undershirt on. Here she thought she'd become so sophisticated, so European, and yet the truth is she's a homesick little girl with goose pimples, and crumbs in her lap, and none of this is lost on Françoise, who peers at her with what Naomi takes for cool sympathy.

Françoise has had about enough, over the years, of Grappone's famous passion, as if that were a scholarly virtue! And now she has to hear it from this girl. Bad enough that the chairman, the dean, the president, the whole Medieval Academy of America do homage to this man, this…slob…who dares to elevate his personal quest to the level of…who does he think he is, Christ Jesus? While no one even takes notice of the work she devotes her life to, the verification of a group of Provençal poets writing in Tours around 1120, a project fully in keeping with the great European tradition. But America is different. There they think he's the brilliant one. Not one annotated edition to his name! At least Naomi is done with him. She can be repaired.

"You're right," Naomi says. "About confusion, I mean. With Kurtzmann, I knew what I was supposed to do. He assumed if I could trace obscure references through the Cornell catalogue, I could find my way in the French educational system. But once you drop out of the system, no one's there to guide you."

"'Drop out'?" Françoise looks into her empty glass, wishing it were full. A Petersen word, no doubt. A Berkeley word. Ridiculous. One doesn't 'drop out.' One is called. One is committed.

Naomi watches Françoise's unreadable eyes, and the little quotation mark between her eyebrows. Under the shelter of thin, arched brows and slightly swollen lids, her eyes are almost as acute as the ten-power eyes of that woman in the café. Five-power eyes, maybe, not so enlarging as the other woman's, but not what Naomi expected from a lady professor. Oh, she should kick herself for slandering her own future that way!

She tries to act as if it's nothing unusual for a waiter to put a steaming bowl of potato-leek soup before her. She dips her spoon, thrilled by the pulse of life in these tantalizing vegetables she's seen every day in the market at Place Painlevé.

"How do you mean, 'drop out'?" Françoise runs her spoon around the perimeter of the soup. "I thought you had a humanities grant.

Cornell is sponsoring you, are we not? We have to approve your work, I'm sure you know."

"What I meant was, I've stopped going to class. Mauriet didn't want anything to do with an American. With me."

"Did you not show him my letter of introduction?"

"No offense, but he seemed not to remember you." Naomi swallows a spoonful of the smooth soup, thinking how professors probably never remember their women students. Their legs maybe, their breasts. No wonder Mauriet had forgotten Françoise. Stop it, Naomi! The soup comforts her throat, and she pictures "la ferme des femmes." Legs won't count at the women's farm. Only strong hands, arms, voice.

Françoise opens her mouth just wider than the spoon, closing her lips around the velvety soup. Bon, he hadn't wanted to remember her, c'est tout. Her career took a horrible turn, for all the wrong reasons, pulling her back to provincial little Alsace. Paris, after that, was outside her possibilities. She landed at Cornell, no thanks to him.

"He acted like he never heard of Cornell," exclaims Naomi. "'Corneille'! As if everything revolves around his pantheonic view of things."

"He could have helped you, regardless of what you might think of him. I had one early success under his tutelage, an article in *Philologische Mitteilungen* that still appears in bibliographies. It gave me some credibility. Cornell hired me. That says something."

"Credibility. That's what has me worried."

Françoise breaks open a piece of bread and tears the soft center. "Credibility. Don't you mean gullibility?" She daubs her front teeth with the corner of her napkin, watching Naomi shrink back against the seat. Françoise dips the bread into her soup, never taking her eyes off Naomi's face, so charmingly vulnerable, so wan and hungry. It's almost a pleasure to rescue her, even if she is Petersen's. He could never teach her the skill of working for years without notice. His office will be crowded with students. He'll get them to do the drudge work while he pursues his pet ideas, in the hallowed tradition of Naomi's first mentor. But a woman could teach her what she needs to know. About submission to authority. About playing the game.

Françoise observes the blood rising in Naomi's bare neck, her cheeks, a rush of pink so fetching she almost hates to push her to the point where that blush will blanche. But a mentor must push. "You are very prone to belief, would you not say?"

Naomi cringes as Françoise smiles at her, one side of her mouth amused, the other bitter. She doesn't want to be read like a text under Françoise's terrible magnifying glass. She wants to tell her own story, even if it is incriminating.

The waiter saves her with a hot ramekin of cassoulet. She spoons up the golden little beans, the carrots. Chunks of sausage and lamb bob to the surface. A stunning dish to set before a starving student! They eat without speaking until, fortified, Naomi decides it's now or never.

"I've been working on a manuscript at the Bibliothèque Ste. Geneviève."

"A bit off the beaten track, if I may say so?"

"Kurtzmann suggested I explore the Mont. I was afraid to go back to Mauriet's class after...we were getting nowhere at all!"

Françoise sits chewing her lamb. Perhaps it is too late. Petersen's Berkeley poison has infected her already. In Europe, one proves oneself by obeying authority. Otherwise it hardly matters what one comes up with.

"And I think I've found something."

"Of Abélard's?"

"No. Something mysterious. Perhaps...Héloïse."

A plateful of curly endive and soft butterhead distracts Naomi from the change in her teacher's face. Françoise spears a forkful of greens, and her lips twist as if the vinaigrette irritated an old canker sore. She studies this girl who fails to understand. Héloïse! Please. She checks her watch.

"But have you lost sight of what you came here for? Abélard?" she asks tartly, stabbing a ring of red onion with her fork.

"No." Naomi wipes dressing off her chin. "I thought the manuscript was Abélard. But underneath, she was there all along. And I finally heard her voice."

"'Her voice'! Miss Weiss, Naomi, please. It is not voice we are interested in. It is text."

"Something else lives. In the stones they walked on, the air they breathed…"

"Enough! Do you want to ruin your chances? I suggest you stop this love affair with stones before you make a fool of yourself."

Naomi dunks her bread in the puddle of dressing, the corners of her mouth turned down, a tear in her eye. Françoise reaches across and touches her hand. Perhaps she has been too harsh.

"Naomi, I was given this advice once myself, to abandon my passion. I didn't like it either. But look how far I've gotten."

"What was your subject?"

"Hildegard," she mutters, hoping the clattering plates will cover her voice.

"…von Bingen? The mystic?" Naomi tries to imagine Françoise young.

"And then he gave me the other work."

"He?"

"My…mentor. He gave me a manuscript to work on. It was publishable. Hildegard wasn't. No one cares about women mystics. Sources and analogues, the work of known thinkers, that is the coin of the scholarly realm."

"Who wants to be a subject in such a realm?"

"Your stipend is not a gift, you understand. You owe on it. It's about time you realized that." Françoise brushes some crumbs into a pile. Perhaps she should go a little easier. Everyone makes mistakes. And she's enjoying this opportunity to rescue a promising career. She will be thanked in the end. "Tell me about this manuscript of yours, then."

"It was the library that first attracted me after I was kicked out of the Sorbonne. Did Petersen tell you about that? The librarian at Ste. Geneviève actually offered me a manuscript. With no credentials."

Françoise folds her napkin to hide the lipstick marks. "Sometimes in these small libraries one deals with a librarian all too eager to get his material out into the world. One must be circumspect."

"Yes. I know. I am. I was. I mean, the manuscript, how can I explain this? I tried to tell Petersen. The librarian said he found it himself. In the cellar of the library."

"And what did our dear Petersen say to that?"

"He sent me off to Chartres!" she laughs. "Listen, I've been wondering why we think history's such a fixed thing. I mean, couldn't a person find something that would change…everything?"

"Bien sûr, all scholars hope to find this!"

"Well, I believe I have! Monsieur LeFrère, that's the librarian, said no one has ever seen…"

"LeFrère?" She beckons to the waiter with a vigor that sways the skin of her neck. "What do you mean, never seen it? If it's there, at least he has entered it into the catalogue."

"No." Naomi wishes she could retract her tale. It does sound implausible.

"Isn't this LeFrère doing his job?"

The waiter brings them each a crème caramel. Firm custard topped with a drizzle of sweet. Naomi's stomach lurches at the smell of bitter black coffee in a tiny white cup. She watches Françoise watching her. She feels forced to continue, if only to justify herself.

"He was saving it for someone he thought would understand. He chose me. I don't know why. I asked for Abélard's *Oeuvres*, and right away he said, 'We have manuscripts, Mademoiselle,' before he even knew I was a paleographer."

"If he had known. That you were Mauriet's student..."

"I'm not."

"You are. You came to Paris to study with Emile Mauriet, not to fiddle around in a little library with a washed-up man from the provinces..."

"Do you know him? Oh, my God,—are you...?" Naomi tries to remember, had LeFrère ever mentioned the name of that woman he loved? Françoise? No, couldn't be. But wait. The fifties?

"Hush, you foolish girl," Françoise says between tight teeth. "Don't oh-my-God me. And what if I do know him? I was in Paris before you were born!"

She watches Naomi fumble with the handle of her demitasse, spilling most of the coffee in the saucer. Perhaps she has pushed too hard. She must be the mentor, after all.

"I'm sorry, Naomi. I am sure you've found something very interesting." She puts her hand on Naomi's. "I'd like to come see it. Tomorrow. Now eat your custard."

Naomi can barely swallow. She'd like to slide her story back down her throat, to hide it in her stomach. The waiter lays the bill between them. Françoise picks it up and opens her purse.

"My treat." She looks into Naomi's troubled eyes. "Think of me as your friend, Naomi. Not your teacher. Let me have a look at this manuscript. I will come to Ste. Geneviève tomorrow at 2 o'clock."

Françoise puts her glasses on. They stand up, straighten their skirts, put on their coats, and part with a wave in the street. Naomi walks the few blocks to the Louvre, and wanders around the galleries for an hour, eyes burning, throat sore, head pounding with fever.

Dubonnet, coffee, and way too much Paris. She wants to weep. She wants to go home. It is dark when she comes out of the museum. She crosses the Pont Neuf to the Left Bank, the river air seeping through her coat, its fingers creeping up inside her cold silk blouse.

At twelve sharp, after a sleepless night and a sick morning, Naomi enters the reading room and sits at the usual table. Only two hours until Françoise arrives. The damaged final folio is scarcely legible except for that "Eloyssa." Worm holes leave *lacunae*, lakes big enough to swim in, pools to be filled by imagination. She's determined that this work be fastidiously executed, but desire could drown her in holes she's dug herself.

Oh, so what? It's not as if reputable scholars never fabricate what they want out of what they can't find. And yet she's paralyzed, sitting at the table studying this smeared folio at ten-power, her future quivering before her, a doctoral dissertation and then a book, the first step on her journey to tenure. Only if Mademoiselle LaTour believes the manuscript's authenticity, only if Petersen will risk his reputation to sponsor her work. Otherwise, what? A work like Helen Waddell's "wonderful little novel," *Peter Abelard*? She can't think about that now. She has only two hours. There's a voice trying to get out. She focuses the big magnifying glass on the last section: is that "vd^{ts}"? Veritas? No, it's a d. Viduitas? She looks in her dictionary: bereavement, or want. Widow or spinster, both called "vidua," both lacking a man. Another example for Marie.

She feels LeFrère's eyes on her back. Her bowels churn, as they had all night, maybe from the lamb and sausage and beans, too rich a feast for a fasting stomach. And a fevered brain. Was Françoise the woman who falsified LeFrère's manuscript and usurped his beloved mentor? Why had she suddenly softened, and agreed to come see this manuscript? She looks over her shoulder at LeFrère. All right, then. She will just ask him. She gets up. He backs into the stacks.

"Wait, Monsieur!"

"Oui, Mademoiselle. A votre service." He brings his hands together.

"Tell me. What was the manuscript you say Mauriet gave to this lady friend of yours?"

LeFrère's face darkens to the color of cooked liver, then fades to lavender. "Oh, Mademoiselle, we French are very sensitive to anything relating to the war, you know. Mauriet was a collaborator, c'est vrai, but now I would discredit him if I were to reveal…"

"What do you care about discrediting him? Look what he did to you!"

"Enfin, Mademoiselle, we French respect our teachers, no matter how they may abuse us."

"You keep their secrets? This woman falsified the manuscript you were cataloguing. You are not the guilty one. They've made their reputations off your silence!"

He steps further into the stacks. Naomi follows him to the back window. "Mademoiselle, before the Nazis would destroy our monasteries, libraries, historical sites, they would retrieve any manuscripts. And give them to Mauriet."

"What did he do in return?" Naomi wants to see if Marie's story is an orphan's exaggerated grief. Could a man really trade human lives for manuscripts?

LeFrère hesitates. "His specialty was to trace the Germanic influences in French monastic culture."

"What Germanic influences?"

"Précisement, Mademoiselle. His work was false. He invented the debt owed by the French to a 'superior' culture. Superior! And I helped him perform this obscenity. I said nothing about her false transcription. He banished me. She made a great success publishing the manuscript."

"And you continued here as curator of Mauriet's acquisitions?"

"Not exactly, Mademoiselle. I went into a sanatorium for a few years. And they met with a small misfortune. A manuscript disappeared from his desk. And he accused her."

"Of stealing it?"

"Oui, and of having her own ambitions. He fired her. Next I knew she was gone to les Etats-Unis."

"The United States? Can you tell me her name?"

"I cannot, Mademoiselle. My cure at the sanatorium, you see. Weeks of shock treatment. I remember very little of what happened before. But I can still work. He lets me stay on as curator, but not of his private collection. The guard, you see…"

Naomi stares at LeFrère's vacant face as he hugs himself and rocks from heel to toe. She goes out to the index, 1940s, 1950s, runs her finger down the L's, and there it is, LaTour, Françoise, "Recherches à propos des influences germaniques sur le monachisme français au moyen âge: un manuscrit inédit." *Philologische Mitteilungen*, 1957, just as she'd said. Funny that Mauriet denied knowing her. But then, he may hold a grudge about the disappeared manuscript that cost her the job.

The clock sounds two bells. One-thirty. How to stop Françoise from coming in? How to warn LeFrère? A cold sweat erupts on her forehead. Is this the manuscript that disappeared? She stares at "vd^{ts}." Viduitas? No—Veriditas? Greenness? A concept developed by Hildegard von Bingen, wasn't it? Hildegard was also "Abbatissa," an abbess in the twelfth century. But no, it couldn't be Hildegard. She was German, and had no connection to Paris, while the manuscript clearly says "in monte sancto geneveso." And besides, "Eloyssa" stares up at her from the last damaged folio. No, this isn't Mauriet's disappeared manuscript. LeFrère found this one undisturbed behind a rock in the cellar, moldy and worm-eaten, not like a manuscript carefully stored in a monastic library until the Nazis grabbed it and delivered it to Mauriet. LeFrère wouldn't lie to her. Would he?

She lowers her hot face onto the parchment, dusty against her cheek. She inhales its earthy smell, like the soil of an open grave. Veriditas? She grabs the dictionary. No such word. Viridis, green. Is it viriditas, then? "Verdure, greenness, freshness." A far cry from widowhood, bereavement, spinsterhood…but whose cry?

The hands of the clock jerk, the bells chime four times, then two loud gongs, and in strides Mademoiselle LaTour, black briefcase in hand, looking—Naomi can't help using the word—like a spinster, certainly not fresh and green.

"Alors, Naomi, let's have a look at your manuscript, shall we?"

Naomi gives Françoise her seat. She turns to see what LeFrère will do when he notices her, but he is still in the stacks. Françoise pushes a stray hair into her tight bun and lowers her glasses to the end of her nose. She turns to the first folio, and picks up the magnifying glass, her finger right on the "Abt^a." Naomi stands over her teacher's chair, inspecting the tightly waved dark hair, the emphatic part down the middle that exposes her white scalp, the strands of gray, the pins that hold her hair in place, the one piece that is out of place. She waits.

"'Abailardus,' do you think, Naomi?"

"No, look again. I see 'Abbatissa' there."

Naomi pushes her long hair behind one ear. She'd expected Françoise would see Abailardus in the squiggled letters. Even with a magnifying glass, one sees what one wants. Françoise, bereft, empty, wants a man on the page before her, to validate her professional performance. Naomi, lonely, wants a woman's voice. A file drawer slams. Both women look toward the sound.

"It *is* you." Françoise's voice is tight, measured, low, as she glares at the librarian.

"Oui. Le même. And you. So I suspected."

Françoise glances up at Naomi, then coldly resumes her critique of the manuscript, ignoring LeFrère's ghostly presence.

"Naomi, it could not be 'Abbatissa.' You see, I have worked on this manuscript, and the authorship is already established as Abélard. You should be happy! He's your man!"

"Non, non, non...," LeFrère whimpered.

"But...he said...it was found here, in the cellar."

Françoise pushes back her chair. She rushes into the stacks after the retreating LeFrère. Naomi ducks out of sight behind a shelf.

"You took it! I knew it!" Françoise corners LeFrère against the grimy window. She stands with her face close to his, like old enemies, or old lovers. "A fine thing. And then off to the sanatorium. I'll have you know I lost my post because of you. I know just when you took it, too, that night we drank wine in Mauriet's office, the last time I ever saw you." She backs off. "One can't trust men. No sooner does one love them, then they use one for their own advancement."

"Non, non, it was not that way. This is not the same manuscript. Mademoiselle has convinced me, much though I have hungered to believe it was Abélard. Look at what your pupil has found. The signature is Héloïse!"

"Outrageous! Never!"

"C'est vrai! This is not your manuscript. You were looking to verify that Abélard wandered to Germany. That his canticles were translations from Middle High German. You could not find that evidence here—or anywhere!"

Françoise grabs a thick book from the shelf and throws it down. Naomi peers through the chink left by the missing book at Françoise's eyes blazing, LeFrère's cheeks sucking in and out.

"You are a madman and a liar! You stole it, you wanted Mauriet to hate me and love you!"

"You are wrong. This is not the same one. This one I found in the cellar..."

"...right where you hid it in the first place, before your supposed breakdown, and conveniently they erased your memory. Now you can claim you found it. And you shamelessly use this innocent girl..."

"Non non non non!" LeFrère keens, smoothing the shiny hair back from his temples with both palms.

"I will go to Mauriet, that's what I will do." Françoise marches toward the reading room. Naomi runs ahead and wedges Françoise's briefcase against the chair rungs with her legs. She grabs her teacher's wrist.

"Please. Mademoiselle LaTour, please don't do that. Don't bring Mauriet into this."

Françoise assesses the strength of Naomi's grip, the danger of it, because if Naomi does bring this thing out, her own work will be overshadowed, diminished. Not to mention the honor that will accrue to Petersen, for sponsoring her. But on the other hand, one might sponsor it oneself. One might guide her through proper channels.

"Naomi. What are you worried about? If Mauriet thinks it is authentic, then your future is assured. If it is specious, your reputation will be saved."

"But Mademoiselle La..., Françoise, he hates me! He hates Monsieur LeFrère. And he hates you, too!"

"Hate has nothing to do with truth. He'll look at it. He'll say what he thinks."

"You don't understand. He ruined Monsieur LeFrère's career, and he'll try to ruin mine!"

Françoise glances at LeFrère's stony face. She leans closer to Naomi. "One can be sure," she says, removing her glasses, "that Mauriet did more for his career than your Monsieur deserved." She steps back. "He stole, he lied!"

"And you didn't? You went along with Mauriet's scheme. Oh, yes, I know all about it. What does that say about your career?"

Naomi is in the blind spot, she knows it, in the place she should not be. Not the detached scholar, observing, investigating. No, she's fighting for the truth, her truth, desperate to protect it from the scrutiny of these others with their own truths to hide. She is wild with hope and fear. The last thing this naked, damaged manuscript needs is a touch of Mauriet's Gallic scorn.

Françoise sees the fear in Naomi's eyes. No point scaring the girl. Let her make her own mistakes. Let her think she's discovered something. Besides, why should she give Mauriet a chance at this find? In Naomi there might be a chance to salvage her own authority. She buttons her sweater.

"I'm returning to the States tomorrow. I don't have much time. I still have to tie up my research. I'll see what I can do."

"Oh, please, don't do anything, Mademoiselle LaTour." Naomi grabs her wrist again. "I'll ask Mauriet myself. Tomorrow. I will bring him here. I promise."

Naomi's voice, beseeching and tight with emotion, fills Françoise with a sense of loss. To be so young, so impassioned. Her own dry research never makes her heart beat fast, as her early work on Hildegard von Bingen had done, before she got caught up in Mauriet's game. He ripped up her thesis, told her not to waste her talents on a nun who saw God in green plants and suffered from fits and visions. No one would ever cite her work, she would never be asked to lecture or sit on commissions. She should help him with his project, if she wanted to succeed. She should put her knowledge of German to good use.

All that is behind her. Her expertise in monastic culture, her native Alsatian affinity to German–French connections, her professional promise, all dashed, and she is—what? a scholar of the courtly love lyric, of all things?—because of one mishap. Whatever happened to that missing manuscript? Is it this one? If so, LeFrère did an ingenious job of it, especially the worm holes. Imagine physically defacing a manuscript for some deranged idea about the past. She shakes her head. There's so little time. Should one protect the girl from her passion? She must position herself correctly in all this. To be the approving mentor, if all goes well. Or the one who told her so, if she fails. She frowns and looks at her watch, then picks up her coat from the back of the chair.

"See you back in Ithaca. I will leave all this for you to tell Petersen. He's the Latin expert, after all."

Her heels click across the marble floor of the rotunda, and the door booms closed behind her. Naomi goes to the front window and watches her teacher walking toward the Panthéon until she is lost behind a kiosk and a line of parked cars.

Naomi turns to LeFrère. They exchange a look that wavers between relief and fear, with a touch of glee in Naomi's blue eyes, a glimmer of copper in LeFrère's black ones. "It is four o'clock," he says.

Naomi returns the manuscript and gathers her things. "Don't worry, Monsieur. We have it right here." She pats her briefcase, and smiles shyly at him, still wondering what, exactly, she has.

"Oui, Mademoiselle. We have it."

Naomi hesitates in front of the counter. LeFrère draws back from the girl, who smiles and raises her hand in farewell. He recoils from the memories her sympathy has released—Mauriet loving him, Mauriet denying him, Mauriet terrorizing him. He withdraws into the one triumph that saves him from the terrible memories: the loose stone, the dusty manuscript hiding behind it, the moment of discovery. He watches the girl walk across the foyer. LeFrère knows, if he ever knew anything, that the manuscript is authentic, valuable. No one can take that knowledge away.

He switches off the lights. Celle-là, she is the one to trust. Naomi turns and smiles at him once more through the grille-work of the door. The guard locks it behind her. The weight of her briefcase carries her down the Mont, past the redolent doorways of dusk, past the fenced-in park at the corner of Rue Monge, and up the spiral stairs to her room where, for some reason, she feels happy and free, sprawling across the bed, her fever gone, her throat clear.

❧ xix ❧

Naomi is late, rushing up the dreary Mont in a steady rain. She has a new hunch about the vexing problem of "deposituram" in the salutation. She pumps her tired legs up the last hump of wet cobbles. Long night last night, that man behind bars weeping as if his salvation lay in the balance, as if his tears were not for one moment only, but for centuries. He kept ranting something like "the men with hoods and the knife Oh Oh Oh!" and then a prayer. "Translate me, O Lord, from this island of silence!"

"Translate me." Carry me across. His plea battered the closed glass doors of Naomi's room. She tossed in her sheets until finally she got out of bed and threw open the doors. No voice. No light behind the bars. She leaned over the iron railing, cold metal pressing against her damp flannel. She looked to the left, drawn by the colored lights emanating into the night from Notre Dame's windows, the shadowy towers against the half-lit city sky. Translate me, translate me from this island of silence.

She glanced to the right at the barred window. She, at least, was not a prisoner. She could cross to that jeweled island, Ile de la Cité. She got dressed and walked down to the Seine, and across, and inside the cathedral, where the tall air was somber and still. No light entered through black windows from the dark outside. A priest walked up and down the nave, swinging his censer and chanting the midnight mass for a few people in coats and hats kneeling on the stone floor near the front. Naomi sat far from the celebrants, enveloped in sickening spice. She leaned her throbbing head back. Far above, the vaulted ribs and pointed arches reached achingly for heaven, as if one breath could float the cathedral upward, to be swallowed by clouds, leaving nothing but an empty island in the middle of a river, snuffing out the centuries and her own tiny life.

"Translate me!" The desperate words of that poor stranger who sought release from the death knell of silence. She knows silence. Unable to speak in defense of her position. Afraid to be skewered like a dead bug on a pin. Out of step with men's swift logic. But her silence is self-inflicted. She's no prisoner. She can translate herself.

He was still weeping when she returned to bed. She lay staring at the crack in her ceiling, vaguely lit by a cloud-covered moon, until she had to get up again to work. And it was the puzzling word "despositu-ram" that jumped off the page of her notebook: "the epistle...*to be deposited* on Mont Ste. Geneviève"? The -ur- that makes the future participle wasn't all that clear. She searched the Latin dictionary. Deponere, *vb. trans.*: to lay down, arrange, put away. Depositum, *n.*: trust, deposit. Depositus, *adj.*: dying, dead, despaired of. Could it be the dative case—"epistulam in monte sancto geneveso deposito," a letter to one dying of despair on Mont Ste. Geneviève? Outside her doors, the man continued to weep until she woke at dawn, cheek down, drooling on the notebook.

And now, shaking her head to clear it, and wiping the rain off her face, Naomi hurries up the hill. Last night recedes like a weird dream as she emerges onto the plateau. But this much remains, an emotional syllogism: if breath can lift a Gothic cathedral off its foundation, then despair can penetrate her doors and make her see new shapes in the abbreviations. She will give tongue and air to the buried words, whether her teachers like it or not. For her own sake. For LeFrère's sake. And also, somehow, for the sad, desperate man behind bars.

She cuts across the slick cobblestones behind the library, past the building that abuts her hotel, where there is or is not a poor creature incarcerated. Is, when she's not looking. Is not, when she looks, like those black letters that squirm away from her scrutiny. As she rounds the bend, she notices Monsieur LeFrère standing in the back window of the stacks. Cold rain runs down her sleeve as she raises a hand in greeting. Still as a statue, brooding, he does not wave back. Another one sentenced to his own silence. Condemned to the hell of no one listening. If the man behind bars and LeFrère could hear each other across this narrow stretch of cobbles, they would not be the lonely prisoners they are.

Naomi touches the cold brass latch in front. The heavy door swings open, just missing her forehead. She stumbles, stunned, raising a hand to her head. A black trenchcoat grazes so close it throws her back a few steps.

Emile Mauriet storms past without looking down at her, clutching a brown valise under his arm, trenchcoat flapping, head bare to the rain. His eyes are fire. His aim is sure. He moves in a fast diagonal across the cobbled plaza, between the parked cars, toward the Sorbonne.

She stands with her thumb on the latch, holding the door open in shock, as rain soaks through to her sweater. "Professeur!" Her voice is drowned out by the splash of rain on cobblestones. The old professor disappears between the Panthéon and a kiosk, just as Mademoiselle LaTour had done yesterday. Mademoiselle LaTour! Naomi rushes into the foyer.

The guard is smoothing his thin white hair, adjusting his gloves. He stoops to retrieve the keys fallen to the floor, and casts his rheumy eyes up at her. She peels off her scarf and hurries to the reading room. LeFrère is not behind the counter waiting for her arrival with lavender hands folded on a manuscript tied with string. She goes into the stacks, and he is still at the window. He droops as if his stem were cut, oozing silent tears as a sliced eggplant sprinkled with salt will shed what little moisture it has.

"What happened?" She steps toward him. He winces. His arms hang down, snipped at the shoulders.

"Mauriet was here," he mumbles, barely audible, "ten years ago…"

"Yes, yes. But what just happened?"

"…and he mocked me, called me a fool, forbade me to…"

"You are not a fool, Monsieur LeFrère. What happened just now?"

"…but he…now he…," LeFrère sobs. Naomi touches his trembling sleeve.

"What did he do? What has he done to you?"

"C'était elle, Françoise…"

"She promised to leave it up to me to contact Mauriet. She was lying, wasn't she! She went right to him. I watched her leave. She wasn't going in the direction of the Métro that would take her back to the BN. She told him! Now he'll want to verify it. He'll want his name on it. He doesn't have a right! These manuscripts belong to France! Even the ones he got for turning in Jews."

"Jews? Non, non, Mademoiselle." LeFrère runs a finger across one temple. "Handing over Jews was only part of it. The Nazis wanted documents. They wanted a new history."

"Okay. Listen. Couldn't this manuscript have been salvaged from the Paraclete, before they burned the library, and given to Mauriet for…"

"Non non non, Mademoiselle, it was just as I described to you. I tripped on the stair, the stone was loose, and it was there. And now…"

"What?"

"Now it is not there."

LeFrère sobs again, and turns to the window as if only in his dismal view of the abandoned building will he be safe. Something lost can be looked for, obsessively, for a whole lifetime. Once something is dead, no one can kill it. Death is as safe as stone. No more hiding, nothing to find. His face goes the color of cut potatoes that have sat too long.

Naomi feels a scream pushing her heart out her mouth. Mauriet took it! She closes her lips hard against her teeth. He tucked it under his arm like a copy of *Le Figaro*, as if the wisdom of the abbess were nothing more important than the news of 9 January 1970. The man who falsified documents, who killed to get them, has stolen the one manuscript innocent of blood. Thief! Murderer!

She grabs LeFrère's elbow. Poor LeFrère, his life wedged between two walls, one with loose foundation stones containing secrets, the other with bars on the windows. She'd hoped to be his swinging gate, to let him out.

Françoise, the prim accomplice scurrying with a briefcase full of ambition to Mauriet's office at the Ecole des Chartes. "I don't have much time," she'd said to Naomi. It doesn't take much time. Betrayal begins deep in the soul, but takes only a single gesture to complete, like Abélard having to pitch his *Theologia christiana* into the fire. It only took a moment for the condemned book to leave his hands and land on the pyre, as the bishops watched the parchment ignite, one folio at a time. Abélard came back from that betrayal. "The indomitable rhinoceros," as he was called, re-wrote the book. What could LeFrère do, weaker by far than his idol? It's up to Naomi to re-write this destroyed book. Rage will save her from silence now, or drive her mad like the man behind bars. What choice does she have? She can't write a meticulous scholarly work, not now. Imagination is all that's left, to fill in that *lacuna* with guesses of the heart.

Mauriet stole the manuscript not to pre-empt her work, but to suppress it. He must avoid the charge of denying LeFrère's remarkable find. Anyway, Mauriet could never see what she saw in the worm-eaten parchment. The words can only be deciphered by someone willing to hear a new Héloïse who thrives, a new Abélard who despairs. The words will sink back into the skin on which they've rested for eight centuries, remaining as cryptic as bones retrieved from a forgotten cellar. Only those willing to descend the ladder with LeFrère will hear the voice Naomi must release through her work.

LeFrère, her friend, her brother. She looks at him with eyes that could heat the whole city of Paris. She takes his icy hand. "Don't worry, Monsieur. We have it right here." She points at her briefcase.

"Oui, Mademoiselle." He draws the side of one long finger under his nose.

She pats him on the shoulderpad, caught up in a vision that flares before her eyes: Mauriet striding toward the Panthéon with the manuscript under his arm, and she flying after him like an arrow shot through the rotunda and past the iron gate and across the plaza, shouting "We will write our own book, just try to stop us!"

LeFrère moves away from her touch. Naomi wipes her eyes. Her work here is done. She puts out her hand, and he shakes it limply.

"Au revoir, Monsieur. I am leaving for the States in just a few days. With the transcription. Don't worry, Monsieur. I will get it out. Somehow."

He stares out the window. She puts on her wet scarf and turns to go. She glances back one last time at her little eggplant man. He raises one sallow hand halfway. "Adieu, Mademoiselle," he whispers to the dirty panes, then lets his hand fall to his side.

third folio

XX

Through the blinding rain she ran, furious and afraid, to stand dripping on the shabby rug in her garret with a briefcase full of useless notes, heavy as grief. Grief that needs so badly to escape that it will do almost anything now, scanning the dark prison within her for some place where the bars are broken. A hideous olive-green light seeps through the gauze curtain, backlighting the vision of Mauriet she will always remember, as a woman who has been raped will always recall the terrible face of her rapist in his throes of violent ecstasy. It is either too late or too soon for tears, or she would certainly weep. Instead she crouches behind the barricade of her grief, listening for some voice to release her.

She scrapes the chair across to the French doors, and sits studying the sad droplets of rain that hang from the railing. "I felt more shame than pain," she repeats Pierre Abélard's words—Oh Oh the knife the knife—that's what the paranoid next door had been wailing—and his words unlock her rage. She bolts out of the chair, knocking it over, but there's no room to run between bed and desk. She opens the armoire and throws handfuls of clothes to the floor, drags her suitcase out from under the dust, slams it down on the bed, loads books into it, until finally she is chilled to the bone with stifled fury. She does not want to be heard way up here on the fifth floor, does not want anyone to know her shame, her pain, as she has heard his, that man who lives beyond her wall. She peels off her wet raincoat and flings it at the wall. She strips off damp clothes, and layers her cold flesh with thermal underwear, and pink flannel nightgown, and turtleneck sweater, and socks, socks, socks. She can barely roll herself up in the bedspread, knocking the suitcase onto the rug and securing herself at last on her bed in a tight cocoon.

More shame than pain. For what he'd done. Loved a woman, this celibate man. But what have I done, or LeFrère, to deserve this defeat, what! LeFrère's hopeless face rises in her vision, a victim, dead at the hands of Mauriet. Dead! He will not have the strength to go on, like Abélard. You, Pierre, you had love to protect the heart as a golden coffer holds a precious relic. And you, Héloïse, a girl like me, in the grip of passion, you trusted that coffer to hold you safe throughout your life, despite the pain. You trusted love even through the nights of thwarted desire as you lay wrapped in nun's cloth. But what does LeFrère have, what do I have, two lonely seekers finding truth in illegible words?

She squeezes her eyes shut and drops over the wall of pain. Those familiar hands that live behind her eyelids caress a glossy eggplant between weathered palms. Cut from the bush where it grew, a flower first and then a fruit, the eggplant is yet alive in its seeds, to make another life in the soil of that walled garden her dreams take her to. In semi-sleep, she hears a hoe scratching, the clang as it hits a rock, the patting hands that firm the soil around a young seedling. She sees the ripe eggplant held in place on the chopping block, the stem sliced off, strips of purple skin in a pile. A big knife splits the bare flesh lengthwise. Quarters, then cubes, pale green, lie on the board.

Out of the blood-red background of her sleeping eyes, a coarse brown frock appears, a stiff white bib, a heavy chain with a cross hanging against the white. The hands rise in front of the cross, working to layer tomato slices, eggplant cubes, green pepper rings, in an earthenware crock rubbed with garlic. The hands gently place a brown-glazed lid on the full crock, and meet palm to palm over the closed dish in benediction of a holy task accomplished. Then, an afterthought, one hand raises the lid again, and a nose bends down to sniff the raw, fragrant ratatouille. The cross swings toward the crock. The head dressed in a wimple, the face framed in white, with green eyes and arched blond brows like Hélène, with the mysterious smile of the café woman. It is Héloïse beyond a doubt. Héloïse the abbess of the Paraclete.

Naomi murmurs in her sleep, and steps toward the chopping block where the middle-aged abbess sets the lid back on the crock and smiles. Her face, reduced by the starched linen to a triangle of eyes, nose, mouth, radiates kindness and intelligence. Furrowed brow, fine lines around the eyes from squinting in the sun or bending to the parchment. Full lips with a deep parenthesis on each side enclosing some small measure of happiness. Her long brown habit skims the stone floor, the glass beads hanging from her waist sway to the rhythm of her steps, as she goes to place the crock in a brick oven. She turns, and the wooden cross swings out and comes to rest against the white bib.

"So," she says, looking at Naomi for the first time. "You've come."

Naomi takes a step back. Come? She closes like a book not wanting to be read. The green eyes study her, waiting for the words that always fail Naomi under the scope of one who knows.

"I, um, you...," she struggles to unlock her voice, as if it were a foreign tongue she were ashamed to mispronounce. "You...?"

"Yes." The abbess smiles, sweeping vegetable scraps off the chopping block into a basket. She herself had been wordless when she first saw the girl. Who wouldn't be, in Paris, where others' words proliferate like yeast? And, for all that, no one listens. She hands Naomi the basket. She owes her at least these scraps, for finding her after all.

"Come. Follow me. The carrots need thinning."

Naomi steps over a warped threshold. Bright sun blinds her, and she nearly trips on some chickens scratching between the flagstones in the yard.

"Feed them," Héloïse says, watching Naomi discover that she, too, is wearing a brown habit. Naomi pushes back one rough sleeve and scatters eggplant peelings and the pulpy seed-cores of peppers on the dirt alongside the stone path. More chickens appear, pecking at the scraps.

"Bring the basket, we'll save them the carrot thinnings, too," Héloïse says over her shoulder as she heads for a high stone wall at the end of a short walkway. Naomi recognizes the wall as the gateless garden of her dreams. But this garden has a wooden gate on iron hinges. Héloïse pulls a large ring and the gate swings open.

Inside the walled garden, the air is earthy and cool. A rising tide of plants unfolds in the dewy morning sun. On the four enclosing walls, espaliered trees swell with fruit along their candelabra branches. Birds swoop over the walls with busy song. Just visible over the top, a field of ripe barley waves toward a road that runs between an aisle of oaks. Beyond the trees, a silver river flashes.

Naomi stands with the basket over her arm. Héloïse hikes her habit up over her ankles and stoops to a row of carrots. Work fits her like a familiar skin. She has found her way back to where she was all along, thanks to the girl.

"Leave the sturdiest," she explains, uprooting most of the ferny seedlings. "They need empty space to grow into. Come. Try it." Her nimble fingers pull these and leave those, selecting by some sense other than sight. She tosses the discards into the basket. Naomi squats down next to her, and they work in silence as the sun rises toward noon. Beads of sweat form under Naomi's habit, the brown frock dragging in the dirt between the carrot rows.

"Héloïse," Naomi addresses her, finding a tentative voice. The woman looks up. "Aren't you hot?"

The abbess smiles at Naomi. "Only my body is." She stands up and wipes what shows of her forehead below the wimple's edge.

Naomi looks up at her, picturing Heloïse naked under her habit, a triangle of pale curls like any other woman, and breasts beginning to sag with age. Naomi stands up, too, stretching her young body under the habit, dark brown hair and full round breasts. This body has a future ahead of it, while Héloïse's is past. The body of a nun, what is it but a rebuke?

"I still remember, Naomi, the day I gave my body to my beloved. You're wondering about my body, aren't you?" Naomi blushes and shrugs, returns to her work.

"We were reading Ovid," Héloïse bends to the baby carrots, "on the bench near the window in my Uncle Fulbert's study, the heavy book on the table in front of us. My pulse was rushing. His was, too. I saw the vein throbbing in his neck as he pointed at the words, keeping his eyes off me. I wasn't looking at the words. I had never been so near a man before, except leaning over my uncle as I put down his soup. Pierre's hair curled in sandy tendrils over his ears. His eyes burned. I was almost glad he didn't look at me. He pointed at words, grabbed the air as he spoke, rubbed his head while thinking. He was not a peaceful man. I wanted to see him find peace. I stared at the vein as he recited Ovid. I couldn't help myself, it was as if I were starving and he was food. I put my face on his neck, breathed his man smell, felt his skin like warm wax under my cheek. I lost myself behind his earlobe. He opened his arms to me, we melted together like two votary candles. Oh, it was everything, it was all, it was..."

The nun raises her eyes to the sky, and they fill with light as if a holy vision had come upon her here in the carrot bed.

"You don't regret it, then? After all that happened?"

"Would I regret a visitation from God? Many women have been tortured for their visions, and I for mine. But would I deny my Lord?"

"Your Lord? You mean God? Or Pierre?"

"God, Pierre, what's the difference?" She throws her head back and laughs, showing straight teeth and tender skin. "Naomi," she turns her soft green eyes toward her, "Pierre is only a name for God. Love is God, the earth is God, the body is God..."

"...mind is God," interjects Naomi.

"Yes, it's all God." She casts her brown-sleeved arm in a wide arc, taking in the garden, the countryside, the stone building they'd come out of, the hen yard. "Mind, though...," she stops, thinking, and goes back to thinning carrots for a long silence. "Mind has a mind of its own." She laughs again.

"Why is mind different?"

"Language. Words. They fill the mind until it cracks open like a chick hatching, and it becomes afraid, and keeps trying to return inside the perfect shell. Here, we give the chickens their eggshells to eat. Our feet grind the shells into the ground as we go collecting eggs. The shells nourish the earth, and the weeds grow, and the hens eat those, too. It's all God, it's all food. It's all Pierre!"

Héloïse looks at Naomi's puzzled face. And why wouldn't she be confused? Héloïse herself had snagged her mind on a branch in a flowing river. It took her eight centuries to cut loose, with Naomi's help, though the girl doesn't know yet what she's done. All that deciphering of text and wondering why. Poor girl. And then to fail. There is no final truth, can't she see that? Maybe this way she'll understand. Through carrots.

"The only way forward is to die."

"Forward?" Naomi tosses the carrot thinnings into the basket, and wipes a muddy hand on her frock. "Die?"

"Look, see these carrots?" Héloïse points down the row. "They live to be eaten, to give us life. And then they become soil again. And so do we. Our life doesn't belong to us, just because we put our name on it. We pass it between us. What happens doesn't matter, only that we live and give others life."

"Are you...dead?"

"Don't get stuck in time, Naomi. Mind talks a straight line. It thinks beginning and end, I and you, mine and yours. But that's all words! I floundered for too long trying to find my name, my story. I disappeared, all but a trace, enough to keep me wandering the streets of Paris looking for something, or someone." She returns to her thinning.

"What else is there, without words?"

"Infinite space. Space is a body, and body speaks another language. Carrots speak it—can't you hear them?" She holds a tiny carrot to the starched wimple that covers Naomi's ear. "It's a round language, not linear. No memory, no possession, no desire, no regret."

"A boring language!" Naomi bites off the crisp root and sputters the mud off her tongue. "What does a carrot have to live for? Nothing to strive for, nothing to finish, just grow till you're eaten, what a mission!"

The parentheses around the nun's mouth deepen at the sound of Naomi's true voice, the one she uses when she is alone. For centuries she wandered the narrow streets, waiting for someone to hear her. And in an instant this girl has done it.

"But Héloïse, come on, tell me the truth. You weren't always serene. What about your suffering?"

"I carried my suffering, yes, and looked for some place to set it down. The story of suffering can only be discovered by one who suffers. Like you."

"I discovered the story? You don't mean…the manuscript? The Abbatissa…was you? Here all along?"

"I was. Here all along. But I needed you, with your pain, to help me recover the words he never responded to. I began to doubt I had ever written them. You showed them to me. Now I see he did receive them, and understood, or why else would he have buried them? Now I can pull away the scaffold of my need. My self stands. Eternally. Thanks to your studious work."

"You know I wanted him to be my teacher, just like you did." Naomi moves the basket along the row. "I wasn't looking for you!"

"No. But I led you here with the work of my hands."

"The vegetables?" Naomi looks more closely at the abbess' hands.

"Yes, it was my hands. You didn't pay attention to anything but words. Only now, when your hope for those words is destroyed, you find me."

She lifts her habit and steps to the other side of the row. She squats across from Naomi and looks directly at her from the depths of her eyes.

"You came for him, but what did you find of him? You studied his words. You thought reading him could penetrate to the man. And because you could not read me, I was absent. A mystery, unsolvable!" She throws her head back and the sun casts the shadow of her nose across her laughing mouth.

"Can't know what you can't prove," Naomi parrots the scholars. "Can't prove what you can't read. The word is God made flesh."

"When nothing could be further from the truth! Words are a prison that keeps him who he was at the moment of writing. And the others who wrote to perpetuate his story lock him behind bars."

Bars? She watches the top of Héloïse's head, the brown veil falling over the nun's shoulders and shading her hands as she deftly thins a patch of carrots. All this time, Naomi'd seen but had not heard Héloïse's hands. She'd heard but not seen the man beyond her wall. Could it be…Pierre?…man of many words, man of history?

"I guess I thought people lived in the texts they left behind. You were the absent one, because what you wrote was lost. See, when I found the manuscript, I hoped I could bring you back by decoding your words. But…"

Héloïse looks up from her work. "I'm saying that I am back because you found my writing and then lost it. I needed to be sure I was ever there. Now I don't need those words. My life is my text. The garden is my text. Earth is my text."

"And him? Do you...see him?"

"I told you, he's still in the prison he forged with his words." She smiles at Naomi's bewildered face. She already hears with her heart, this one. How long before she breaks the habit of text and learns to see with her hands?

"And nothing could bring him back except to destroy those words?"

Héloïse shakes her head sadly. "You're the paleographer. You know his words will never be allowed to rot in peace as old bones do. They are preserved, a substitute for the life that created them."

"But, Héloïse, couldn't he be...alive...like you? Why would he just...die?" They move into the cool shadow of the stone wall at the end of the row.

"Come. Bring the basket."

Naomi turns to pick up the basket, her habit twisting around her ankles. She kicks to get free, tangling, in her sleep, the bedspread more tightly around her, sweating in the heat of the garden of her dream. She opens her eyes once, twice, in the twilit hotel room, then sighs and sleeps again.

XXI

"Héloïse?" Naomi stumbles over the worn threshold of the stone chapterhouse, into a large dim room with a flagstone floor. She sets the basket down and lets her eyes adjust to the low ceiling with dark oak beams, two long slant-top tables with ink wells, a high lectern up front with a wooden crucifix on the wall. A schoolroom, perhaps, or a scriptorium.

She is hot, very hot, just as she was the first day she set foot inside the lecture hall at the Ecole des Chartes, a lifetime ago. So hot she might faint, her body encased in heavy cloth, a rope around her waist. She closes then opens her eyes. The dark crucifix jumps out against the white wall. She squeezes them shut again, swooning, and squints just enough to stagger to one of the tables. She slides in along the bench, her hem dragging, bare feet on cool stones. She puts her cheek down on the slanted desk and pulls the habit up over her knees. A breeze wafts through the iron grille of the window, the sound of a distant river, the fragrance of lavender and thyme.

She could sleep here forever, sleep until her skin cools and her face melds with the worn grain of the desktop. Sleep until the Middle Ages, as long as the river keeps flowing, until the book is written. The book? She raises her head and looks around. She is alone enough to write. She reaches under the desk and finds a composition book, the one she'd bought in Paris, with the marbled cover. She opens to the first page. "Pensées de la Nuit, 1969 – " written in her own blue cursive. She closes the book. How embarrassing. Was she ever that romantic, that young? She looks at her hands. Healthy and brown, with dirt under her nails. Is she older now? She inspects her palms and finds them still uncallused, fingertips smooth except for the familiar ink-stained bump on the middle right finger. She reaches into the desk and finds a quill. She opens the book. She dips into the dry ink well and moves the quill across the empty page. No words appear as the rhythm of writing carries her through several pages.

Heavy oak against flat stone. Chair scraping on floor. She closes the book. Héloïse? Or...that man? He seems to scrape his chair especially when she's writing. But that's in Paris. She looks at the cover of her notebook and up at the crucifix. Paris? She slips her "Pensées" back under the desk, trying to remember what she'd just written. It seemed important.

She slides out along the bench. Hem drops down and swirls around her ankles. Nice, really, to be all hidden by cloth. Legs move freely under the frock in the private darkness, carrying her along a white-washed corridor. Fingers reach out to touch the rough walls. Nice here. Stay here until the Middle Ages, as long as the river keeps flowing.

An oak door stands open. Stark against the wooden walls, a shrunken figure in a white wimple and brown veil sits bent over a table, writing. Naomi crosses the threshold and stands watching the old nun, her bony knuckles laboring to guide the quill. She reaches to dip into the ink. Naomi sees that she is more habit than body, with a very wrinkled face peeking out, forehead deeply grooved, mouth pulled by gravity into a slight frown. At the next dip of the quill, she looks up and raises her arched white eyebrows. Naomi is looking once again into the green eyes of Héloïse.

"You're so old!" Naomi gasps. The nun laughs, deepening the crescents that enclose full lips, showing straight, yellowing teeth. "And so beautiful!" Naomi approaches the table when Héloïse sets down her quill. She wants to kneel and touch the walnut face, to put her head in the lap of this gentle soul, and feel the weight of those weathered hands on her hair. But starched linen constrains her own head and neck, and so she remains on the other side of the desk in a position familiar from a lifetime of discipleship. A lifetime? Is she old, then, too? She can't tell, with the frock covering her body. She feels very young, the way she always feels with professors. But this is no arrogant Mauriet, no dignified Kurtzmann, tortured Grappone, cocky Petersen. This is not a mentor who will inject his knowledge into her emptiness, and reward her intelligence with his lust. This is a woman who can't give anything but what Naomi already has, who can't be anything but what Naomi already is.

"Sit down," Héloïse gestures with her quill toward a chair of leather straps slung between a crude wooden frame. "Don't be afraid, Naomi. Don't be shy with me. I'll teach you." She pats Naomi's hand. "We're all women here, and girls who come for the day. I can teach you, too. Afternoons we do the work of words. Mornings there's the garden, as you saw, and the kitchen. Evenings we pray. So you see, we make a life together, and that is God."

"Together...it sounds nice! Not austere like a monastery."

"Our first Latin lesson, then: the origins of the word 'convent.'"

"Con-venire?"

"That's right. Come together." She smiles. "And monastery?"

"Hmm, I don't know. Mono. One? Alone?"

"Yes. A monk forsakes others to seek one truth. For us, God is the multiplicity of a working community."

"No wonder!" Naomi begins to laugh. "Life is a battleground, to men. Of course they'd have to separate to find God. It's that or kill each other!"

Héloïse laughs, too, reading the inside of Naomi's mind. She watches the green shadow of their morning work in the garden settle over the labyrinth this young woman has constructed for herself. Too difficult a path, to forsake all human company in order to find something she can defend, something the men will accept her for.

Naomi relaxes into the leather sling, eye to eye with the old woman, willing to be read by her gaze. She shudders at the memory of Mademoiselle LaTour's way of reading the book of Naomi through a lens distorted by bitter disappointment. But here, the old abbess looks right into her face and magnifies the beauty in every pore of her skin, the bewildered eyes that can hide nothing, the hesitant mouth that envelopes her desire to speak, the heart swelling with something found at last.

A shaft of light falls across Héloïse's interrupted writing, her neat lines of careful minuscule. Naomi thinks of her own "Pensées de la Nuit," and how words eluded her night after night in Paris. The notebook remains another empty promise to take back to Ithaca along with the notes from the illegible, and now stolen, manuscript. Out there in the scriptorium, she was able to express the way it felt inside her own skin, as if she were a secret garden to which writing was the key. Writing—but not words. She always thought she had to be alone to unlock the gate. The presence of that man on the other side of her wall had put a chill on her writing. Just now, words flowed from her quill, invisible but palpable. She isn't alone here. There are women quietly at work in every corner of this convent. Could that be the key? La clé, la clé...a little melody comes into her head, and she smiles.

Héloïse watches the young woman looking at the parchment on her desk. "There is more going on than what gets written down, Naomi." The surface under Héloïse's dripping quill lacks worm holes and mold. She waits for the size and shape to register on Naomi's face. Finally, she sees her blue eyes quaver with recognition, and confusion.

"Yes. This is it. The manuscript you found."

Naomi's mouth drops open. If she's writing it right now, then is this 1137? Did she sleep until the Middle Ages after all? Or is it 1970?

But then where are the holes in the parchment? What about Abélard hiding it, and LeFrère finding it, and LaTour tattling and Mauriet stealing? And herself, laboring over it with that café woman's ten-power glass? If the ink is wet, then the whole story that transports an object from one place to another never happened, and these are the words, and this is the scene of writing.

And what about Héloïse saying it was lost for good, and that's how she'd been able to find her way back to the garden after so many centuries?

Héloïse laughs, watching Naomi's face change. "The roads of history converge here, at the river, the beautiful Ardusson that runs by our convent. And I am always here, writing the same lesson."

Naomi squirms in the chair and rubs her eyes. Héloïse instructed her to forget about words so she could find this place. If she tries to read them, will she end up back in Paris where she's always dissatisfied and afraid? She runs a finger under the edge of the wimple, which is choking her.

Héloïse pushes the parchment toward Naomi. "Look." She points with a bent finger at the last line, still wet. "This is the part you could not decipher. You had to leave it blank because you needed to come here, and stop using the library. You needed a woman to teach you."

Naomi leans closer to look where she's pointing, but the wimple cuts into her throat and all she can see is the map of blue veins on Héloïse's hand, the soil-caked fingernail obscuring the letters. She sits back against the leather seat, exhausted with the effort. She tries to swallow.

"I've really never had a woman teacher," she says, erasing Françoise LaTour from her mental roster. A real teacher wouldn't sweet-talk her into submission, then betray her. "I've only had men."

"You need a teacher to be your partner in change."

"Change! My teachers never change. They have all the answers!

And I'm supposed to find the answers in the back of the book. Their book!"

"Exactly. They give knowledge, and you receive it. They write the book, and you read it. Who will go with you to discover the knowledge within yourself?"

Naomi manages to swallow past the lump in her throat. "I feel so alone."

"And that is the danger. You want a companion—your teacher, a man—this can be very complicated! Look where I ended up!"

"A nun!" Naomi glances down at her own brown habit. "But Pierre…"

"After he was castrated, he did become a true teacher. We worked together to rebuild love's body through words of counsel and consolation. We gave each other strength, me to direct this convent, him to continue his fight in the world of men."

"You can't mean that only a woman or a eunuch can teach a woman?"

"No," she laughs, "no. But a woman needs her own strength before she can learn from a man. You have to make your own choices and not be swayed by desire. Desire obscures your intentions, and this leads to great suffering." She takes Naomi's ink-stained hand and smoothes the soft palm with her leathery one. Sometimes a great learning can come of passionate attraction, she knows that. But the price is very high. She wants to spare Naomi that pain. "I never meant to be a nun, Naomi! This has been my tribulation, that I came here out of circumstance. I lived a lie, and only I knew it, only I and God."

"Héloïse, no! You lived a worthy life. Look at all the good you've done. You built this place up to a great convent, with six daughter-houses before you…died. You shaped the Benedictine Rule, to guide nuns in their communities. You taught girls and women to read and write. You gave Pierre Abélard a reason to go on living."

"All that is true. And so I don't regret my life. It's not what you choose, it's what you do with what happens. Look, I know what your real questions are—about belief, and the power to choose. Not one of your teachers has ever answered you!"

Naomi nods. Even Petersen only sends her back to what he knows. Which doesn't help her at all. Is he even really listening?

"Let me try. To talk about choice, I mean. Sometimes an action has a consequence you don't intend. I never meant to hurt my Uncle Fulbert, or give up Astralabe, my son. I never meant that my golden-haired lover would force me to marry him, and later force me to take the veil. Love was our intention, a love that joined two minds. We became students of each other. But the result of choosing love was a secret marriage, an abandoned son, a damaged career, a mutilation. Naomi, don't you see? The learned abbess with her outward piety—what praises she earned! I simply made the best of what came my way."

Naomi opens her mouth to defend her, but Héloïse raises one hand. They study each other's eyes. The room grows dim, and their wimples glow in the lavender afterlight of the dying day.

"You're saying that choices plunge you into a moving river where you lose control. But...I'm afraid I'll end up where I didn't choose to go."

"Just go. Live. Find your own voice in the world."

Tears well up in Naomi's eyes. She blinks and they cascade down her face. The old woman blurs to a voice, a warm breath on Naomi's cheek as they lean together. Héloïse picks up her quill, dips it, and bends close to the place where Naomi had interrupted her. She comes to the end of the line and looks up.

"First you must learn to plant and harvest. First you must write a book without words." She laughs and sprinkles a pinch of sand on the wet ink. Her white bib, with the dark crucifix, pulsates in the fading light. Outside in the courtyard a bell rings, calling the nuns to

Compline, but Héloïse does not rise from her chair. Only the sound of their breathing stirs the resonant silence after the bell.

"And Pierre?" Naomi wipes her eyes with a sleeve. "Is he…dead? I mean, if you're still around, is he?"

A sudden knocking interrupts them. Héloïse presses a gnarled hand down on Naomi's shoulder to push herself up from the chair. A breeze crosses Naomi's cheek as the crucifix swings out from between what would be the nun's shriveled breasts. The frantic knocking goes on. Naomi looks all around at the dark walls of the room, the grey square of window, the open door that leads down the corridor to the scriptorium, and the other door, closed, where someone is pounding harder and harder, as hard as the blood in her ears.

"There he is now," Héloïse says, groping for her applewood cane. She hobbles away from Naomi, her frock blending with the darkness. He? Here? Now? Naomi straightens her back against the leather thongs of the chair, bathed in fearful joy. To meet Pierre Abélard at last!

She tries to turn toward the door. The stiff wimple presses into her neck, and the sleeves catch on the frame of her chair. She turns and turns, looking for the door where Héloïse has disappeared in her dark habit. She glimpses the silver streak of the mirror, the hump of her suit-case on the floor, and she is strangling in the bedspread. Someone is banging. On the pink wall? Someone is banging. Oh, God, who could it be? That man? She struggles to unwrap herself and find the light switch. The banging continues, and voices in the hall.

xxii

"Moment, s'il vous plaît!" She unwraps herself from the bundled bedspread. The door, someone is banging on the door, not the wall. Not him, then. Him? She flicks on the light and a neon pain sears her eyes. She rushes the two steps across the rug, not thinking how she must look in all her rumpled clothes. She pulls open the door and in tumble Hélène and Marie.

"We finally found you," Marie says breathlessly. "Your concierge down there, we woke her. She did not want to let us come up, she would not tell us what is your room. But we remembered you said the top floor. Et voilà, here you are!"

"I guess."

"She guesses she is here! How do you like that, Hélène? Come back from the dead to join us, eh? Naomi, there's a demonstration, right now, at the Jardin. Women are gathering to march to the Ecole Polytechnique, on the other side of Mont Ste. Geneviève. We want you to march with us, this once, before you go home. Don't give me those frightened American eyes. Listen to me!"

From the half-crazed Marie, Naomi looks to Hélène, hoping to find the usual serenity in her…green eyes…familiar…as if she'd just been talking to her…? She rubs her hot forehead, shakes her head. No, no.

Hélène nods vehemently. "Yes. Naomi. Listen to her!"

"The Ecole Polytechnique, Naomi. They don't admit women there! We are not going to let those swine tell us what our rights are. You have to come with us!"

"But…," Naomi begins her excuses, the old pattern of objection she'd practiced on Sharon at Cornell. I have to study, is what she used to say. I have to sleep, went the cadence. I have to pack. I'm leaving. I have to remember something, a dream I just had. I have to think about it. I have to forget about it, or else I'm going to go crazy, like my lunatic neighbor.

"I...," Naomi stammers, still not knowing what to say, just wishing, even though they're her only friends in Paris, that they would go away. It's easier to be lonely, easier to ignore other people's pain, easier to cry over spilled history than to clean up the present. It's easier to wish someone would come. But someone never does come just to give comfort, without demands.

"You must," says Hélène. She leads her by the elbow and sits her down on the bed. "It is very important, you know, because the college it was founded by a woman, Jeanne de Navarre, the wife of King Philippe le Bel, in 1304..."

"I don't care, I don't care," Naomi starts to cry, her head splitting open. Her brain feels all wrong, one side lashing out and the other holding back, one shrieking with pain and the other glazing over with denial, neither here nor...where? As if she'd just been wrenched away from a long-desired embrace and thrown to her doctoral committee, expected to perform, to know everything, to defend, to argue, to prove. Her friends go on as if none of that matters.

"...for 'poor students'!" Marie finishes. "That was her founding mission."

"And who are the poorest of the poor students, if not women? Even now. Look at you, living in this garret!" Hélène looks around the dingy room with sympathy. "How can you stand this place? It's even worse than you told us."

"And remember how hungry you've been," adds Marie, stepping closer to the bed, touching Naomi's shoulder. Immediately the garlicky memory of a ratatouille she never got to eat fills Naomi's nose, and she can almost hear the tearing of a crusty baguette, and she realizes she has not eaten since this morning's croissant. Or is it garlic on Marie's breath as she demands, "Do you think your Mauriet ever goes hungry?"

Mauriet. The name resounds like a bell in her head. The manuscript, her inconclusive notes, LeFrère's limp arms, their defeat! She'd held the damn door open for the thief and just watched him, stunned, watched him walk off with the treasured piece of skin, the evocative black marks that mean nothing at all now. Black bars on parchment, a figment of her imagination, a story to tell Petersen before getting on with some other work that means even less than nothing. Mauriet. The name burns in red letters on her retina, as with a magnifying glass in the sun. She slumps further into the edge of the bed, her back wilting until her face hangs over the threadbare rug. It is strangely calming to study the faded pattern, the dust, her socks.

"In the name of Jeanne de Navarre, get dressed!" Hélène commands, and props her up by the shoulder.

"She's already dressed, can't you see, Hélène?" Marie laughs.

Naomi glimpses herself in the streaked mirror. A disheveled, very young, woman with a round body layered like a cabbage. She touches her frizzy hair. No wimple. Awake now from a dream that plays on in her mind. There she is, and here she is.

"I dreamed I was a nun!" she exclaims, rubbing her temples. She should be grateful her friends have roused her from that fate. Instead, she wishes to droop back down and continue her study of the rug. To forget how hungry she is. To avoid the life stretching before her as Naomi Weiss, whom she recognizes now in the mirror. She collapses back onto the lumpy mattress.

"A nun, our little Jew!" giggles Hélène. She kneels by Naomi and tousles her damp curls.

"There was some kind of crucifix," she says, looking at the crack in the ceiling as if the dream were projected there, "and vegetables, and a walled garden I've seen in dreams before, but with a gate. A stone building with two doors, one open and the other closed. And he was banging on the closed one."

"He who?" asks Hélène.

"That's what I want to know. There was an old abbess. Héloïse. She looked like you, Hélène. And like that woman in the café who gave me the magnifying glass. But it was clearly Héloïse. And I was a novice. I had a habit on."

"No wonder you dreamt that," laughs Hélène, poking Naomi's garments.

"Well, if you can be a nun, then you can be an activist, too, there's a first time for everything," declares the practical Marie. "Enough of this cloistered life. Get dressed!" She bangs the glass doors open to the chilly night. "Just listen to those sirens. Ahh! Music to my ears."

The siren song comes from the direction of Boul' Mich. A call to action for Hélène and Marie, for Naomi a call to hiding. To think she tried to escape the annoying turbulence at Cornell by coming here! She stayed in her room at night, unwrapping the pink paper from around a cream horn, while these two and so many others were stirred by the call of a bull horn.

But why, oh why, do they insist she come with them tonight? She's an American. She's leaving in two days. She can't help them solve their coeducation problem. If women can't go to the Polytech, let them go someplace else. It's not her business. Cornell was coed from the very start, from 1860-something.

Wait. Did they say 1304? What a little fool she is! Six centuries of exclusion! Such an ancient scheme ensnares all women. Without them, without us, half of history remains untold. She sees Mauriet striding across the Place du Panthéon with the manuscript in his valise and "Yes!" she yells, a surge of power rising from belly to throat, "Yes!" To her friends' amazement, she furiously peels off her damp layers right down to the thermal undershirt.

"Leave that on," says Hélène. "It's cold in the Black Marias."

Black Marias. She hesitates. It's those police wagons she fears, parked along the curb of the Jardin du Luxembourg every night, just waiting for a recurrence of "the events of May" like a pack of police dogs trained to savor young radical flesh. She's through with fear! Yes! She pulls on her brown sweater. Mauriet! Old men like him stride past those threatening vehicles, and no one dares interfere with them whatever harm they might do. No one denies them their birthright, the wine and meat that await them on the Right Bank, a book-lined study to retire to with a snifter of cognac. Yes! She buttons her wool skirt. And young men, too, the ones who led the historic rebellion, students and workers marching through the streets—even these young men will inherit rights denied to women for hundreds of years. She pulls on one boot. And now it's up to women—including herself, Yes!—to unveil the oppression at the core of the precious revolution. Writing is not enough. The other boot goes on and she stands up. Those young radicals, those purveyors of leaflets, had simply walked all over a muddied feminist pamphlet she found in the gutter on Rue St. Jacques, "Lettre ouverte aux hommes," an open letter to men. It's time to take to the streets, to break the laws of Mauriet and his ilk, to make men listen, so Yes!, headlong into the Black Marias it is, with these women at her side.

"What's the plan?" asks Naomi, looking for her coat.

"We'll occupy the Ecole," Marie explains, "so be prepared for the gas."

Occupy. Tear gas. A shadow of doubt cools her heat. On the other side of the Atlantic, she's heard these terms casually bandied about. But in France a year ago, hundreds of French students occupied the Sorbonne, protesting the Minister of Education's threat to draft every dissenter. They set fire to police motorcycles and threw rocks at the paddy wagons. They were gassed and arrested. A week later, she read in the *New York Times*, the students were expelled without a hearing and drafted the very next day. Two hundred professors denounced the move. More protesters were arrested at the Gare de l'Est as the draftees' train departed. Occupation was serious business, here in France.

At home, student protests seemed more like a wild party. Dogs, balloons, placards, flowers, joints, and a few haggard radicals in Navy pea jackets haranguing the crowd. Frustrated administrators, dispersing them with bull horns, were live entertainment for the stoned students with flowers in their hair. As for their demands, some were important, like more black professors, more "relevance" in the curriculum. But some were frivolous: end curfews, drop drinking restrictions, eliminate required courses. The faculty would meet late into the night, voting yes to free speech, no to unbridled dissipation, issuing their inevitable "statement of outrage" by morning. Naomi suddenly realizes, the last of her doubt burning off, that if women alone had occupied campus buildings, had demanded equal rights on campus, equal numbers of tenured faculty, equal access to graduate school fellowships, imagine what the professors' "statement" would have been then! Something a lot more than "outrage" would be needed to keep those women down.

"What's a little tear gas," she grins, "after all the tears we've shed. Now where's that coat of mine?"

Marie claps her on the back. Hélène walks around to the other side of the bed and picks Naomi's wrinkled coat out from the heap lying along the faded pink wall. Naomi fumbles her many-layered arms into the damp sleeves.

"Vite, alors! En avant!" Hélène says, taking a beret out of her pocket and molding it over Naomi's curls.

"À la Bastille!" shouts Marie, as they pull Naomi from her room and out into the treacherous night.

Running faster than she's ever run before, running with fear in her mouth through the narrow streets of a foreign city, dark and terrifying, not knowing if *les flics* will be patrolling the back of the Bibliothèque this night, not knowing if she will be safe there from the gas, from arrest, but running, alone now, to hide there. Yes, to hide. Again. Her old habit. But this time it was Hélène who'd shouted "Run!" as they pushed her out of the paddy wagon that swallowed the women. "Run!" Hélène's command, her face disappearing in the dark commotion, made it seem like the brave thing, to take off down the alley behind the hellish scene at Place du Panthéon. Naomi had shouted Yes! with the best of them when the march began, peacefully, in the Jardin du Luxembourg. Yes! to solidarity, to action, Yes! to refusing a system that excluded women. But No! and Run! once she saw how easily women's strength could be crushed and dispersed by gas, the smashing of billy clubs, the powerful stampede of law.

She runs over the familiar cobblestones until tears stream down her cheeks, nearly tripping over a torn banner with the smeared letters, "Psych et Po." She knows this plaza as well as any part of Paris. She knows its hiding places, and what terrible things can happen here in the shadow of the Panthéon where great men are entombed. "Psych et Po." Just an hour ago the trampled banner waved proudly aloft. "What does it mean?" she'd asked Marie as they approached the Jardin arm-in-arm to join the excited crowd inside the gates.

"Psychoanalysis and politics, ma chérie. The theoretical core of our feminism." Naomi's blank face made Marie say more. "Psychosexual

difference determines women's political position. The men, our com-
patriots in struggle, they preach Freud. We women are missing something, they say. But what would we want with that piece dangling
between our legs? We have nothing to lose, nothing to fear, no 'castration complex'! And yet they use it to…Bpf! You already know what they
do with our difference, if you've been listening to me at all!"

The torch-light made Marie's face glow, her square shoulders powerful as she strode over to where placards were stacked against the iron
fence.

"Different, to them, says we can only be helpers, you know,"
Hélène added. "Which means stay out of it. Our womb, they say, makes
us fragile. Au contraire! Everything we have, all our power, we keep
tucked safe inside. We must direct our own revolution. Here. Carry
this!"

Hélène thrust a sign at Naomi. They lined up along the path across
the street from the dark Sorbonne, its cold surface marked by the flicker of torches reflected on closed windowpanes. Naomi, too ashamed
and aggrieved to tell why they'd found her in her room wrapped in a
shroud, still had the story of Mauriet stuck in her throat. Standing there
waiting in the noisy and joyous line, she knew she had to tell before she
could march. She needed that rush of rage to give her courage.

And now look at her, running alone along Rue Clovis away from
swarming gendarmes in riot gear, running around the side of St.
Etienne du Mont, crouching in the shadow of the church to avoid the
horrible gas and the women's screams. She'd told them her story, to
make herself brave. "You see?" Marie shouted over the din. "He is filth!
He must be stopped! And we shall do it, Naomi, we shall!"

"How?" she asked, tears welling behind her eyes.

"Do you see that building?" Marie demanded, pointing her placard
toward the dark Ecole des Chartes. "That is no fortress. I worked there,
I know the hallways and doorways. I know how he stashes his precious

manuscripts. He may be above the law, Naomi, but he is not immune to our…"

And then the march began. The long line of women streamed past the Sorbonne, up Rue Soufflot, their chants bouncing off the stones of the Panthéon: "Voltaire, Rousseau, Victor Hugo, NON NON!" They cheered as they approached the top of the Mont, the flat open plaza where now, an hour later, Naomi finds herself running from kiosk to kiosk in the ominous dark, police motorcycles rushing up the Rue de la Montagne Ste. Geneviève, paddy wagons weaving their way around the alley to the other side of the Panthéon.

But she had been brave. She had carried a placard high over her head–"VIVE LA DIFFERENCE???"–and pushed confidently across the plaza, toward the embattled Ecole Polytechnique. The advance group of women, well-trained in these tactics from May '68, already had cobblestones piled as a barricade before the main doors. She pressed forward as a crowd of women forced open the doors. Rocks began to fly and sirens wailed and hundreds of police with tear gas stormed the gates that had denied entrance to women, the gates they now seized with courage. "Allons-y!" she herself had shouted, the lump in her throat released at last. The body of women surged forward and entered the opened doors.

She'd been brave even when police charged with swinging batons, grabbing them by the arms and dragging them to the waiting Black Marias. Hélène held fast to Naomi's sleeve, smiling through it all, and never lost her nerve, and never let go of Naomi even as they were pushed toward the wagon. Only when a club hit Hélène's arm did she let go. She disappeared behind the armored door, but her voice held on, yelling, "Run!"

And so Naomi runs, her eyes squeezed shut against the stinging gas. Her running spreads a flame inside her, a fury kindled from fear and fanned by joy. This is the history her parents kept from her. This is what it feels like to be a Jew. They tried to escape that history by hiding their daughter in a white-carpeted bedroom. "Don't be afraid," they commanded. But the "don't" was lost like a breath in a hurricane. "Be afraid" lives in her muscles, her bones, the ancient will to flee.

She stays low, darting behind parked cars, until she reaches her haven, the familiar Bibliothèque Ste. Geneviève, sand-pale in the moonlight. She scoots around the back, under the ledge of LeFrère's darkened window. She crouches against the wall with the black beret pulled all the way down over her ears to muffle the horrific sirens. Gasping to catch her breath, she wishes now she hadn't run, foolish girl, afraid of what? She'd been brave, for once, and now here she is again, hiding in the shadows. When black students with guns occupied the Cornell student union after Martin Luther King's assassination, she had scurried across the street with her briefcase, a little mouse caught in broad daylight. Sure, of course, the takeover was terrible. And so was assassination, so was war, and the draft. Yet she couldn't join their rage. She fled from the serious black warriors, and hid from the exuberant whites whose rebellion she judged to originate more from the budding of elm trees, the flowering forsythia. She fled from herself, hiding like a Jew in a convent, rooting herself like an orphan in someone else's history.

This war in the French streets on a January night, this angry darkness of Mars, is someone else's revolution, and also her own. Not Mars only, but Venus coming out of her shell, claiming the dignity of her own body after all these millennia. Yes, Venus throwing blame in the face of all those gods of antiquity who pinned their folly on her. And all those sneering professors lecturing their misogyny to smug young men—Mauriet! His image enflames her and she roars into the circle of her arms as she huddles, shivering, against the wall, her head tucked till only the black nub of the beret sticks up. She lifts her face toward the mysterious dark façade across the way.

"ROARRRRRR!" she yells, testing the echo.

"…ting for, or?" bounces off the side of the building whose identity still eludes her.

"RRRROARRRRRRRR!"

"…waiting for?" comes the question she'd yelled at the wall just before New Year's, and got scared right down the hill by the returning echo. The night of her fever. The night LeFrère was so angry with her for reading "Eloyssa" as the author of his sacred text.

"What proof are you waiting for!" she repeats now, as if to LeFrère. She lifts the beret off of her ears to listen. Nothing wails back but the sirens.

LeFrère's pain penetrates her, as if her shoulder against the foundation stones of Ste. Geneviève were a lightning rod for his disappointment. In the dream she had last fall, he was younger, his olive face suffused with a lavender blush, his eyes lustrous as a cleaned windowpane. They were waiting in the cellar for their *magister* to be seated on the wooden chair. Would he come, the brilliant teacher he and she both waited for like students in a seminar impatient to try out their teacher's words in their own mouths for the first time, words that taste like luxuriously tentative first kisses? She was waiting with him, her brother in this shared and careful passion that savors the withholding of flesh, a love held safe and eternal as mind. But now their master will never come. The chair in the cellar is broken. Her brother is destroyed. Now there are sirens and she is roaring her rage, and hiding, and nothing is safe.

Mauriet's theft surely proves something—

—that her whole reason for coming to Paris, her desire to hear the master's silence flicker into speech, was a mistake. Her whole education, in fact, a giant mistake, leading her away from herself. LeFrère, as good as dead now, haunts the window above her head. Perhaps he, too, had been a dream. And even the manuscript—the "Eloyssa" damaged by a worm—a dream?

But just because you can't see something doesn't mean it's not there. "RIGHT?" she yells, holding back tears by force of pride. The sirens have made her deaf to all but the sound of her own voice inside the beret that cups her head. Just because you can't hear something...? She cranes her neck to look at LeFrère's window over her head. Oh, yeah, the happy ending. LeFrère there, a young LeFrère, and he loves her, of course, and has the manuscript, of course, and they know for sure it is a priceless text that proves...

"WHAT? WHAT AM I TRYING TO PROVE?"

No echo of her voice. Only fading sirens as the Black Marias recede down Boul' Mich, across the bridge to the Préfecture de Police, carrying her friends to jail. Alone now in the quiet darkness, body shoved against the stones, she shuts her eyes under the edge of the beret. Everything is wasted. Even Marie's "We will get it back!" That does no good now. If she'd gone to jail with them, she'd be a criminal with nothing left to lose. She'd miss her plane back to the States, and be saved from Cornell, saved from the Latin poetry seminar with Petersen, saved from facing LaTour. She'd be a safe nothing, an absence—anomie, not Naomi.

When is a "nothing" a something, dangerous and explosive? Did "nothing" happen in Paris? She has "nothing" to show for her semester here. That's a lie. But the net result of her work is an absent manuscript. A *lacuna* where there had been solid ground, as if some glacier had hollowed out what was her life. But a gorge is not just an empty space between two walls of rock. A gorge is evidence of violent motion, of something that was crushed and carried off. Shall she go down in the gorge, then, as they did at Cornell for sunbathing or suicide? Follow the trail of what's gone, to where it's been deposited someplace else? Shall she crawl out from the center of the zero where she's spent her life in hiding, and speak?

Yes. A wrinkled face answers with a nod as Naomi closes her eyes, nearly asleep with her head against the library wall. Gentle green eyes, weathered hands—Naomi opens her eyes, her throat constricted by all she's swallowed in this cold, mean city, from all the crying she has kept herself from. How, Héloïse, tell me, how shall I begin?

The old nun leans her wimpled head back and looks down at Naomi, as if to shake a finger, as if to say, You know. You already know. You know it's the garden, the young green shoots, without which no learning, no study, without which no life at all. You know it's the book without words. Only then, only then, in the knowledge of green, will belief sprout in your quickened soil. Only then will you have begun the work you are always only beginning. Only then…now…whenever you are ready…from now on…

Naomi presses her eyes into the damp sleeve of her raincoat, crying at last in the privacy of the deserted night, crying as one who's had no bread for months, released from a prison cell, walking out into the sun, would cry. Crying as one would cry before a single crumb has passed her lips, even as she breaks the crusty loaf. Crying as one who needs tenderness would cry when strong arms fold her against a warm heart, the nurturing arms of one who has been crying all along, even with a smile on her old, wise face.

Monsieur Montreux watches the girl fix her eyes on the little white plate with a golden croissant in the middle of it. Dirty hair hangs over her cheeks until it almost meets at her chin. He waits for her to take the first bite. He's gone out especially to get this croissant at the market for her, since the corner boulangerie is closed today. And now she just leans over the plate without picking it up, and the *demi* of chocolate steams at her elbow untouched. Where is that rose he has so admired in the Mademoiselle's cheek? Perhaps she is ill.

"Ça va?" he asks, softly. "Mademoiselle?" She jerks her head up, and he sees her troubled blue eyes. "Vous êtes malade?"

She shakes her head, no, not sick, and tries to smile. She wants to tell him everything. How all is wasted. Even this croissant he placed before her. Her stomach hurts, her head throbs, but she doesn't want to offend him. He's the only one left who cares.

The abbess cares. But Naomi wants someone alive. After last night, her head lolling against the stones of Ste. Geneviève, crying till she was dry, then staggering down the Mont in the dark and climbing the spiral stairs to her room without giving the light-timer a single twist, after all that, can she still be sure she is alive?

She takes a sip of the thick cocoa. He is watching her, and there is something in his watching that heals her, a grandfather's tender awe. What is it about her he admires? She's nothing. A coward. Two days to go, then back to Cornell, where she can hide in a library carrel for a few more years and emerge with a Ph.D. in medieval nothingness, equipped for what? She should just go plant a garden somewhere. She sticks one end of the buttery crescent in her mouth, not tasting anything, but savoring the nice man's gentle eyes as he watches her eat the cherished offering.

"Merci, Monsieur," she says, putting the half-eaten croissant down. He gestures for her to finish it. She obeys, but leaves the flaky crumbs on the plate. She pulls her coat on and tilts the beret over one eye as she's seen Hélène do.

"Le béret, c'est nouveau? C'est charmant."

"Oui, merci," she answers, embarrassed. And she's back out on the street dimly lit by a January half-sun. In her mind's eye, she sees a silver river. Rows of carrots glistening with dew. Plant a garden. That sounds good. Now, what to do with these last two days in Paris?

She crosses the street and walks by the Café des Etoiles. Pointless to be looking for Marie and Hélène. She knows where they are this morning. Locked up on the Ile de la Cité. She looks inside the café at men and women drinking coffee as if nothing out of the ordinary happened last night. She watches an old professor lick his thumb and turn the page of his newspaper, not even bothering to stop at the headline "LES FEMMES ARMÉES AU QUARTIER LATIN." Naomi stands there staring at the white-haired man, unconsciously humming a medieval ballad, "L'homme l'homme l'homme armé, l'homme armé, l'homme armé doit-on douter, doit-on douter…"

She hears herself, and laughs. One should doubt the armed man! No, doesn't "douter" mean fear in Old French? Fear and doubt. Her specialty. She smirks at herself in the glass. Just beyond her reflection, she sees the writing woman again. She'll go in and talk with her. Yes. Before she leaves this dreadful city for good. Just as she puts her hand on the knob, the door flies open and out bursts Alain Lévi with a load of books under his arm.

"Bon jour, ma petite soeur juive!" His dark eyes twinkle, his curly hair awry.

"I am not your sister," Naomi stammers, glad in spite of herself to see a familiar face.

"But Jew you do not deny?"

"What're you, an emissary from my mother, prodding me to be the Jew…anyway, we say Jew-*ish* in America."

"Jew-ish. Ha ha. 'Resembling a Jew.' The way a fool is fool-ish? You can't escape with the turn of an adjective, Naomi. Henceforth you are a noun! Jew!"

She tugs the beret over her ears, hoping it will make her immune to his jovial ranting, or better yet, invisible. But this circle of black wool appears to signal the world that she is…what? a proper noun? It amplifies her hearing, and lights the dark tunnel she must crawl through to get back to—Ithaca!—like Odysseus. Anonymity is no longer an option. "Nobody" ever escapes this place alive.

"Where are your fuming feminist friends this morning? Usually they inhabit this café late and early."

"Didn't you hear the sirens last night? The demonstration at the Ecole Polytechnique?"

"Oh. That."

"Yes, that. They're in jail!"

"Brava! Why not you? They took only naughty Frenchwomen over their knee?"

"Well, I…ran, and they didn't catch me."

Alain makes a triumphant fist and leans his head against the building next to the café. His Adam's apple rises and falls as he laughs. For once it is not a mocking laugh, but a tender one, and she feels proud and warm, facing him this close. The overcast sky breaks open and drops more sunlight onto the Rue des Ecoles. The woman inside the café looks up from her writing just in time to see Naomi grin. Enfin, her bruises are healing. Which, after all, is in the nature of things. A bruise gives flavor, as when I lay a clove of garlic on the block and knock once with the side of a big knife and let it bleed into the simmering lentils. Lentils need garlic the way we all need pain.

Naomi laughs so hard her beret slips down over one flushed cheek. "Alors, Naomi," Alain finally says, "show me this monstrous Ecole Polytechnique by the light of day. Explain to me what you women were rallying about last night."

She stops laughing, and the hard knot of fear returns to the place in her stomach where the croissant would have gone if it had made it past the lump in her throat. She presses her waist and breathes deeply. Yes, there it is, the old fear, even though laughing reminded her that the slim daylight available at this latitude offers safety. And Alain offers friendship, here in the Latin Quarter on the cusp of the rest of her life.

"Okay," she says, and they head for the Rue de la Montagne Ste. Geneviève. So many times she's climbed this hill on her way to the manuscript. Keeping up with Alain's quick pace, she's out of breath. It's hard to talk. But she wants to log the story in Alain's mind, so that Mauriet will not go free when she leaves.

"There was a manuscript," she says, looking sideways at him with his armload of books, quiet for once, head down.

"Ah oui, there is always a manuscript, Mademoiselle la Médiéviste!"

"Yes, but one that hadn't been seen. Not by the scholarly world. You know."

"Here's the turn," Alain says, interested only in seeing the remains of the night. Some broken glass, deranged cobblestones, crushed placards. Getting there fast is all he cares about. But the manuscript story is a winding alley that encircles the why of her joining up last night. She needs him to walk through the story with her. She needs him to carry it after she goes.

"Come on, Alain, I listened to you talk all through Christmas dinner in Chartres. You owe me."

He stops and shifts his books to the other arm. "Dis-moi, alors."

"If someone steals something, do you think that proves it was of value?"

He appears to be considering her question. Then a snide light flickers in his dark brown eyes, and she knows he's cooking up a come-back.

"Bien sûr, Mademoiselle." He bows and steps toward her. "We Frenchmen are excellent judges of value, you know." He moves in on her until she's backed up to the building at the turn onto the Rue de l'Ecole Polytechnique. The sharp edge of its corner pushes into her spine.

"'We Frenchmen'? You align yourself with the old professors, then? What happened to all your radical talk?" She wriggles away and dashes to the other end of the short street.

"Where are you going?" he shouts, following after her. "This whole block is the Ecole. Come on, Naomi, I was just trying to get you to touch the building, so you wouldn't be afraid."

Naomi stops and turns around.

"Come on, tout va bien," he reassures her as he hurries toward her. She wants to believe him, but when he cornered her just now, with his talk of value, she felt like some bottle of wine that The Great Frenchman will now sample. Yes, she supposes she is a bottle of young wine, stored in the cellar for just long enough to give a light bouquet. And maybe it is time to drink that wine. But it's not for him to assess her flavor. "We Frenchmen" indeed!

She waits for him to catch up, the weak sun now filling the narrow street. Scattered pamphlets litter the gutters, some of them partially burned. That must have happened after she ran. She doesn't remember any fires. But she'll never forget the sirens.

"You see?" Alain says, reaching her side, gripping his books with one arm. He reminds her of the nice Jewish boys back home who carried her books home from high school. They were a sweaty and earnest lot. Alain Lévi as nice Jewish boy? The "nice" kind must be an American breed, Jew-ish. This one is a war orphan, which turns a nice Jewish boy into a revolutionary pretty quick. "You see, Naomi," he says, reaching over and patting the stones, "it's just a building. All of Paris is just a construction, which means it can be deconstructed."

"Deconstructed?" She hates the way these radicals are always making up new words. It's hard enough to follow their French in the first place. "What do you mean? Destruction?"

"Yes, in a sense. But without physical force. That's where you women went wrong last night, storming the doors. That's what they do in America. You see, here we can no longer afford force. The police, they're just waiting for one false move. And so we must undermine the structure in other ways. We must fight them with intellect—not their strongest weapon!"

"L'homme l'homme l'homme armé..." Naomi sings as they continue walking along the street toward the entrance of the school, "l'homme armé doit-on douter, doit-on douter!" The tune bounces off the grimy walls of the Ecole.

"Now your Hélène and Marie, they go about things the wrong way. They should listen more to me and Louis."

"I don't suppose you consider that women know something you don't know about revolution? We have our own voice. We have community."

"Oo-là-là, la ferme des femmes, you must mean. One season on the land and you'll all be back in Paris. We will be waiting for you at the café. You and your roofless barn. Now that's what I call deconstruction!"

The Ecole Polytechnique runs the length of the cobbled street, which now has patches of bare sand where they pried up the stones for a barricade. The glass doors are all smashed in. What a lovely sight. She'd like to see the Ecole des Chartes vandalized like this, even destroyed, and old Mauriet out wandering the streets. It would mean the final loss of her manuscript, but wasn't it already as good as dead? Some things must be sacrificed for the sake of others.

What is she talking about? The idea of Paris burning, where people have lived and walked and thought, all this beauty and history—Notre Dame!—No! There must be another way, without destroying these structures. Where is Alain? She twirls in the street, looking for him, just as two gendarmes crunch over broken glass and take her by the elbow. And there he is, around the corner—he's just going to stand there and watch her get busted?

"Mademoiselle, venez avec nous."

"Je suis américaine, Monsieur, je ne sais rien, je vous en prie!"

"Mademoiselle, do you know anything about what happened here last night?"

"Non, Monsieur. I am a visitor here. I was just curious."

"Were you not with that man over there? We recognize him. That is Alain Lévi. Were you not with him?"

"Um, non, Monsieur. I am a student at the Ecole des Chartes, you see."

They look at each other and then at her. They let go of her elbow. "Paleographers make no trouble," one says, smiling at her crooked beret. "It's those socialists, those philosophers, we watch out for! You can go. Just stay away from here, if you want to keep out of trouble. You Americans have a lot to learn about life in Paris. We invented law and order!"

The other one takes her by the shoulders and points her in the direction of the Ecole des Chartes, the Sorbonne, the Jardin. What she wants is to run the other way, back to the Hôtel Plaisant, where she won't see Alain, or anyone, again. The gendarmes are watching to see where she goes. She passes the corner of the building and sees Alain crouching in the shadow, grinning at her, ready to pounce. She scowls at him, keeps walking in the direction she does not want to go, toward the Ecole des Chartes, toward…yes! That's it! Toward Mauriet! She will pay him a little visit this morning.

Her strides become longer as she approaches the Panthéon, retracing last night's march. This is where they took Hélène and Marie. And this is where she ran up the hill to hide behind the Bibliothèque. She passes the Panthéon, not even glancing at her tiny library with its charming green dome, trying not to wonder what LeFrère is doing today. She marches along the path LaTour took to go tattling to Mauriet. It's her turn to tattle now. She laughs out loud and starts singing as she approaches Rue Soufflot, "Les femmes armées doit-on douter, doit-on douter!"

"Naomi!" Behind her, the sound of feet running. "Naomi, yes," Alain gasps as he reaches her, "if something is stolen, it means it was worth something." He droops against the railing that encloses the Sorbonne.

"You forgot your books," she says, noticing his empty arms. "You almost got me in big trouble! I see now why you didn't try to help me out, though, merci beaucoup. You are infamous! Get away, I can't be seen with you, they may be following to make sure I go to my school."

"Don't worry about them. They're probably already sipping cognac at the nearest café. Come to my room instead. It's on Rue Thenard, near here. You can meet me there. Come on!"

"So you think the manuscript must be valuable if he took it?"

"Who?"

"Mauriet. Professor Mauriet. I was trying to tell you. Is that proof of something?"

"No, probably nothing. Just forget it. Come with me instead."

"But even a nothing is something. To me anyway. A nothing marks the place where there was once something. Do you know what I mean?"

"Yes, yes. Come on, come home with me."

"Alain, I'm nothing to you, and you know it."

He smiles broadly. "Even a nothing is something, Naomi." He steps toward her. "And if I steal...something...from you, doesn't that mean you have...a certain value?"

Naomi rolls her eyes, but she can't help it, she's smiling at him. The clever Jewish boy has dropped his books and now he's using her own arguments on her. It isn't going to work, though. She's got to get to Mauriet.

The stairwell is dark. She drags her hot hand up the cold banister and creeps past the lecture hall crowded with black berets. From the podium, the old professor addresses immortal words to his tie-clip, interrupted by a yellow cough. The berets sway slightly. Mauriet resumes his droning.

She could walk down this dark corridor, stand pressed to the wall until the lecture ends, invisible with her dark hair, dark beret, dark raincoat. Then? He'll shuffle down the hall, he'll reach for the big knob on this door right here, and just as he's about to disappear into his sacred privacy, she'll pop out of the woodwork. She'll startle the frail old man with his sheaf of notes. She'll interrupt his habits and challenge his confidence.

She checks her watch and looks toward the square of light at the head of the corridor. She listens, but can't tell from the monotone whether the lecture is almost finished or just begun. Sometimes at Cornell, she'd waited out in the hall for Sharon, who sat right in front at the big Brit Lit lecture. She could tell when the professor was coming to a close. His voice would rise, his pace would quicken, he'd rush to get in just one more joke, and the two hundred students would laugh, not writing it down in their notebooks but chances are remembering it forever, though it would not be on the exam. And then there would be shuffling and rustling as they gathered their books. The professor's voice would rise even higher to give an extra assignment, and they would stream out into the hall. She looks down the corridor at this other scene, berets framed by the doorway, tiny old man at the lectern, a tableau as lifeless as a stained glass window.

She puts her head back against the wall, exhausted, then jerks to attention at the thought of Marie's "We will get it!" as they slammed her into the paddy wagon. What the hell is she waiting for? "It" is what she wants to get, not "him." Mauriet striding across the plaza with his briefcase that terrible rainy day—just two days ago?—had swept right past her as she stood there in a dripping scarf like some poor immigrant, holding the door for that criminal. He just took off with her manuscript! She tries the knob. It turns. The hinges creak. She listens for the drone from the lecture hall. She opens his office door just enough to slip through. And she's in.

The second she hits the stale air thick with decades of cigarette smoke, she knows she'll never find it here. It. The thing she wants more than revenge. Seeing the mess of books and papers, empty wine bottles, stale cheese on various plates here and there, the old typewriter, she thinks revenge might be easier to find than the manuscript. But how to undermine this man whose power comes from—where? To subvert him without physical force, Alain would say. She could deconstruct his tangled mess by making it so neat in here he can't find a thing. Or, perhaps she could just unnerve him? She steps toward the typewriter and scrolls in a blank sheet of paper, then thinks better of it. The noise, after all, of typing. What would Marie do? Her eyes fall on an ashtray filled with old butts. Matches. She would? "We will get it!" Right, and what good would fire do, if she wants that manuscript alive? Her head swims as the stuffy air nearly overcomes her. She sits down in the hard chair by the typewriter. To wait. Yes. She'll just wait right here. She closes her eyes.

Not fire. File. Yes, Marie had once said something about a file where he hid all his treasures. She opens her eyes and looks around. No bookcases, strange for a professor's study. Stacks of books on two work tables, a desk, and three chairs. She opens the cover of one. Université de Paris. Library books, checked out fifteen years ago. Doesn't need bookcases. Owns the library. Owns the whole damn university. She ducks beneath one of the tables. Dust kitties, and a dented safe, dark green, with a combination lock. She rattles the handle. Darn. Would Marie know the combination? He doesn't seem like someone who would ever change a combination, or anything else. She rattles it again, then listens toward the hall. People moving! Quick, back to her plan of hiding against the wall out in the corridor. Too late! She remembers the routine: Mauriet's processional past the students' benches and out the door before they even so much as cap their pens.

All right then. I'll scare the old codger to death. Death? What are you talking about? You just want that manuscript! He has no right to take something from a library. Demand the manuscript back!

She pushes the door closed so he won't be suspicious. Voices in the hall, but still no Mauriet. Her resolve is shrinking, she's becoming tiny but can't seem to disappear. Her hands are shaking as she reaches for the lock just below the big doorknob and turns it. The bolt hits home. She expands in size, big again, and strong, locked in here, disrupting his routine, confusing him.

Footsteps, and the knob turns, back and forth, the door rattles against the frame. She sees his keys here, on her side of the door, thrown onto the desk. She stifles a laugh. The door jiggles back and forth, and then stops. Footsteps recede. She waits. She grabs the keys and lets herself out. Empty corridor. Dark lecture hall. She pulls his door shut and locks it, shoves the keys into her raincoat pocket along with her lucky chestnut. When she hears the outside door slam, she goes down, out, and spots him on St. Jacques, heading toward St. Germain. She walks the other way. Having accomplished what— retrieved the manuscript? Scared the old man's pants off? Neither, nor. She swings her arms, listening to the keys clanking against the chestnut. The best thing to come of this adventure was managing to stay out of Alain's room. Rue Thenard is back in Mauriet's direction, so it's out of the question. She strides on, as elated as if the key to the city were in her pocket.

Up Rue Cujas, across the Place du Panthéon toward the Bibliothèque, around behind it to go home the back way. She faces the big sooty building with its annoying "Défense d'entrer" painted over the door. La clé, la clé...I have the key. She grins. An ambulance screams across the plaza, lights flashing, and swerves to a stop right in front of the abandoned building. Is LeFrère watching out his window in the stacks? She turns to see the big panes reflecting nothing but grey sky, breaking clouds.

Two men go up into the building with an empty stretcher. Not a hospital, then. Could still be a prison, or an insane asylum. "All of Paris is just buildings," Alain had said, "just a construction." Just one huge insane asylum. And I have the keys. She walks right under the "Défense d'entrer" sign and enters the building.

It's too dark to see the men coming down with the stretcher. Their voices echo in the deserted hallway. She hides in the shadow of the staircase. The first man comes down backwards, the patient's head at his waist. A long greenish face, eyes closed, sheet drawn up to the hairless chin. It's LeFrère they are carrying. Her hand reaches out. Chrome slides under her fingertips, and the coarse cloth of the other attendant's pantleg, and they pass without seeing her, heading for the open doorway. They shove the stretcher in and shut the ambulance doors. She hears the words "mort, il est mort." Dead! Mauriet really did it this time! She rushes toward the patch of light just as the ambulance pulls away.

She pries loose a cobblestone to prop the door open, then enters the building again. She may have the key to the city, but she's not taking any chances of getting locked in here. She gropes her way to the wide staircase, reaches down to touch the slate steps rounded with wear. She climbs, counting twenty shallow steps. Another even darker corridor, with a dirty skylight at the very top of the stairwell. She climbs, another twenty, forty. To the top. To see, once and for all, if there is a room perpendicular to her balcony at the Hôtel Plaisant, where she's seen a light coming through the barred window from a corridor, where she's certainly heard a man crying. Just because you can't see something doesn't mean it's not there. Is the corollary: Just because you can see something, doesn't mean it is there? Her head spins with hunger. Monsieur Montreux's blessed croissant could hardly be expected to carry her through all that's happened since early this morning. She steps toward the row of doors on the side nearest the Hôtel Plaisant. Pleasant except for what those faded pink walls are hiding. Does pink always hide black, smeared like a thick swath of oil paint over the horrors of history? Is that what pink is for? She tries a few doors and finds them locked. She tries the next one, and it opens.

It would make a nice story if the room held someone who could tell her she'd been right all along. Isn't that the fantasy, of reaching the core, of finding closure, the answer, a truth above which there is no other authority? She pulls the string to an overhead lightbulb. Broken glass is everywhere on the floor, and a rumpled bed, a single chair pulled up to the window at an angle. The shards of thin glass, like crushed lightbulbs, crisp into dust under her feet. She sits down in the chair. Her right shoulder touches the cold bars, the window open just a crack with chilly air streaming in. A large book rests on edge against the wall. She reaches down for it, but it's too heavy for one hand. She extends the other. As she does, her eyes glance out the window, and yes, indeed, there is a balcony—hers? The railing is close enough to touch. The French doors are closed so she can't see if it's her room. Then she recognizes the stone crest carved on the façade, a lion's head surrounded by a garland of leaves. And, yes, she spots the nearly empty cider bottle and two apples she left on the balcony to keep them cold. She stands and leans into the bars, trying to make out how much someone could see in, trying, in a way, to see herself, the pink girl living her pink life in the shadow of black. She bangs on the wall. She listens. So this is what it's like, banging, wailing, watching, waiting. Was it LeFrère all along?

She walks over to the bed and feels the sheets. Clammy, just like hers. No other sign of life. No plate, no crumbs. She remembers LeFrère's little crate in the stacks, his plate and tumbler. She'd never seen him eat, or drink. She'd only seen him watch, wait. She'd seen his fear. Maybe even, was it love she'd seen? More like hope. And then despair. And now nothing. She sniffs the musty bolster. A little piece of glass just here, at the edge of the mattress. She shivers.

For a long time she stands in the doorway facing out onto the dark corridor, knowing even less than before, thinking she'd found the core, and having it crushed like a broken lightbulb. Now it seems both more important and also meaningless to get the manuscript back. She pulls the keys out of her pocket, wondering how much time she's bought herself by taking them, how long till Mauriet returns with another set. She studies the keys by the light of the hanging bulb. One for the office door, that one she knew. One, this big one, was probably the front door. This one looks like the kind that opens an apartment. A Citroën key. And a little round key. Suddenly she remembers her locker in high school. There was a master key the janitor carried on his belt that fit into the center of the lock, in case the combination failed. Like this one!

She runs down the sixty stairs, clutching the keys in her hand.

☞ XXVI ☜

Professors in Paris are notoriously unavailable in the afternoons. They say they're doing research, but Naomi has seen the younger ones smoking in the cafés, surrounded by students, or the reclusive ones reading alone at a tiny table. Today, for once, their absence is an advantage. She looks up and down Rue St. Jacques, lectures finished for the day, students dispersed to wherever they go, she wouldn't know. She fingers the keys in her pocket, warm by now from contact with her nervous hand. Relax, Naomi. Just act like you're going to meet with your tutor. Just climb these steps and open the front door. She looks toward the bookshop across the street, closed for lunch, and steps over the marble threshold into the Ecole des Chartes, perhaps for the last time. The heavy door booms shut, and she stands alone in the quiet foyer.

She watches her feet climb the stairs to the dim landing, then turn and climb the last half-flight. LeFrère once climbed these very stairs, perhaps with the same fear that damps the fire in her chest. He smoldered for ten or fifteen years, and finally his fire choked out. She jumps at the sight of someone in a dark turtleneck leaning over the rail.

"Marie!" she gasps with relief. "You're out of jail!"

"Ah, oui. They only keep you overnight, unless you are the leader. They let us out just in time to not feed us. Moi, I have much hunger."

"Why are you here, then? Nothing to eat here."

"I don't have any money. Besides, I was looking for you, ma chérie, or, failing that, I was going in alone. We have our little promise to keep, n'est-ce pas?"

"How will you get in?" Naomi baits her friend, who can't see the twinkle in her eye.

"He used to leave his door unlocked, and I knew by now he would be halfway through his afternoon carafe. But, zut!—the door is locked, I don't know why. His habits have changed since I worked here."

Naomi dangles the keys in front of Marie's glasses. "I'm the one who locked it! And I have the key!"

Marie gives Naomi's shoulder a friendly punch, and they head down the dim corridor. Naomi fits the key in the hole, turns the bolt, and the odor of cigarettes envelopes them. She scoots right under the table and fits the little key in the center of the combination lock.

"You waste no time!" praises Marie. Naomi grins up at her. The key won't budge. She jiggles it, pushes less hard, tries again.

"Here, let me. It sticks. I remember." Marie crawls under and gives the key a knowing twist. The lock clicks. She pulls the handle down, and the dented door creaks open.

"Do you think it's in here?" asks Naomi. "Is this where he'd be most likely to put it?"

"Who knows? Once I found a stale crust of bread in here! I wouldn't put it past him to leave a burning cigarette here and forget where he put it. He's in his own world. But I'm going to drag him out and make him pay for what he's done."

"I know how you feel, but I just want to find the manuscript and get the hell out of here before we're caught."

"Before we're caught! He's the one who stole your manuscript, and far worse. We must expose him! That newspaper where I first learned of his link to the Nazis—bpf!—they write all they want about our countrymen's war crimes, but what is done to punish them? 'Let's forget the war,' everyone says. How can I forget, while he lives in luxury and prominence? He had my parents put to death—for his ambition! I'm going to get him, Naomi, and you should want to, too, being a Jew."

"You said, 'We will get it,' not him. That's all I want. I'm afraid, Marie! I'm a coward."

"Some coward, who steals keys from His Eminence! Come on, chicken, let's see what you've unlocked."

Marie sticks her hand into the safe and pulls out a wad of manuscripts. Film capsules go rolling across the dusty floor. She tugs at a huge volume wedged in the opening. A long strip of microfilm caught in the pages uncoils as she frees the volume and reaches for more papers.

"Whoa! It's probably right on top anyway, from just two days ago. Let's take some of this stuff up into the light," says Naomi, crawling out from under the table with a bunch of manuscripts pressed to her chest.

Never has she seen such carelessly stored documents. At Cornell, when she worked in the Rare Books Department one summer, she'd meticulously placed each manuscript in an acid-free folder, and stacked them in special binders tied with straps. The air in the vaults was controlled for humidity and insects, and a complicated alarm system guarded everything. Each manuscript was labeled, the known ones photographed and described in beautifully produced catalogues, the unknown ones coded and filed, awaiting some future scholar who might make sense of them. She was hoping some day to be that scholar. But the likes of this! Shameful, horrifying. You'd think he would have more respect for his own history.

If she weren't looking for one thing in particular, if she weren't afraid of Mauriet returning at any moment despite Marie's assurances that he had his nose in a tumbler, she would be admiring the variety of handwriting styles in the bundles now lying on the cluttered tabletop, from the simple early scripts to the later, ornate curlicues. Instead she shuffles through unwanted debris. He can have all this! There is just one thing she wants, and so far she sees nothing like her manuscript, its crumbling leather cover tied with LeFrère's careful string, poor man.

"These manuscripts, Naomi," Marie hands up another pile, "these parchments are the traded skins of innocent French people. These words you see are the last testament of my mother, my father, the Jewish orphans they worked so hard to save!"

Naomi shivers as she grabs the manuscripts from Marie's frantic hands. Little Jewish children whom pink could not bring protect. Too late now to look for anything but her own stolen work. Nothing. Nothing. She raises the next pile to the light, and sees a corner sticking out that looks the right shade of brown. She yanks on it, and yes, this is the cover, with the string untied. She wants to rush joyously down the stairs and out onto the street with the manuscript under her raincoat, up the hill to the Bibliothèque to tell LeFrère—but oh, he is dead—then who?—Kurtzmann? dead, too—the woman in the café who lent her the magnifying glass, Monsieur Montreux who fed her, Petersen, everyone, and most especially that Françoise LaTour. She opens the soft, brown cover. The folios are gone. All three folios are gone. The cover is empty.

"Marie," she says flatly. "Marie. Look." She holds up the shell. Marie's face clouds with rage. She crawls out and sweeps an outstretched arm across the shaky piles. Books slide to the floor in a whirl of dust. She spins around and sweeps the other table, raises her knee under it, and it tips, sending a thunder of volumes to the floor.

"Shhh!" Naomi hisses, blocking Marie's attempt to throw the typewriter. "Quiet!" She grabs the empty folio cover and holds it to her chest, looking from Marie to the door and back. She had purposely confused Mauriet's routine by locking him out. What makes Marie think he will follow his usual pattern and stay away? And what point is there in remaining here now, endangering themselves for nothing? Here is the cover. This is all there is. If Marie has some other goal to accomplish here…the front door booms, and they hear doddering footsteps on the stairs.

"Come on! Let's get out of here!"

"I will not run. I've had enough running. What can he take from me that hasn't already been taken? We will get it back, Naomi. I swear we will." She stands squarely in the middle of the office, arms crossed over her chest.

"Marie! Come on! The folios aren't here. I don't care! Let's just go!" She grabs Marie's arm and pulls her out the door before realizing it makes no difference, they are trapped, in the office or in the hall. Unless there's another door open. The footsteps, painfully slow, climb the stairs. But there's no time. Unless they press themselves against the wall in that shadow down there. But Marie is too volatile for hiding. All that's left is to stand their ground. Naomi freezes in the middle of the hall, still clutching the leather cover, looking this way and that, until Marie pulls her away from the approaching footsteps.

"This way! The back stairs!" They tear down the corridor and turn a corner just as the footsteps shuffle to the top of the stairs and stumble drunkenly toward them, then come to an abrupt stop. Naomi peeks around the corner and sees Mauriet standing aghast before his violated office. She giggles, and they race down the stairs and out a side door into a small green park facing the Musée de Cluny.

The fierce look in Marie's eye when they reach the daylight frightens Naomi. Confounding an old man will never satisfy a revolutionary, she should have known that. "Come on," Marie says, and leads them back behind the school in the direction of the Panthéon. Of course she's not worried that they are passing right below Mauriet's window, and Naomi doesn't dare say a word as they cross the plaza. She just pulls her beret way down and hunches her shoulders as they head over the top of Mont Ste. Geneviève and down the other side, past the medieval wall that kept students in and barbarians out. They are barbarians, then, as they exit past the mossy remains of the old wall at the Place de la Contrescarpe, the marker lost among restaurants and cafés, swarms of students and shoppers, Arabic and French signs, spice shops and fruit stands, banners, kiosks, cinémas.

Marie finally slows down. She turns to see Naomi gawking at everything, the high Mansard roofs that loom over the narrow street, the little urchins begging for a franc. Brown faces among the white. Gorgeous flowers and vegetables, racks of exotic clothes, carved gourds and woven baskets.

"The world of the Other, ma chérie. Have you not been here, over the top of your precious Montagne and down the other side? Look, here is my street, Cardinal Lemoine. I live right up here, where it runs into Rue Monge. Just a few blocks from your familiar *quartier*!"

All those cars she'd watched streaming along Rue Monge from her perch on the balcony, all those walkers, all those people on the Métro who kept riding when she got off at Maubert-Mutualité, this is where they were going. And she had stayed put behind her railing, just like the prisoner behind bars who had undoubtedly been watching her step onto the balcony for an apple or a breath of damp night air. But she did not have to die in a rumpled bed. She could go, she could live. She follows Marie up Cardinal Lemoine to an arched doorway decorated with blue tiles, and up a dark stair that smells of urine and onions, to the second floor. Marie pulls a key out of her back pocket and lets them in. A tiny room, six steps across, littered with newspapers like a hamster cage. A small window looks down into a courtyard where, in summer, those earthen pots must overflow with herbs and flowers, those floor tiles must be home to lazy cats. Naomi smiles to see how such a poor, run-down place could yet be beautiful, enclosed upon the richness of growing things.

"Where have I been all this time?" she exclaims to Marie, who is pawing through papers like a nervous cat. Naomi paces the room's perimeter, rustling over magazine clippings, past towers of books with notes sticking out of them. She runs her finger along the edge of the table, a coffee-stained mug weighting down a stack of paper filled with Marie's black scratching, an open wine bottle, half full, no glass in sight. A gas ring and small cast iron skillet, wooden spoon, water jug, pepper mill, some matches, a head of garlic, a cruet of oil, cutting board, knife.

"Where do you sleep?" she asks, coming full circle back to where Marie still searches her piles, and then Naomi sees a thin mattress rolled up under the table with a blanket thrown on the floor. The chair is an overturned barrel with Arabic lettering on it. A towel, once white, now grey, hangs on a nail.

"Et voilà." Marie stands up, knocks her head into a hanging light-bulb that goes on swaying as she studies two pieces of writing. One, a blue paper with lots of numbers on it. The other, a parchment with burned edges. "The *Theologia christiana*, Naomi," she waves the burned parchment. "Of Abélard. You know him." She flashes a sly smile at her friend who looks so clean and pure against the backdrop of her unholy mess. So young and hopeful. What does she know about revenge? It won't be possible. Naomi is not stunted, like her. Naomi will grow.

"This?" Naomi takes the parchment. "Condemned by the Pope at the Council of Soissons? How do you know? Where did this come from?"

"I have it by accident. When Mauriet threw me out—remember I told you? I was his assistant, but then I read about his Nazi deal, which clarified some questions I had about this other piece." She brandishes the blue paper. "This is the list, Naomi. The list of manuscripts he traded Jews for. When he threw me out, and all my books, he didn't know I had the list inside one of the books! And this scrap of Abélard, too. You can still identify it, and so, of course, it's worth a career!"

"Françoise LaTour's career. That explains where her falsified manuscript went. Mauriet fired her for losing it, unfairly, I see. But wait. Didn't you come to work there after she was gone?"

"Yes, two or three years after. Naomi, you wouldn't believe. I told you he was a slob. I found this priceless relic in the safe, stuck with what smelled like spilled Chambord to the back of some completely worthless manuscript he sacrificed a Jewish life for. But this, ha! For the loss of this one he accused his lady, and sacrificed his love."

"Chambord?"

"Raspberry liqueur, my sweet. How he loved to sip of an evening!"

"And the list? Why haven't you done anything with it all these years?"

"To tell you the truth, I tried to forget all about him. I got involved in the radical politics of the Latin Quarter, and the strike of '68. And then feminism, too, and realizing I am a lesbian. I mean, who cares about a Mauriet when there's such revolution? But then, when I met you, I was reminded that some Jews don't know why they survived— don't even know there is danger."

Now Naomi does know the danger of what people can do to each other, Jew or not. She stares down at the burned parchment in her one hand, the blue list in the other. Amazing finds, but what good are they to her, really? Going after an old man and exonerating LaTour, her betrayer, isn't going to eradicate that danger. Could this list be useful, though, to verify LeFrère's story of unearthing the manuscript in the cellar—or at least to eliminate the possibility that Mauriet was the one who stashed it there? She scans the columns, but nothing fits the description of her manuscript. Anyway, she wants to let LeFrère's story stand. That's the least she can do for him, as the one who survived. Sometimes love leads to better choices than revenge. But why has Mauriet removed the three folios from their cover, and where are they?

"Here, come on," Marie says, grabbing the documents from Naomi's hands and yanking open the warped door to the hall. "Come on, I'll show you the Arènes."

Naomi follows her down the stairs. The Arènes? They come out into the busy street filled with the delicious smell of mint and wood-grilled lamb. Marie gets far ahead of Naomi, zigzagging around vendors' wagons, until Naomi catches up with her at a Tabac where Marie stops for cigarettes. This is what a radical eats? Naomi's stomach growls painfully.

"Come on," Marie calls over her shoulder, starting off again before Naomi can say she wants lunch. She sees the street sign, Rue Monge, and yearns to turn left, to return to her familiar end of the *quartier*, perhaps to the Café des Etoiles for an onion soup. To see if Hélène got out of jail, or to sit with that woman, as she had intended so many hours ago when Alain came tearing out the door and started her on this unbelievable chase. Maybe if she turns left and goes back, the day will happen differently, and better. But there's no going back. Marie turns right, and Naomi runs to keep up with her fierce pace.

"Here it is," Marie points just ahead.

They come to an amphitheater she hadn't even known about, a Roman ruin, so close to where she's been staying all these months. She follows Marie past the sign, "Arènes de Lutèce," down concentric rows of stone bleachers, down onto the circle where the decadent spectacles of the Roman Empire were once performed. Yes, she remembers now, reading in a guidebook that Rue Mouffetard, with all those wonderful markets, was once the main route from Paris (Lutetia) to Rome, and that this arena had been excavated and restored when they built Rue Monge.

"Marie, wait!" Naomi struggles to keep her balance on the seemingly endless descent into the pit, wishing she'd stopped for a loaf of bread at least. Her legs ache, and she's not sure she really wants to spend her second-to-last day in Paris chasing a feminist gladiator into the center of a Roman arena. "Wait!" Her voice echoes impressively off the stone tiers.

Marie reaches the bottom and lights a cigarette. Pulls the papers out of her deep jacket pocket. Holds her cigarette to the edge of the burned parchment until it smolders.

"No!" Naomi tries to pull the cigarette away. Could this really be a surviving piece of the book Abélard himself tossed into the flames? "Don't!" If it is, it's an unbelievable find. How could you tell for sure what it was? Only by careful study and comparison, only by great scholarly good luck. "STOP!"

Marie holds the burning parchment away from her body and the fire catches. She drops it onto the sandy floor of the arena. Naomi lunges for it, but the heat keeps her back.

"What do you want it for? You thought it was already burned, you and the whole historical enterprise which values words more than life itself. Don't ally yourself with those who will do anything for a piece of ancient skin. Look what is burning here. Nothing! Nothing that matters as much as my parents' life. What do you want it for? Let what you thought was burned be burned once and for all."

Naomi watches the flames. What does Marie think she's accomplishing? There is retrieval, and there is revenge, and this fire does neither. "At least return enough of it to him that he knows what's been done," she says.

"Now you are thinking." Marie smiles at her, and stamps a boot on the smoldering parchment. Maybe the American understands more about revenge than her sweet face lets on. Maybe there is a game we can play in order to get her manuscript back. Then we will both have what we want. Marie pockets the blue list she'd been about to toss into the flames along with the scrap, and grins at her young friend. "Very smart. And I will keep this list—for blackmail, non? For you to get your manuscript back. For me to get even."

There is another way, then, another chance. Naomi could still return with something verified inside this empty brown cover. And blackmail would be justified, wouldn't it? After what he did? To the

Jews and the resisters, to LeFrère, and yes, even to LaTour. And of course, to her own fragile beginnings. But—she can't believe how caught up she is in this whole drama—how could she possibly have forgotten? The whole point is the abbess, isn't it, the words of Héloïse that history has been only too ready to swallow up? She's got to get those words back from Mauriet, and release them from their silence, and she has only one more day. She squats down and picks up the charred parchment. It weighs almost nothing, a black leaf with a tiny white center, only half a line still legible, "et jhesum christum…"

She drops the blackened piece again, overcome by a wave of dizziness. "Et jhesum christum" is what's left of the opus that brought Abélard to his last punishment. Excommunication, isolation, illness, and death. If she were to leave a record of her life somewhere, say the notebook she writes in her room at night, and it burned, and two or three words were saved from decay, what meaning would her work have, distilled into a few drops? "…wonder why…" might be those words. If she's learned anything, it's that you can wonder all you want, but you can never know. There's always more to a story than the Q.E.D. "Quod erat demonstrandum" is only The End until the ink dries. Wonder is green, and puts down roots, and produces seeds.

She turns to Marie. "No," she says. "I don't have time for blackmail. And anyway, it doesn't matter. Maybe you are right. Words matter much less than life. Your parents—they saved your life. Mine, I guess they saved me, too. From too much grief before I was ready. They never told me, you know, about the Jews in Europe—our relatives! They let me grow up unburdened. Now, thanks to you and…the abbess…I can handle it."

Marie stoops to retrieve the "jhesum christum" that Naomi dropped. She stands up and puts her hand on her friend's shoulder. She's helped Naomi learn a lesson she herself has yet to learn. Because, true, what is the point of revenge? Her parents are gone. She is alive. Messing with the old man will only distract her from the real work of revolution—to make everyone free. You live not to rectify the past, but to leave a new mark. Which clearly Abélard did, despite the burned work. And Mauriet did not. Did she, bitter orphan that she is? Marie looks into Naomi's blue eyes and recalls their bewildered innocence last December. Now she sees a deeper shade, which she has contributed to, having loved Naomi's purity even as she tried to mold it otherwise, and having allowed herself to be changed by it.

She'd imagined waving the blue list under Mauriet's nose, threatening to expose him now that leftists were prodding the French to pursue their Nazi sympathizers. But no. She pulls the list from her pocket and hands it to Naomi. She lights a match to its corner. Naomi drops the burning evidence of genocide, and the two women watch it flare and curl and blacken. Marie grinds it into the sand with her heel, still holding onto the charred scrap of Abélard's work.

"Au revoir, then, my little sister," she says, tightening her grip on Naomi's shoulder and releasing it.

"And thanks for showing me, you know, the other end of Rue Monge."

Marie nods. She squeezes her fist around the crisp scrap and lets the black flakes fall. A swirling wind picks them up, along with some old chestnut leaves, and drops them into the litter against the circular wall of the stadium. They walk out of the arena, Naomi heading north, Marie south.

⸙ XXVII ⸙

The heat from the yellow lamp is all that exists. And her two hands rubbing each other in the circle of light cast by the lamp. Why would she want any knowledge other than the indisputable fact of a night? The plastic tablecloth has a worn-out pattern of roses, once probably deep pink, as the wallpaper was once the deeper pink that shows behind the bed. The bedspread was never anything but grey, though the threadbare rug might have been. She flips the corner of the rug for a hint of former color, but the light is too dim. Besides, what does it matter? What does anything matter?

She slumps into the chair. Her notebook lies open to the inconclusive transcription of the manuscript which now, she is sure, remains out of reach. *Her voice must speak of loss, as water must fill a well. Drawing a bucket from that well, I bring life to the surface, and I drink, and give you to drink.* That much is clear. But what about the spoiled final folio, the worm-eaten "Eloyssa"? Irretrievably lost to that beastly old man. Oh, forget it, Naomi, just forget it! Abysmal, abominable, abhorrent, her inability to just hang onto what's important here, not the words but the voice, a woman's pain without apology or guilt. She's heard it, regardless of where the folios are now. And she must hold onto it, and not get swirled in the rapids that drag water up her nose and gag her. She will drink this voice of life, and she will live.

I mourn a memory left unspoken.

Naomi picks at the heel of bread she bought this afternoon at the boulangerie. After leaving Marie, she went right to the Café des Etoiles. She knew just what she wanted. But when she saw Alain at the espresso bar, and no sign of Hélène or that woman, she decided to skip the onion soup. It was conversation she hungered for. Alain argues, Alain flirts, but Alain never listens. If she couldn't talk of the one thing, she did not want to talk at all. The one thing? Oh, God, she doesn't even know what that is. Did she ever know?

Know know know know know know knowknowknow no no no no

She doodles in the margin of her notebook. One thing's for sure, she's no good detective. Kicks herself for not looking to see what that big book was, in the barred room. Dumb move. Got distracted by the view onto her own damn balcony, and trying to peer into her life behind these glass doors. She had her hand right on it, the only piece of evidence in that disheveled cell. Then she looked up and saw herself, the young woman with long hair parted in the middle, pinned back below the ears, pale face, leaning out over a balcony and watching the cars on Rue Monge. Now she has seen where those cars go, seen what lies beyond the little park below her balcony, another world entirely, which is more than he saw from behind those bars. But surely he had a life before those bars, was put there for something?

The book is the key.

The keys. Left in Mauriet's office. Another sloppy act. Not that they'd done her any good. Got her a trip to the Arènes de Lutèce, to stand where Romans once gored animals for sport, where orators spoke, where, today, two women burned something and then parted. And nothing is left of those events. *There*, the place, the arena is what remains.

Didn't the café woman once tell her the mysterious building was part of the medieval wall? Today she'd laid a hand on the mossy ruin of the wall, at Place de la Contrescarpe. The sooty bastion next door will never be a ruin. It will stand forever, getting blacker and blacker but never giving way to moss. Maybe the building is not part of the wall, but in the same place as the wall? *There* remains, holding invisible captives effaced by time.

She chews the last of the loaf, braiding her knuckles together as she stares at the notebook. She brushes the crumbs off *replace my mistaken desire with the strength of iron*. She remembers cider on the balcony, and opens the doors to fetch it. There's a light on in the room behind bars! She steps toward the window, which is open a crack. If only she could reach just a little further, raise the window, get ahold of that book she knows is leaning under the windowsill.

"Hell-o!" she calls, sure now that someone is there, never having seen a light on before, only a trace of light coming from the hallway. She missed the chance to check the evidence, but now something more than a book entices her. A hunch, something to do with LeFrère, or his beloved Abélard. "Bon soir!" she calls across the rail. "Vous êtes là?"

No answer. She uncorks the cider, swigs what's left, and waits. In the dark, her vision fills with the image of LeFrère on the stretcher, a skeleton really, gaunt, as if dead already for hundreds of years. An eerie chill creeps up through her socks as she stands on the cold iron, holding the empty bottle. LeFrère…is…Abélard? Uh-huh. Soon they'll be putting her behind bars for real. She shivers, picturing herself on the balcony as he saw her. It's fear that imprisons her. Fear keeps her from entering the arena of life, to love, to fight, sometimes to lose. Was it LeFrère who screamed LET ME OUT, as if she alone held the key? LET ME OUT—or was the cry she heard really her own?

She'd held the key that could retrieve the manuscript LeFrère so carefully saved for her. But she can't retrieve what isn't there. "Hall-oo-oo!" Someone must be in that room! The light is on!

Her voice echoes off the sooty wall. She waits. Watches to see if the shadows change. Listens. She squats down and peers through the crack. Door to the hallway standing open, outline of the banister. They brought LeFrère down the stairs. She ran down the same stairs, and kicked away the stone that held the door open. It locked behind her. She can't go back. But the light is on. She has to know who is there!

But of course. She sinks to her knees and presses her forehead against the railing. Ridiculous. Absurd. She left the light on herself. She stands up and goes inside.

Her face is flushed, hands ice-cold, the yellow lamp all that exists. She opens the "Pensées" in the small circle of light. She writes, just to prove she is here. *A man can be imprisoned by his own words and all the words written about him, while a woman remains haunted by unsaid words and can only be freed by voicing them. I came for Pierre Abélard. I wanted the man behind the story. The man's own story, and not the story others tell of him, which is history. And then I found her, and the stories men never told about her because they didn't know. I lost them both. Found me instead?*

He burned it, I bet. Mauriet burned those folios—

Despair fills the hungry pit of her stomach. She puts her head down on the notebook. She sniffs. The pages smell like...what? Sage? The garden of her dream, not the gateless one where she saw her own skeleton lying in the grass, clover growing up through the eye sockets, and a nun singing "la clé, la clé." Not that one. The one where she and Héloïse thinned carrots. Those orange roots must have grown to fill the space by now—as if that dream place is real, as if time here equals time there, two eddies in a silver river. Is that the problem with history? It flows to the end of time, and then it's too late to tell. She turns her face on the page, sniffing sage behind the ink and paper.

Grey-green with a woody stalk, soft leaves, fragrant in the heat. Here. Crush a leaf against your cheek. You can't know what you seek. You can't lose what you only guessed at. What's burned is burned. What's gone, gone. A scent remains. Smell it. That much is true.

It's her, isn't it. "La très sage Héloïse." That woman in the café. Naomi's lips move in sleep. The clay, the clay...sun, rain, time...I am the root. The root is the key. She turns her face again on the green-tint notebook page, her cheek indented by the spiral that holds together "Pensées de la Nuit."

— XXVIii —

It's early, very early, dew on the iron gates and only a few stalls open in the marketplace. Leaflets, posters, headlines tell of disturbances in the *quartier*. In the chilly café, a few young professors lean over their cups, angry at the foolish risk the women took in occupying the Ecole Polytechnique, which has never admitted women, and why should it, a demonstration that puts the whole movement in jeopardy, just now when the Ministry was beginning to unclamp its hold on political activity. Haven't the women done enough harm already, alienating men on the left? Don't they know allies when they see them? An outrage, *vraiment*.

The one woman in the café tries to ignore their fists banging the tabletop, rattling the spoons. She sits staring out at the sleepy Rue des Ecoles. She opens her notebook and takes a sip of strong coffee.

Feathery lentil bushes bend with the weight of blossoms on slender stalks. The white petals drop, and stubby pods lengthen, swell, and dry in the short autumn days. The pods hold a secret, two flat seeds each. One, grown in light and gathered into dark, will live again in kettle steam with garlic, celeriac, bay, and thyme. The other seed is saved, to sprout again in garden heat.

She watches for the girl to come around the corner of Rue des Bernardins and open the door to Chez Montreux on this, her last morning in Paris. The men's loud voices impinge on her thoughts.

They dip their spoons into thick potage, but do not taste these unrecorded secrets. Silence, to them, means absence. I have suffered in silence. The unforgotten story waited, and did not rot, but sprouted in her. When they dip their spoons, they do not hear the voice of steam. Presence needs no name, because it is life itself.

And now here she comes, a beret pulled over long brown hair, a few childish curls crowning her forehead. Coat smudged with Paris grime, high boots that leave an inch of pink knee showing, hands deep in her pockets, no briefcase. There's a faint rose in each pallid cheek, a hint of that blue-eyed girl who used to pick up chestnuts. A new kind of smile plays at her lips, as if inside the coat she glows with the coming spring. She turns at her café, where the Monsieur will admire, for the last time, the smooth skin under her chin as she tips back the last drop of cocoa. Regret will pierce him, that such a girl should grow up and go off into a woman's life. The sun slowly rises over the chimneypots, sending up trails of steam from sidewalks and lamp posts. The girl comes out, buttoning her coat, and hesitates at the curb.

Naomi glimpses the woman who watches her through the window, deeply satisfied lines around the mouth, wedge of wrinkles at the eyes. The face, fully revealed by hair tucked into a beret, is pensive, high forehead furrowed like garden rows marked out with string. A "nouvelle Héloïse" in beret and trenchcoat. Naomi laughs at herself. This woman with startling green eyes looks nothing like the one in the dream. Héloïse's eyes were more grey-green, like sage. Naomi grasps the handle of the ten-power magnifying glass in her pocket, which she means to return, and heads toward the reflection of her own face shining in the glass as the sun burns through the mist. She pulls open the café door, brushing past a group of departing professors, and comes to stand at the little window table.

"Your magnifying glass, Madame, and thank you very much for the loan."

"A coffee?" asks the woman, taking the lens and motioning with it toward the other chair. Naomi shakes her head, but sits anyway, drawn to the jade in her eyes. "Your work, it has gone well?"

Naomi nods, yes, then frowns. No. It has not gone well at all. She has nothing to show for her comings and goings, which she is well aware this woman has been watching with interest, who knows why. She has nothing for her committee that will confirm their faith in her, and their funding. Still, she does feel something has been settled. The woman folds her hands on the open page, and studies the changes in Naomi's face, happy, angry, shy, puzzled, scared.

"Yes, I suppose it went well," Naomi concludes. Something about a book without words. The language of green. "Now I must go back. To write. Like you."

The woman picks up the magnifying glass and peers idly at her own script. It looms huge and dark in the circle of glass against grainy white paper. She lowers it, blurring the words, making them tiny. "Tiens. Here." She thrusts the wooden handle back into Naomi's hand. "I have no more need of this glass."

She examines Naomi's startled face. "My research is finished, you see." She closes the notebook and lays both hands flat on the mottled cover. She's found her buried treasure. The girl has only begun to probe the soil.

Naomi stares at the brown hands veined with deep knowledge, not writer's hands at all. They look out of place resting on the notebook, as if they should be grasping the handle of a hoe. She slips the glass back into her pocket. "Merci," she says, "merci beaucoup." She'd like to raise the magnifying glass to the woman's face and read the lines and wrinkles, a text whose syntax is pain and joy.

"So." The woman keeps her hands on the closed notebook. "Do you still want to know?"

"Know?"

"No? Well, you're better off, then." She swirls the remains of her coffee in the bottom of the cup.

"Know what?"

"That building. You asked me once, remember, the night I gave you the glass?"

Naomi's heart knocks against her rib cage like someone pounding on a locked door. It had been Hélène and Marie at the door. They took her from her room, and everything that happened in the last two days has swept her along only to deposit her here, back in an interrupted conversation as if nothing...as if time...as if waking and sleeping were...but she can't remember what she asked the woman. How much else has she known and forgotten? This morning she read the words she wrote last night, smeared with drool yet still legible, *found me instead?*, but she's already forgotten what she meant.

"You said it was the old wall? I'm sorry, was it something about Abélard? He's the subject of my research. Or was. I wanted to find him alive, you know, not just in books."

"Alive and growing, like a plant. Of course books prevent that. Like a flower pressed between pages. You have the knowledge, codified, but it is brittle, yes?"

"And the thing is, are there only two choices—alive or dead? That's only logical," Naomi says, looking into the jade eyes, "isn't it?"

The woman smiles at the girl's modulations, sure, unsure. Even knowing does not quiet this pulse which is life itself. Knowledge can't be held in the palm of your hand. It must be planted in the dark, like a lentil, to sprout again.

"Let me buy you a pastry." She gets up from the table and leaves Naomi alone by the window, where a ray of sun squeezes past a chimney across the street and falls on her smooth hands. She puts them down flat on the woman's notebook, which is cool and a little damp. She twirls the notebook around to face her, and opens the cover. Neat black script, letters very close together, difficult to decipher. Maybe with the glass...but she shouldn't. She looks toward the pastry cart. The woman is returning, carrying a little white plate.

"Oreilles," she announces, setting it down between them. "Two, of course." She pulls on her earlobes.

Two ears. Two eyes. Naomi bites into the flaky, sticky, chewy pastry. Funny how the body favors pairs. Two hands, two feet. Is logic modeled on the body, the balance of two, the either-or?

"Two ears, but only one heart," says the woman, reading Naomi's blue eyes.

"And many minds!" adds Naomi. "Way too many!"

"So many that you have to ignore them. You just have to jump in, and not try to navigate a straight line. Listen with your heart, think with your hands, let your mind take a ride."

"But I can't make any sense of it. Time and death and truth and... I just can't explain..."

"Then don't. Who's asking?"

"Them. My professors. And, I mean, I have to make choices in my life that make sense to me."

"The only choice that's yours to make is how you think about things. Life's not an either-or proposition! Listen, you like Notre Dame cathedral, non?"

"You know so much about me! You sit in this café, and yet it's as if you've been following me."

"It is because you are so like me."

"How?" Naomi licks her finger and picks up the crumbs of her pastry.

"I came here to find something. Like you. The difference is, you started by reading. I started from a blank book, and no Carte d'Identité!"

"I remember seeing you in the Jardin last fall, my first day at the Ecole des Chartes. I wondered what was in your notebook. I wished to be more like you, with something interesting to write about."

"I had only this." She nudges the notebook toward Naomi.

"Nothing but a voice traveling along the edge between vegetable and mind. The merest wisp led me back along the trail of my choices. You're lost, too."

"Yeah, and I think I know just where I left me. In the seminar room on the fourth floor of Goldwin Smith, in the middle of Dante's 'Purgatorio'!"

The woman laughs. "It was a teacher, non? And you thought the teacher's way was the only way. I made the same mistake."

Naomi, finished with her oreille, sits tracing her finger around the border of the woman's notebook. She looks up. "What were you going to say about Notre Dame? About life isn't an either-or thing?"

"The rose window. With the Virgin in the center."

"Is that who that is? I could never make out the image. It was blocked by the light streaming through the colors."

"Yes. The carved spokes, the colored pathways, lead you to her. It's the woman who holds the center."

"I always figured the towers held the lesson about life: two towers, either, or. But the lesson is inside! All that stone frames a space for light to shine through. It's the rose, not the towers. Wow."

"Wow," the woman grins. She screws the cap on her pen. "Here," she pushes the notebook at Naomi. "I'm finished with this. You take it. There are still a lot of blank pages left. Return to purgatory where you lost your way."

Back in her room, Naomi packs the last few things. She tucks her *Petit Larousse* into the side pocket, along with the magnifying glass wrapped in a wool sock. She folds the thermal underwear, the pink flannel nightgown, onto the top of books and presses her knee down to zip the suitcase. Her briefcase she will carry on the plane, with the manuscript transcription tied inside the empty brown leather cover which is nothing more than a souvenir. "Pensées de la Nuit" goes in next, and then the notebook that woman gave her. She opens to the first page of tight cursive and runs her fingertips over the coarse paper. Yes, it will take a magnifying glass to read this. But she gave her the notebook for these blank pages at the end, to write in herself. She closes the cover and catches a whiff of something like garlic, or maybe it's lentils, and her mouth waters at the thought of all the wonderful soups she'll make in Ithaca. If she could only take back vegetables from the markets of Paris. She slides the notebook into her briefcase. Her ticket and the last traveler's cheque, the key to her apartment.

Now all that's left to do is look around the dim room, made even more stark without her things. How could she have lived in this awful garret all these months, in this grey cell with its washed-out pink wallpaper and bed hard as a rock? This will not be an easy room to forget. The crack in the ceiling, the streaked mirror, and oh! the bidet, which, after all, made a decent foot bath. She unplugs the yellow lamp and leaves it as a gift for her landlady. She snaps shut her briefcase, and steps out onto the balcony for one last view of the little park, quiet in the late winter sun, and the stream of noon traffic on Rue Monge. Pigeons peck for crumbs along the short length of Rue des Bernardins. Cobblestones, they'll never be the same, now that she's seen them dug up for barricades, leaving only the sandy underlayment that's even harder to run on. Nothing will ever be the same, now that she's tasted the fearful joy of her youth. She clings to the railing, and sighs. Paris will just have to go on without her, pigeons and professors, paddy wagons and pâtisseries.

She cranes her neck to the left for one last view of Notre Dame. Paris is so regimented, so cold. Yet in the center of the city, in the middle of the Seine, at the heart of the cathedral, a woman reigns supreme. All those conversations with Hélène—"the woman, she is central"—finally make sense, in light of the rose. Naomi smiles as all the colors pour right through her. The virgin, c'est moi.

She takes one last deep breath before going back in. Cigarette smoke. She turns toward the abandoned building. The light she'd left on had burned all through the night. She steps toward the window, and quickly steps back, bumping her shoulder into the doorframe. Just inches beyond her railing, a man in a white T-shirt smokes at the open window, looking out from behind the bars.

"Au revoir, Mademoiselle," he says. "Bon voyage."

F i n

Dear Reader,

Where does a story begin? Something scarcely remembered clings like the residue on the inside of a coffee cup. It's an empty cup, ours to fill with hope and imagination. Everyone has a story. The trick is, how do we tell our stories to others?

I founded About Time Press in 1996 to publish *Carrying Water as a Way of Life*, because I had a full cup, and wanted to share. Next came *Writer on the Rocks*, in 2000. Without your support for About Time Press, I could never have persevered to complete *Yes and No*, a project begun in 1987. Your positive reception of each new book gives me the heart to continue.

Distribution is the biggest challenge for a small publisher in a corporate industry. If you found this book in a bookstore, library, or on-line, just think of all the busy hands it had to pass through without ever being read! Or, more simply, maybe you ordered directly from me, and I slipped it into an envelope and took it to the post office.

Where does a story end? No matter how this book gets to you, it's the story that opens a channel from author to reader. Forget about all those middlemen! Let me know about friends who'd like the book. Give it to someone else who loves to read. Use it in a book group. Show it to your local bookseller or librarian. Suggest it to your students or your teachers. Pass the words.

Linda

Hand to hand, heart to heart,

a book can move the world.

ABOUT
TIME
PRESS

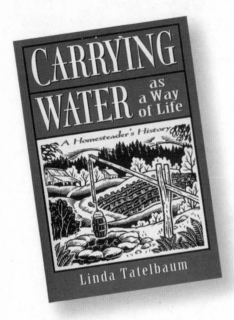

CARRYING WATER
AS A WAY OF LIFE:
A Homesteader's History

with photographs
by Bonnie Farmer
and others

$9.95

I went to live in the woods with the dean of students after the
college where I had my first job as an English professor went
bankrupt. In 1977, we moved to Maine to build a solar house
and plant a garden. I assigned myself three sentences a day, even
if only "Nothing. Nothing. Nothing." Writing about life on the
land didn't keep the world from changing, and the "simple life"
became quaintly outmoded. But a curmudgeon keeps on. By
the time this book appeared in 1997, simplicity was back in
fashion, though nothing is ever simple, least of all simplicity.

"If you're thinking about trying homesteading, read Thoreau to get enthusiastic and the Nearings for assurance that anyone can do it. But read *Carrying Water as a Way of Life* first, for the plain, complex facts."

—*Yes! A Journal of Positive Futures*

"Her observations draw on a sense of place and history that's growing rare. The book stands as testimonial to the changes inflicted on many once-rural places."

—*Washington Post Book World*

"The book tells stories that are broader than Tatelbaum's alone. It is sad, noble, and beautifully written. It is a book to re-read, one that teaches."

—*Colby Magazine*

"a book Thoreau (or his sister) might have written"

—William Carpenter, poet and novelist

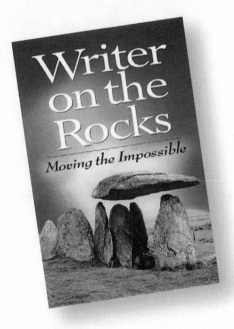

WRITER ON
THE ROCKS—
Moving the Impossible

with photographs
by Paul Caponigro
and others

$12.95

*We had a drought, and the well went dry. My words went dry,
too. Who wants to write about middle age, how your child leaves
home, friends start dying, work seems futile? Who wants to read
about a writer on the rocks? So I started moving rocks instead,
building stone walls and steps. It takes physics to move rocks—
leverage, momentum, friction, inertia. Emotional physics is what
it takes to move words—ambition, joy, grief, frustration. It's all
a dance of body and words, whether writing, gardening, building,
or moving heavy things. Rocks showed me the way back to words.*

"A celebration of the body and nature, and a deeply moving meditation on loss and redemption. Alone, each essay shines; together, they positively glow, forming a deceptively simple story of a writer in despair who finds her voice again. The story is inspiring, instructive, and memorable, and each line is a lesson in elegance."

—Monica Wood, author of *My Only Story* and *Ernie's Ark*

"a lovely, inspiring, galvanizing book"

—Letty Cottin Pogrebin, President, The Authors Guild

"Tatelbaum is a lyrical correspondent from the rock-strewn edges of the American landscape. These frank, playful essays should inspire anyone building a stone wall or re-learning the leverage of language."

—Amazon.com, *Best Picks of the Independent Publishers*

YES AND NO
A Novel
$14.95

I was once a shy graduate student on a fruitless semester in Paris. Two decades later, I wondered how the trip might have gone if I'd mingled with French students in the cafés, if I'd kept a journal, if I'd been more curious and less studious. If, if, if…should I return to try again? You can never go back. So I sent a fictional young woman to Paris, and let Naomi do it her way. She led me into unfamiliar places, remaining forever 21 years old (a trick that fictional doubles have perfected) while I grew wise under her tutelage. What a good teacher a student can be!

"As in her nonfiction, Linda Tatelbaum layers an intimate chronicle with history, philosophical musing, and complicated emotion. *Yes and No* is both a coming of age story and a tale of coming to terms with mortality. It is elegantly written, playful and deeply serious, full of youthful passion and mature wisdom: a beautiful book."

—Deborah Weisgall, author of *A Joyful Noise*

"Compelling and provocative, *Yes and No* calls into question the notion of historical 'facts.' Naomi's studies, and the people she encounters, past and present, set her on a journey of mystery and discovery. The parallels between medieval Paris and 1969, both times that disrupted the status quo, are deftly woven into a young woman's quest for self-understanding. The result is a fiction that delights and challenges, a book you simply can't put down."

—Larissa Taylor, professor of history, Colby College

PRAISE FOR LINDA TATELBAUM'S NONFICTION BOOKS

Carrying Water as a Way of Life: A Homesteader's History
"Spiked with humor, this engaging, true-grit memoir of a self-described 'old hippie' is graced with homespun yet unsentimental observations. Her strenuous personal quest for the simple life rings true and sincere, and her lyrical log sounds a passionate plea for ecological sanity."

—*Publishers Weekly*

Writer on the Rocks—Moving the Impossible
"*Writer on the Rocks* is both charming and vehement (yes, at the same time). Tatelbaum is a master of metaphor and metaphysics, writing as much about life, death, and the spirit as about digging wells, moving rocks, and writing."

—John Cole, author and journalist